# Phantom

# Traces

## Jessica Hawke

Mighty Fine Books, LLC

PO Box 956

Evans, GA  30809

Editing by Rhonda Helms

Cover Design by Clarissa Yeo

Book Design by Jessica Hawke

ISBN:  978-1-944142-07-0

First Edition: February 2016

Second Edition: April 2018

10 9 8 7 6 5 4 3 2

# ALSO BY JESSICA HAWKE

**Phantoms Series**

Phantom Touch

Phantom Traces

Phantom Whispers

Visit www.jessicahawke.com to download
your <u>free</u> prequel novella, *Phantom Light*.

*For everyone who's ever chased a dream — keep running.*

# CHAPTER ONE

IT WAS ONLY FITTING that my little brother was an angel, an actual messenger of God, complete with sparkling white robe and a halo wrapped in dollar-store tinsel. If my mother had forced me to participate in the Christmas play instead of just using me as free labor for the costumes, I probably would have been cast as a lowly shepherd. Or maybe an ass.

Definitely an ass.

I turned to tell my friend Sal as much. He laughed.

"Bridget, watch your language," Lena May said. "You can't say…a-s-s in church."

"What? They definitely said it in the Bible," I told her. And that made it even funnier.

Besides, it wasn't as if anyone was going to hear us. We had the dusty balcony of the Parkland United Methodist Church all to ourselves. The red-upholstered cushions smelled like old books and mothballs, and the wooden benches creaked in protest every time I shifted my weight. Sal and Lena May didn't have that problem, what with them being ghosts and all. There were certain benefits to death, I supposed.

Piled in my lap was a heap of scratchy brown fabric that would eventually be a Wise Man's robe. Mom didn't trust me with her sewing machine, which was sort of a running theme these days. But she'd deemed me suitable for the task of sewing on the snaps and hooks that she didn't have the patience for.

"Bridget. Young ladies shouldn't use such coarse language," Lena May said primly. She folded her hands atop her crossed legs. Her gray hair was neatly curled, and her best pearls lay on translucent skin. If I looked hard enough, I could see through her like a sheer curtain to the dark stained glass on the opposite wall.

There were certain advantages to speaking to the dearly departed. For one, Lena May had overheard Mom telling her friend Donna that what she really wanted for Christmas was a day at the spa. Consider it done. I'd used some of my birthday money from my dad to get her a gift certificate for a massage. Honestly, I had to admit that I had ulterior motives. I mean, I really did want to make her happy, but getting Mom a good Christmas gift would go a long way toward ending her reign of terror over my free time.

Then again, there were drawbacks to counting the dead among your bosom companions. For one, most teenage girls didn't have the ghost of a ninety-eight-year-old woman constantly criticizing their behavior, all of which was appalling by her standards. Since I'd first encountered Lena May, I'd given up on arguing about how things were nowadays, because she stopped all of my arguments dead with, "Well, just because that's how it's done doesn't mean it's being done right."

I mean, how could you argue with that?

Lena May leaned over, passing one translucent hand through my pile of fabric. She made a *tsk* sound. "You need to double the thread up before you sew on the hook. Like I showed you."

I fumbled the brown thread through the eye of the needle and looped it. "Like this?"

"Very good," she said. "A young lady should know how to sew on a button at the very least. It's a good skill for when you get married and have to take care of a husband."

I wasn't touching that one with a ten foot pole.

Sal snorted a laugh. "I can see it now. Housewife of the century."

"Shut up," I told him. As I said, speaking to the dead had its drawbacks, most notably a never-ending commentary on my life.

Lena May ignored him as she watched me sew the first stitches onto the little wire hook. She gave me a little nod of approval, then turned her attention back to the choir rehearsal. "This is just lovely," Lena May told me. "They sound like angels. You know that's my—"

"Great-granddaughter, I know," I said gently. She only reminded me every time I saw her that the little redhead with the adorable pigtails on the third row of angels was her great-granddaughter. I didn't get irritated, though. The dead had their own particular kind of senility, so it wasn't Lena May's fault she was fixated on her family. She was so attached that she had literally held on beyond death.

The church was in a state of festive chaos, with big plastic storage tubs all over the pews and sparkling tinsel stretched out on the floor down the aisles. Ladders stood near each of the two half-decorated Christmas trees. Volunteers fastened lengths of spiky pine garland to the wooden bannisters around the altar. Mom knelt by teenage Mary's feet to pin up the hem of her robe while Mary took a selfie on a pink rhinestoned phone.

"Hark! I bring you glad tides and—" my brother shouted. I winced. He was good at a lot of things, but acting wasn't high on the list.

"Glad tidings," the choir director corrected. Colin sighed. "Glad tidings, Colin."

"Oh, look," Lena May said. She pointed to the Christmas tree on the right side of the church. "I sewed the dress for the angel. Goodness, it had to be forty years ago now." Her translucent features gleamed as she watched a woman in a Santa sweatshirt carefully unwrap the tissue paper from the figurine and place it on top of the tree. "They've put it up every year since."

I'd met Lena May a few weeks earlier, when Mom had insisted on me helping her with the costumes for the annual Christmas play. Before then, I hadn't known a whip-stitch from a bullwhip, but she'd told me that she'd find something for me to do. Church wasn't really my thing, though I came along when Mom heavily insisted. She usually only put down her foot on Christmas and Easter, but things had changed recently.

I wasn't stupid. After what happened to my best friend, Emily, Mom didn't want to let me out of her sight. When Natalie Fullmer, a girl from my school, had disappeared a few months ago, most people thought she'd just run away yet again. They were wrong. Natalie's angry spirit had come to me to make sure I knew it, too. When Emily had disappeared soon after, I'd known Natalie's killer had taken her. No one else took me seriously, so I'd taken matters into my own hands. Emily had survived, but Mom still had questions I couldn't—or *wouldn't*—answer for her.

Her response had been predictable, but completely unhelpful. Now she was keeping me on a tight leash. No, it didn't even qualify as a leash. Imagine when you didn't have a leash handy, so you just grabbed the dog's collar so he kept choking himself every time he tried to take off. That was more like it.

So here I was, sewing snaps onto Wise Man robes with pointers from a woman who'd been dead for four years. As far as I could tell, she'd attended the church since it was built, and despite teaching Sunday school for fifty years, she hadn't gotten the memo that she was supposed to go elsewhere when she died. I still hadn't figured out what she wanted. Most spirits lingered for a reason, and they usually weren't shy about letting you know what it was. But Lena May was different. I'd tried to ask her several times, and she'd just waved me off and changed the subject. It had even occurred to me that she might have passed along without realizing it. When I'd broached the topic, she rolled her eyes and said, "Bridget, I'm dead, not senile. I know." I'd left it alone since then, which was probably just as well, considering I could barely get away from Mom long enough to handle any kind of ghost business for the last few weeks.

"What do you think of some nice earrings?" Sal asked suddenly. "She loves jewelry."

I frowned and turned to him. "Earrings?"

"For Veronica," he said. "Christmas? I was thinking diamonds."

"Right," I said. "I mean, I guess that would be nice."

He sighed, his golden features creasing in dismay. "You think it's stupid."

"Not stupid," I said. "I swear."

"Then what? You've shot down everything I've suggested."

I winced at his choice of words. Sal was a former police officer who'd been killed in the line of duty almost ten months ago. The neat bullet hole and accompanying trickle of blood still stained the faded blue of his uniform shirt. I'd met him on a trip to the police station while snooping around for information on Natalie's disappearance.

"It's just a little weird," I told him. "I mean, try to see it from her point of view. If you walked out your front door and found a random gift on your doorstep that happened to be the exact thing your dead boyfriend would have picked out, wouldn't that freak you out?"

Not to mention there was no way I could afford diamonds. Sal seemed to forget that he couldn't show up at the jewelry store with his credit card, so he was relying on my meager bank account. And they weren't about to give me his police discount.

"But I just wanted to—"

"Bridget? Who are you talking to?"

My stomach leaped into my throat, and I turned to see my mother standing

5

at the top of the balcony stairs. "Uh, I was talking to Emily on speakerphone," I said. *Please tell me you didn't hear the dead boyfriend part.*

"Why are you up here all by yourself?" Her hands were planted on her hips, which meant she was in full-on Disapproving Mom mode. A pincushion was strapped to her wrist, and she had a measuring tape strung around her neck. She still wore her bright pink scrubs from work.

*Because it's exhausting to pretend I don't hear all these ghosts chattering around me.* "I don't know."

Mom sighed. I caught the eye roll, though I'm sure she'd deny it if I called her on it. Apparently it was only rude when I did it. "Rehearsal is over soon. Did you finish?"

I held up the robe. "Close."

"Well, try to finish it up quickly. We're going home soon."

# CHAPTER TWO

O N THE DRIVE HOME, Colin instantly whipped out his phone to play some Nerds of War game with all his middle school friends. He put on his headphones, leaving me to entertain Mom the entire way.

Traitor.

I checked my own phone to find a dozen notifications about likes and new follows on Instagram. For someone who used to be able to count her friends without taking off either shoe, it was still too strange to wrap my head around. Right after the news had broken about Natalie's killer, along with my involvement in rescuing Emily from him, I'd been crowned princess of the Fall Court. This wasn't because I was secretly gorgeous or popular, but most likely because Emily's friend Hachi had plastered the school with Photoshopped posters of me fighting Chuck Norris. If anything, I represented the average crowd, those of us who weren't particularly cool but also didn't fit into any of the labeled groups like band nerds, theater kids, or Goths. Freaky Ghost Girls was still a clique of one.

In any case, I was just shocked that people had actually applauded, instead of awkward silence while my mom did a slow clap. The crown was unexpected sparkly icing. And as much as I'd protested participating in the whole silly show, even I couldn't resist the appeal of a tiara. Ever since then, I'd been on this weird upward social climb.

"Ugh," I muttered. I'd been tagged in Allie Williams' Throwback Thursday picture. Wonderful. The same Allie Williams who'd been my middle school BFF and had used me as a stepstool to the social ladder in ninth grade, when she'd told everyone I'd gone off the deep end after Valerie had died. Now that it was cool, she was suddenly trying to be my best friend again, as if the last two years hadn't happened. She was the personification of all things terrible.

Case in point. Her Throwback Thursday picture was a grainy shot of us in neon pink Field Day shirts from eighth grade. I still had my braces and hadn't yet gotten the memo that neon green rubber bands were objectively awful and would never be cute. Yet Allie looked perfect, which I suspected was due to genetic engineering or a bargain with Satan himself. And just to be clear, there were plenty of pictures of us where I didn't look like a surgically modified cave troll, so I knew she'd picked it for the utmost strategic value in scaling the social ladder. It subtly said, *Look how I was friends with her back when she was a sad little loser with radioactive snot-colored braces!*

The caption was *Middle school besties! #lovethisgirl #sobrave #tbt*

I snorted a laugh. Emily had commented under the picture: *Oh, how the times have changed…* If Allie had picked up on Emily's pointed barb, she hadn't deigned to reply.

I contemplated reporting the picture as offensive but decided against it. I did, however, wish I had a picture of Allie right after I'd punched her in ninth grade. She'd been holding court in the girl's bathroom, telling her new crowd about how sad and pathetic I'd become, not realizing I was in the last stall trying to clear my head before homeroom. Sure, clocking her hadn't done much to counter the rumors that I'd lost it, but it was worth it to see the look on her face. The mental picture was beautiful, but I'd have loved to see Allie's black eye and bloody nose in high definition on every smartphone in school.

"Bridget, I really wish you wouldn't be so antisocial," Mom said finally.

"I'm totally social," I said. "According to Facebook I have three hundred friends." Of course, that was about five real friends and two hundred and ninety-five people who'd been intrigued by the whole Runaway Killer thing.

"That's not what I mean. The women's group put on a really nice potluck, and people were asking about you, but you were nowhere to be found."

"Well, I'm sure you filled them in on everything they needed to know," I said. And plenty they didn't.

I was no longer Bridget, Whose Sister Had Died Tragically. I was now Bridget, Who'd Rescued Her Best Friend from a Serial Killer. And while the distinction might have seemed impressive on the surface, the result was still the same. Sidelong glances, conversations that abruptly stopped when I walked up, and a lot of questions that could all be answered the same way: *none of your business*.

We stopped at an intersection in front of Target. With the holidays looming large, traffic was congested and snarled near the shopping center. The light was green, but we were stuck thanks to a line of impatient drivers who'd run the red light and blocked the intersection. Mom drummed her nails against the steering wheel and muttered under her breath. I couldn't make it all out, but I was pretty sure Lena May would have something to say about my mother's language.

In the tangled knot of traffic, a woman slowly shuffled across the crosswalk. Headlights passed through her body uninterrupted. Her yellow sundress was far too light and thin for the weather, and it was stained and dark up the back. My skin crawled with the familiar sensation that accompanied the presence of the unsettled dead. I didn't want to notice the dark stains, but my brain leaped into action immediately. Car accident, maybe, or a house fire somewhere nearby? Her hair was matted, covering her face like tattered curtains. As she looked up, I dropped my eyes to focus on the glowing screen of my phone.

*Don't look, don't look, don't look. You can't do this now.*

I hadn't really dealt with a ghost case since Natalie, and frankly, I didn't want to. I'd taken a risk to help her and crossed a line I couldn't come back from. Before Natalie, I'd only ever seen the spirits of the wrongfully dead, people who'd been killed before their time by the actions of others. It had been a lot to deal with, but it had been a pretty small sector of the ghost world, relatively speaking.

Now I saw them all, no matter how they'd died or how long ago. And they were everywhere: in the stacks at the library, the aisles at the grocery store, even the pews of the church. There was nowhere sacred or quiet for me anymore. Many were shy and skittish as feral cats, but I felt the weight of sad, dead eyes on me everywhere I went.

*That* was why I was antisocial, but I certainly couldn't tell Mom that.

The intersection finally cleared, and Mom stomped the gas through the yellow light. The car passed through the woman's incorporeal form. I squeezed my eyes shut and told myself the cold chill running down my spine was just in my head. When a few seconds had passed, I sneaked a glance in the rearview mirror. The ghostly woman paused and looked over her shoulder like she'd heard something in the distance. But if she'd noticed me, she forgot me quickly and resumed her sad journey across the busy road.

Mom sighed. "I wish you wouldn't keep everyone at a distance like this."

Well, some people—ghost pedestrian included—needed to be kept at a distance. "And I wish everyone would quit asking me about what happened."

"Honey, the story was all over the news. You can't blame people for being curious."

"Is curious the polite version of nosy?"

"Bridget," Mom said. She shook her head. "One of these days, you're going to have to quit hiding and give people a chance."

"Maybe so," I said. "But not today."

I stuck in my headphones and scrolled through my phone. I knew Mom meant well, but she didn't get it. What she wanted was for everything to be normal, but things were never going to be normal for our family. My sister was dead, and I saw dead people.

I mean, really? On what planet would we ever be normal? And I'd tried to tell her what was going on once before. She'd done everything except have me committed. Keeping my personal life on lockdown was a matter of survival.

When we got home, Colin ran for the Xbox, but Mom headed him off and told him to go to bed. Like the precious little angel he was, he didn't argue a bit, hugged her goodnight, and went upstairs to brush his teeth.

I waited at the foot of the stairs, fiddling with my backpack. "I need to study for my Spanish final."

"Okay," Mom said. "I love you."

"I love you too."

As she hugged me, I tensed, then slowly put my arms around her. It was nice for a moment, but I hoped she wasn't going to start another one of her Heartfelt Talks. She'd been doing that a lot since everything that had happened with Emily and Natalie. Somewhere in her mind, she probably meant well, but it always cycled back to the same old tough-love, "let's discuss everything wrong with Bridget" tune.

We were nearing the critical period where staying longer would set off the Talk. I pulled away from her and said, "Goodnight."

She smiled faintly, but there was tension around her eyes. "Don't stay up too late."

I trudged up the stairs and into my bedroom. At the sight of my familiar room, with its smooth hardwood floors and purple decorations, the tension flowed out of my body. I flopped onto my bed and let out a heavy sigh. The lavender comforter smelled like fresh laundry. I inhaled deeply and felt at home. Finally, solitude.

Coiled in a neat pile on my nightstand was the silver dragonfly necklace that had belonged to my sister, Valerie. I brushed my fingers over the fine silver links. Part of me still hoped it would bring her back, like a genie's lamp. I wouldn't even need three wishes. One would be plenty. But it was only a necklace, and she was still gone.

"Long day?"

I peeked to see Kale sitting cross-legged on the end of my bed. "Hey there."

Just to be clear, I didn't make a habit of having attractive teenage boys showing up in my bed, but Kale was an exception. And considering he was both not alive, and probably a few hundred years old, he didn't count as teenaged or a boy.

Still, he was nice to look at. He was pale, but more in a 'never saw the sun' kind of way than corpse-like. He had thick dark hair that was always a little windblown, and eyes the color of a summer sky. His light linen clothes made him look like he'd walked off of an exotic beach photoshoot and into my boring little bedroom.

Kale was the one spirit I was never sad to see. Unlike the others, I wasn't sure he'd ever been human. And if he had been human at one point, it wasn't unfinished business or injustice keeping him here now. It was me.

Kale was a Guardian, and I was his responsibility. I still didn't know what that meant, despite asking him enough times over the last two years to qualify as thoroughly obnoxious. He always gave me the supernatural equivalent of a Mom answer: "Because I say so."

"Hard day at the office," I replied.

"I know, being a teenage girl is really tough," he said. He threw one pale hand dramatically over his glittering blue eyes. Ugh, those eyes belonged on a magazine cover. He set a pretty tough standard for living boys to measure up to.

"You speak from experience?"

"I do have my secrets," he said. He disappeared for a second, then reappeared, lying flat on his back next to me. I got a whiff of him, a clean smell of green, growing things. For a moment, it was like being a normal girl, until I noticed the way the bed didn't shift at all. The blankets didn't crease under him, since there was no body to weigh them down. He could interact with the physical world occasionally, but it seemed that he did it as he wished, and not as a rule. "Your mom is ticked about something."

"My mom is always ticked about something," I replied. "Phone?"

He nodded. "She just told your father she's worried about you."

"Shocker," I said. "She's talking to Dad?"

"Yeah, they're discussing what to buy you and your brother for Christmas," he said. He smirked. "Do you want me to tell you?"

"Let me guess," I said. "Electric fence system or a year's supply of therapy."

Kale gave me a disapproving look. "You know, you need to take it easy on her."

I sighed and turned onto my side. "What is this? Ghosts-correcting-Bridget day?"

"I don't understand your reference, but I assume it means someone else is trying to mold you into less of a pain in the ass," he replied. He propped his head up on his hand, fingers disappearing into his thick hair. I was suddenly overcome with the urge to touch it. It had to be kitten soft. *Focus.* "She's your mother, and she worries about you. With good reason."

"What does that mean?" It was too bad Mom couldn't walk upstairs right now and see me lying in bed with my smoking-hot ghost BFF. That would probably send her right over the edge, but it was probably the most normal thing I could do, at least if Kale was a real boy and not a spirit of unknown origins.

"What happened with Emily," he said. "You know, reckless and dangerous and—"

"Ugh, you too?"

"Try to see it from her point of view," Kale said. "She thought you were safe at school, and then she found out you were trying to stop a serial killer all on your own and nearly got yourself killed."

"Okay, one, it's not like I didn't try all the other options first. It's not my fault people don't take me seriously. And two, are you saying I shouldn't have?"

"No," Kale said. He gave me a little smile and brushed one finger over my cheek. His touch was cool and electric. It sent a tingle that was icy and hot at the same time, sizzling down my spine. I swallowed hard and desperately hoped the heat didn't show on my cheeks. "I'm just saying anyone with an ounce of sense would worry. Your mother in particular, because she's already lost one daughter. She doesn't want to lose you, too." His finger grazed down to my chin, trailing up nearly to my lip. My breath caught in my throat as he withdrew his touch. "Just have a little compassion."

I let out a breath, carefully exhaling so he didn't notice the way my heart was racing. "You know, you're awfully annoying sometimes with all your logic and nonsense." *And being so delicious.*

"I'm going to take that as acknowledgement that I'm right," he said. "And besides, that's my job."

# CHAPTER THREE

A YUDA ME, POR FAVOR," I repeated, trying to imitate Sal's crisp pronunciation. *Ayuda me* was right. I had a final in ten minutes, and I needed all the help I could get.

"So you can actually hear him?" Emily said, dark-shadowed eyes wide. She leaned in and whispered, "Where is he?"

Sal laughed. "*Aquí, hermana.*"

"Why are you whispering?" I asked her. I gestured around the noisy lunchroom. Fox Lake High School was in the final countdown to Christmas break, so there was even more of a roar than usual. Besides, Emily and I sat at our own table with at least five empty seats between us and the group of freshman boys who played *Magic: The Gathering* all through lunch period. We weren't in prime eavesdropping territory. "It's not like anyone can hear us. And he's right next to you." I pointed to the empty seat next to Emily.

She slowly looked at the round plastic seat, then back at me. She cautiously waved one green-nailed hand through what she saw as empty space. I winced a little as her nails passed harmlessly through Sal's face. "Here?"

"Right there," I said. "Oh God, you poked him in the eye."

"Bridget," Sal scolded. "That's just mean."

"Oh shit, I'm so sorry," she said, yanking her hand back. I chuckled as she examined it, like she was expecting it to be dripping with ectoplasm a la Ghostbusters. Emily still hadn't gotten a grasp on my ability. To be fair, it had taken me months to get over the weirdness, so I tried not to get too annoyed with her lack of progress.

"She does understand I'm already dead, right?" Sal asked. He watched in amusement as Emily patted the air around him.

"You're not hurting him," I told her.

Emily raised one perfectly groomed eyebrow. She hid her hands under the table. "Okay, how many fingers am I holding up?"

"*Cuatro*," Sal said.

"Five," I said.

Emily's brow furrowed and she shook her head. "Wrong."

"Four," Sal corrected. "We just covered numbers. Are you paying attention at all?"

"Four," I said. "It's not his fault I suck at Spanish."

"Damn," Emily said. "Bridget, I'm not gonna lie. This is epic levels of weird. Even for us."

After I rescued Emily from the Runaway Killer, as the papers called him, I'd told her my secret. Of everyone I knew, she was the right one to tell. Not that I had a lot of friends to choose from, but that was beside the point.

At first she simply didn't believe me and thought I was pulling an epic prank on her. Then we'd gone through a short stage of denial. She'd been diplomatic about it; she didn't believe me, but she respected my beliefs, which was a really polite way of saying I was crazy but she'd love me anyway. And honestly, that would have been okay. It was a lot more than my supposed BFF Allie had done. But her curiosity had gotten the best of her, so with a little help from Kale and a subsequent freak-out, I'd finally convinced her I was telling the truth.

"Tell me about it," I replied.

"So why don't you just have him help you on the test?"

"Well, for one, that's cheating," I said. Emily rolled her eyes. "Two, even if I wanted to, Sal is a cop. He has a code of honor or something."

"Was," Sal said, his face going uncharacteristically solemn. "Not anymore."

And there was the great big elephant in the room. No matter how much Sal and I laughed and studied for Spanish, we would eventually circle back to the same unavoidable truth.

Dead. Finished. Life-challenged. *Muerto.*

I envied the fact that Emily avoided the painfully awkward silence I was experiencing. She shook her head and said, "I think you're going about this all wrong. You should be getting lottery numbers and sports bets and shit."

"She does know I'm dead, not psychic, right?"

I laughed. "He can't tell the future."

Emily shrugged. "We could have a reality show."

"We?"

"Yeah," she said. "I mean, we're kind of in this together now."

"I guess we are," I said. I couldn't help but smile at the thought of it. I didn't have too many friends with heartbeats. So it meant a lot for Emily to stick it out even with my little curse complicating our lives. Unfortunately, her friendship wasn't going to help too much on my Spanish final. I consulted my study guide and sighed. Surely we hadn't even learned half of this. Irregular verbs? I was so screwed. "Okay, Sal. Preterite verbs. *Ayuda me.*"

Sal smirked. "*El pretérito.* The preterite is for completed actions, *–ar* verbs. Let's say, *caminar,* to walk. *Yo caminé.*"

"*Yo caminé,*" I repeated.

"*Tu caminaste, él o usted—*"

"Hey, Bridget?"

I looked up from the study guide to see Brady Thomas sliding into the seat Sal occupied. The sight of him knocked the preterite verbs right out of my brain. My stomach fluttered in anxiety.

Brady was in my AP Literature class with Mrs. McDaniel and held some swim team record. His *Parkland Summer Swim League* T-shirt was tight enough to show off a champion swimmer's body, as if he was saying *oops, did I shrink my shirt, or did my muscles get magically delicious over the summer?*

What the heck was he doing over here? He must have gotten lost.

As if the nerves weren't enough, Sal's translucent form combined with Brady's very solid one to create a bizarre two-headed monster across the table from me. Sal leaned to one side to examine Brady. Now it looked like his curly-haired head was sprouting from Brady's shoulder. And I'd thought it was hard to keep a poker face with Lena May critiquing my sewing skills.

"Hey, Brady," I said. *Hey, Brady?* What was I thinking?

"Hey." He gave a little shiver and smiled. "It's kind of cold over here. That's weird. It's, like, crazy hot everywhere else," he said. He glanced up at the ceiling.

If I was smooth, I might have said something like, "Maybe the heat is just you," but all I managed was, "This spot gets a draft." I hoped it didn't sound as stupid to him as it did in my head. Yeah, there was a draft, all right. A draft named Officer Luis Salazar. "It's great in August."

Sal burst out laughing. "'It's great in August,'" he said, mimicking my voice. One of these days I was going to find a ghost who was one hundred percent Team Bridget. I widened my eyes at him, then plastered on a smile for Brady. I was the absolute worst at this.

Brady laughed a little, his gaze sliding away and over my shoulder. "So, how's it going?" Was he nervous? I glanced over my shoulder. Was someone recording this to post online or something?

"Fine," I said hesitantly. I didn't see anyone around, but I'd seen Emily quickdraw her phone for a selfie in three seconds flat. All it would take was a minor disturbance to turn fourth period lunch into a full-on paparazzi scene.

"So, I was wondering," he said, folding his hands and unfolding them rhythmically. I couldn't help but notice the way the muscles in his forearms shifted as he did it. Somehow, he was still tan even in December. "Are you going to the Christmas dance?"

"No," I said. "Why?"

"Oh, good."

"Good?"

Sal laughed. "Jesus, Mary, and Joseph, you're so clueless."

"No, I mean, I was just, uh, wondering if you would go with me," Brady said. "I know it's kind of late notice."

"Seriously?"

Emily kicked my foot under the table. I scowled at her.

Brady's smile faltered as he gave her a nervous glance. "Uh...yeah?"

"Oh my gosh. Sorry," I said. My cheeks heated. "I didn't mean it like that. I'm not going because I have to do something Saturday night. It's not you. Really. My mom roped me into this play, and I can't get out of it now."

I knew perfectly well that if I told my mother someone like Brady had asked me out, she'd practically trip over herself making sure I had a dress and shoes to match. There'd be a tight curfew to observe, but things like dances and games were what normal kids did. It'd be a sign that I was okay. No, the thing standing in my way wasn't the fearsome Barbara Young. It was me.

To be honest, there were a lot worse ways a girl could spend an evening than wrapped up in Brady's chiseled arms. But I wasn't ready. No matter what the all-powerful Instagram numbers may have said, I was still weird Bridget, Girl Interrupted, the one who'd lost her shit after her sister had died, and most recently the one who'd gone toe to toe with a bona fide serial killer. Not to mention that any date now ran the very high risk of ghostly third wheels.

19

No thanks.

"It's cool," he said. His shoulders slumped a little, but he smiled and nodded. "Maybe another time, then."

"Sure," I said. I watched in disbelief as Brady and his tight shirt walked away. When he'd disappeared again into the crowd of kids, leaving behind the distant alien planet of Bridget and Friends, I turned to Emily and said, "Did that really just happen?"

"Okay, really?" Emily said. "How many is that?"

"Just two, but that's two more than I've gotten in a long time. We are officially in Bizarro World." Along with my newfound social media windfall, I'd apparently become at least marginally dateable. Last week, Justin Marsh from my gym class had asked me to the dance, but I'd given him the same excuse I'd given Brady. It was all too weird.

"You really should go. At least you'll get a free dinner out of it and probably make out with the dude of your choice."

"I'm glad you see the opportunity in everything," I said. I turned to Sal. "And you! What's with the running commentary?"

"I'm just a casual observer," he said.

"Observers don't talk," I muttered. He laughed. "Anyway, I really did promise Mom I'd help her with the play Saturday night."

"Seriously? You've been looking for any excuse to get out of it. Come on, do it for me," Emily said. "Mom won't let me go, and I want to know who shows up drunk and who makes the most questionable fashion choices."

The fifth period bell rang, a chime that barely rose over the lunchroom din. "Oh look, time for class."

"You're lame," Emily said. "I love you like a fat kid loves cake, but you're so lame."

"Guilty as charged," I replied. "Thanks for the study help, Sal." I took Valerie's necklace out of the small pocket on the front of my backpack and held it up. "I need some peace and quiet for a couple of hours, okay?"

He gave me a snappy salute. "I'm going shopping."

I shook my head and latched the fine silver chain around my neck. As a consolation for being stuck with this curse forever, Kale had put his own touch on Valerie's dragonfly necklace. Now when I wore it, I couldn't see the dead. I wasn't sure if it drove them away or just dropped a filter over my eyes, like putting on sunglasses.

He'd warned me then not to wear it too long, and I understood why. As soon as the silver chain touched my skin, I felt as if I'd stepped into an elevator that shot up fifty stories in two seconds flat. Pressure swelled inside my head, making my ears pop painfully. And my vision wasn't quite right; all the colors were faded and washed out. Once I took it off, I'd have a killer headache.

Still, it was nice to feel relatively normal for a while. As I inched down the crowded hallway, I didn't worry that a spirit was going to materialize in front of me. School was hard enough without a needy ghost wailing about his problems when I was trying to take notes in Spanish class. And quite often, that was literal wailing. Talk about distracting.

The crowd of students around me was unusually happy, even though it was exam week. People were walking around with candy canes hanging out of their mouths. Candygrams had been delivered this morning in homeroom. I'd actually gotten a few, and they weren't all from Emily, who had a tradition of always sending me one signed, *Your Secret Lovahhhhh <3*.

Unfortunately, the necklace did nothing about opportunistic vultures like Allie Williams materializing in front of me. Ugh, she was like a cockroach, squirming out of some invisible crack in the wall. She flipped her long, dark hair over her shoulder, her face set in a smile too big to be real. "Bridge! Hey, girl!"

"Hi," I said flatly as I kept walking. The nickname made my skin crawl, doubly so coming out of Allie's mouth. She hurried to walk next to me. If she linked her arm in mine, I was going to shove her into the nearest trash can and pray that someone got it on video.

"Are you going to the Christmas dance?"

"Sorry," I said. "I told my mom I'd help her with something Saturday night."

"Oh, are you sure?"

"Yep," I said flatly. "Totally sure."

"That super sucks. But it's so cool that you're helping your mom. I bet you guys have bonded really well. How is she doing? You know..."

I felt my PB&J turn to lava in my stomach. After the way Allie had ditched me when my sister had died, I couldn't tolerate her bringing it up. She didn't know anything about me or my mom. "What do you mean?"

"Uh, I..." Allie stammered. Her smile faltered as if she'd realized she was nearing dangerous territory. I wouldn't have thought she was self-aware enough to notice. "You know, just in general."

For a minute, I considered dumping the biggest pile of awkward guilt imaginable on her. *I'm not sure what you'd be talking about, Allie. Are you referring to the fact that my sister—her eldest child—died tragically? Or maybe the time when I got brained by a serial killer? To which of these situations are you referring?*

Instead, I forced a smile. "She's fantastic."

"Oh, that's so good to hear," Allie said. "So good." She nodded rapidly and looked like she wanted to crawl out of her own skin. Her smile was actually twitching at the corners. Her discomfort brought me a tiny bit of joy, enough to make the encounter worth it. Her eyes went manically wide as she shook off the awkwardness. "So, yeah! You'd better put the Valentine's Ball on your calendar! We're going to get a limo and go to the Red Door for dinner first. We can double date it! Wouldn't that be super-fun?"

"We'll see," I said. It was a cruel twist of fate that I had three of my six classes with Allie. I'd been able to ignore her for the better part of a year, but recent developments had made me the target of her fickle attention. I wished I had Emily's backbone. I talked a big game about Allie, but I didn't have it in me to shut her down hard, even though she totally deserved it.

"*Hola, Señorita Young,*" Mrs. Chavez said as I walked in. "*Señorita Williams.*"

"*Hola, Señora Chavez,*" I said. How did you say "liar" in Spanish?

"*¿Ya están listos para tomar el examen?*"

Something about taking the exam. I smiled and hoped for the best. "*Sí, Señora.*"

I sat down behind John Chang, who immediately turned around to fix me with a disapproving look. At some point in the last month or so, John had made it his personal goal to drag me out of the house to hang out with his friends. So far, he'd been unsuccessful, but to be fair, I'd had a pretty intense couple of weeks. He seemed nice enough, but I hadn't quite broken through the mental block yet. "What's this I hear about you not going to the Christmas dance?" he asked. His dark eyes narrowed at me, but his lips were curved up in a sneaky smile. "I thought Brady actually had a chance."

"How did you already—"

"You're a heartbreaker, Bridget," John said with a wry smile. He held up his phone. "Age of the iPhone."

"*Señor Chang, guardó su teléfono,*" Mrs. Chavez said.

"*Sí, Señora,*" he said, grinning as he shoved his phone into his backpack. He gave me a mock-serious expression. "This discussion is not over, young lady."

Mrs. Chavez started handing out the answer sheets and reminding us about the honor code. As she passed out the exam packets and told us for the tenth time not to write on it, I wondered if it would really be so bad to go to the Christmas dance after all. I'd fought Mom and Emily kicking and screaming over the Fall Court, but I'd actually sort of had fun wearing a fancy dress and feeling pretty for a night.

Then again, hanging out with Brady meant hanging out with his best friend, Sumir, who was taking Allie to the dance. That crowd was something I wanted no part of. If Natalie's older brother, Michael, had asked me, it would have been another story. But going to a high school dance was probably the last thing he wanted to do after burying his sister barely three weeks before.

That was life, wasn't it? The perfect, cute senior boy came along, but plot twist: his sister had been abducted, brutally murdered, and then lingered after death as a vengeful spirit intent on using me to solve her own murder. And I'd lied through my teeth about it the whole time and eventually kicked him in the balls so I could steal his car to go find Emily. It wasn't the stuff of which rom-coms were made, to say the least.

I sighed and returned my attention to the Spanish exam. My grades had sucked for the last few years, but I'd been trying to recover a little. Still, I probably should have done more than ten minutes of cramming on the day of the test. Maybe I'd add it to my New Year's Resolution.

My heart thumped as I scanned the first page. Instinctively, I looked over my shoulder for my sister but had the chilling realization that she was gone for real this time. I sighed and brushed my fingers across the dragonfly necklace. I was tempted to take it off and ask for Sal's help after all.

*Okay, you know this*, I told myself. *You just faced a serial killer. A Spanish exam is nothing.*

# CHAPTER FOUR

**W**HAT ABOUT A NEW STROLLER for Reina?" Sal asked. I struggled to lift the huge plastic bin of costumes out of Mom's trunk while the strapping policeman's ghost watched. Kale could lift small objects if he focused, but it would be really great if more spirits could get on the whole physical-interaction bandwagon. We could clean the house *The Sorcerer's Apprentice* style, and hopefully with a better outcome than poor Mickey.

"Again, Sal," I said, stumbling under the weight. "It's going to be super creepy. Finding a brand-new stroller on the porch sounds like the beginning of a horror movie." I made a scary face and did my best dramatic movie trailer voice. "You woke the baby, and now he's out for blood. Coming to theaters near you."

He stared at me with a blank expression. "That's not funny."

The humor dried up like sand on my tongue. "I'm sorry."

"I can't just sit around and do nothing. This is my family," he said. For a second, his form flared as though a light had flashed inside him. I could have sworn I saw fresh blood bubble from the neat puncture over his breast pocket. Sal was a relatively calm spirit, but his dedication to his girlfriend was keeping him here. As his first Christmas after death approached, he'd been getting progressively more on edge.

The church parking lot was filling up with cars for the evening's rehearsal. Families trickled through the parking lot, bundled in heavy jackets to block out the sharp chill. A damp wind blew, giving credence to the rumors of snow on the way this weekend.

"What if we do an anonymous gift?" I suggested.

"But I want her to know it's from me. She needs to know I'm still watching out for her."

"Sal, that's going to terrify her."

Instead of going up the main steps, where I'd have to pass through the gauntlet of church moms, I walked around to the side entrance. Past the main steps, the sidewalk branched off, with one path ending at the side door and the other leading into a small cemetery surrounded by a waist-high brick wall. Two metal benches flanked the entryway to the cemetery.

"I miss her so much," he said suddenly. I paused and put the bin down on the closer of the two benches. "I go see them all the time, but I can't smell Reina anymore. I can't touch her hair. And Veronica cries, and I can't do anything about it."

My eyes stung, and I sat down on the bench, looking up at him. I preferred the light-hearted Sal, but this was the pain hiding behind the smile and jokes. "I know. It totally sucks."

"Yeah, it does. I would give anything to make her smile again."

"She will," I said. "One of these days."

I held out my hand, and Sal put his in mine, or as close as he could manage. Even in his state of grief, he didn't have the intense anguish or rage that made some spirits strong. He couldn't touch me at all. His hand passed through mine like water.

His face creased as his warm brown eyes squeezed shut. "And when she does, it'll be because she's put me behind her. Then she'll find someone else to make her smile. And I'll just be a memory she tries not to think about anymore."

I didn't often wish to touch the ghosts I encountered, but I wished I could give Sal a hug right then. It would take a power far greater than what I had to make him feel better. I couldn't fix his problem, because his problem was being unquestionably, irreversibly dead. No amount of positive thinking would change it.

Instead, I settled for putting my hand on the bench where his rested. We made no contact, but in our way, we occupied the same space. It was the best I could do.

"Young lady, you shouldn't be out here alone," an unfamiliar voice said. I looked up to see a middle-aged man shuffle out of the graveyard. I sighed. He wore an old-fashioned blue-and-white seersucker suit, well-tailored to his slender frame. With his dark hair slicked back, he looked like he'd stepped off the cover of a magazine from the fifties. Either he was really old-fashioned, or he was really dead.

Not tonight.

"I'm fine," I said. "Just getting some fresh air."

"She's all right," Sal said, giving the newcomer a suspicious look.

"No offense, son, but in your condition, I don't think you can do much to protect her," the man said. Well, that answered that question.

Sal's face fell, and he faded away into the night. Probably to go shopping for more potentially creepy Christmas gifts. A flare of irritation swelled in my chest like a gas bubble.

"Wrong time, dude," I said. "And you're not exactly Mr. Protector yourself, either."

The man shrugged and sat next to me on the bench. Apparently unfazed by my biting wit, he draped one arm over the back of the bench. A chilly breeze accompanied him. "I suppose I don't need to tell you how unusual it is that you can see me."

"No, you don't," I said. "I'm Bridget."

"A pleasure, my dear. I'm Peter," he said. "Like the disciple."

"Or Cottontail," I replied. "Is there something I can help you with, Peter?"

Peter shook his head and tipped his head to look up at the sky. "Oh, I'm just enjoying the evening."

I looked around. It was cold and damp outside, not that those things had any effect on Peter. "What exactly are you enjoying about it?"

Peter gestured overhead. "Dead or not, I can still appreciate a night sky, blanketed in stars. I used to be quite the astronomy buff. If I'm not mistaken, there's Venus." He pointed up, which didn't really help the search. All I saw was the expanse of black, pinpointed with stars barely peeking through the haze of clouds.

"How long ago was that? Because depending on your answer, we might have to have a difficult discussion about Pluto."

"Well, I was part of the Greatest Generation," Peter said. "We fought in the—"

"Blah, blah, blah," a female voice interrupted. A pretty woman in a swingy red dress and glittering high heels materialized in front of me. "We survived the Depression and two World Wars," she mimicked. "And here we all are. We all end up six feet under the same dirt."

Peter shook his head. "There's no need to be rude, Annette."

"There is when you're talking this poor girl's ear off," she said. Her platinum hair was styled in sleek finger waves with a red rose pinned behind her ear. "I know a girl trying to avoid being chatted up when I see one." Like it had only just hit her, she cocked her head. "You can see us?"

I nodded.

"How unusual. I'm Annette. But I suppose you figured that out. You strike me as a sharp girl."

It still felt strange to communicate with the dead so openly. Before, I'd had to find some kind of conduit to let me communicate directly with the spirits. Usually, it had been electronics. Natalie had spoken to me through my sister's old laptop. Sal had spoken through a stolen police radio. With most spirits, I never figured it out, but instead relied on awkward charades and a lot of games of Twenty Questions. As it turned out, that had been a sort of natural protection to keep the spirits from getting too close to me.

But I'd given up that protection in order to help Natalie, and in turn, I'd gained the ability to talk to ghosts directly. When Lena May had shown up, she'd started chatting as if it was the most normal thing in the world. She'd been my first spirit since Natalie, and it had taken me a few minutes of conversation to realize she was dead and not a particularly ancient church lady. Peter and Annette made two more for whom the communication gap simply didn't exist.

"Bridget!"

Who now?

I looked up to see the very alive silhouette of my mother standing in the open side door of the church. Little clouds of fog puffed out of her nose as she scolded. "What's the holdup?"

"Oh, hello, ma'am," Peter said, giving a crisp salute. Mom ignored him, and Annette snickered. "Never mind. Doesn't run in the family, I suppose."

"Sorry, I lost my balance and dropped the box. It took me a couple of minutes to put everything back in," I lied. "I was just resting for a second."

Mom sighed and gestured to hurry up. "Well, come on, we need those costumes."

"Coming," I said. I hurried after her, bumping my hip on the box as I turned to fit through the narrow doorway. Peter and Annette followed, passing through me in a cold breeze to walk into the sanctuary.

I left the box on the floor near the altar, then hurried for the stairs to the balcony.

"Bridget!"

The familiar voice sent a wave of dread washing over me. Damn. I'd almost made it. I turned slowly to see Mom's friend Donna. I tried not to wince as I said, "Yes ma'am?"

The jingle bells on the sleeves of her Christmas sweater tinkled as she gestured for me to come over. I trudged over to her, hoping my displeasure didn't show on my face. Donna folded me in a perfumed hug. "I've been meaning to check on you and see how you're doing. You know, after everything." The way she leaned on the word *everything* was loaded with meaning. She wasn't going to come right out and say it. At least not to my face; it would be easier when she was surrounded by a circle of other gossipy women to spread my business.

"I'm fine," I said mechanically. "Really."

Her blue eyes were wide and concerned under her thin, penciled brows. "Are you worried about him...coming back?"

My eyes widened. *Good Lord, lady.* "Well, if I wasn't before, I might be now," I said before I could hold the words back. "Really, I'm fine."

Donna nodded. "Well, I want you to know I'm praying for you."

*Save it.* I forced my dry lips into a smile that felt like it would split open and break off the bottom half of my face. "I sure do appreciate it," I said, hoping I sounded as sincere as Mom did. "Sorry to run off, but I need to go study. Bye!"

I rushed to the stairs at the back of the sanctuary and took them two at a time, trying to escape before any more of Mom's busybody friends caught me. Peter and Annette were close behind me, while Lena May was already upstairs, sitting in the center of the front pew. Her translucent hands were folded in her lap as she watched the bustle in the sanctuary below.

"You're late," Lena May said. She looked up. "Oh, hello, Peter!" she added. She arched one eyebrow. "Miss Moore."

Great. Ghost drama. The living were bad enough without sitting through my own episode of *Days of our Afterlives.*

I shrugged off my puffy purple jacket and tossed it onto the pew. One sleeve dangled to the dusty floor below. Lena May gave it a pointed look. I silently straightened it and laid it over the back of the pew, then looked to her for approval. The corner of her red-lipsticked mouth quirked up. I sat next to her. "Lena May, can I ask you a question?"

"Of course, dear," she said. She reached out to pat my hand, but like Sal, she was a relatively weak spirit. Her hand passed through mine, but she held it in position as if she was touching my hand. There was no physical contact, but I could feel the cold pressing against my skin, like putting my hand up to the air conditioning vent in the car. Even though she was mimicking the motions of being alive, it was comforting.

"My friend Sal," I said. "He wants to do something for his girlfriend and their son."

"I gathered as much."

"He does realize he's dead?" Annette said. "Hard to do much from the grave."

"He just wants to provide for them," I said defensively. "He's trying to be a good man."

"Annette didn't know many of those," Peter said, settling into place at the end of the pew. "No wonder it's hard for her to recognize one."

"Still don't," Annette snapped. She crossed her arms over a generous chest

31

and leaned against the wall. "Not that it's any of your business."

"It's rather difficult at first," Lena May said, ignoring their argument. "To detach, I mean."

"What do you mean?"

"I lingered here first because I simply wanted to make sure my family would be all right. But secretly, I believed the world would end with me. Imagine my surprise when it didn't, and my family managed to keep on living without me. Of course, they shed tears. There was no shortage of love. But I learned there's not a one of us so important that our loss would stop the world from turning." She turned and gave me a sad smile. "If he wants to help his lady love, then he must be willing not only to let her go, but for her to let *him* go."

I nodded slowly. "That's a lot easier said than done."

"Most things worth doing are," Lena May said. "But it's the only way he'll ever find peace."

"So you don't think we should do anything for her?"

"I never said that," Lena May replied. "Everyone needs to know they're loved. And Christmas is the perfect time for it. I trust you'll figure it out."

"You didn't really answer my question," I said. Downstairs, the choir gathered on stage as the director ushered them to their places. I watched the cute pigtailed redhead take her place in the front row. She wore a tinsel halo and a long white robe. Lena May's green eyes glittered, her pale face actually glowing as she watched her great-granddaughter. "Lena, why do you stay, then?"

"Hmm?"

"You said at first you stayed because you were worried about your family. But you said they were all right without you. And you don't seem angry, so I'm assuming you don't have something left to resolve. So why do you stay?"

Lena May shrugged. "What can I say? I spent my whole life in this church, and I can't think of a better place to linger." But something pulled at her eyes. I wasn't about to say *bullshit* in the balcony of a church, but that was exactly what Lena May was dumping in my lap.

"Well, that's a load of malarkey if I ever heard one," Annette muttered. I liked her.

"Mind your business, you brazen hussy," Lena May said, her politeness dissolving into a sharp tone that told me she'd run a tight ship when she'd been alive.

"Maybe you should buy a guard dog," Peter said. "German shepherds are solid dogs."

"Huh?" Annette said.

Peter pointed to me. "The copper's Christmas dilemma."

Annette rolled her eyes. "Typical."

As they bickered, I tuned them out and opened Facebook on my phone. It was still startling to open the app and see the notifications about people who had liked my posts. For years, my only real friend had been Emily. I had a few other friends on Facebook, but they were the kind of people who added everyone they knew so they could count their friends and followers like it was some sort of Awesomeness rating.

I scrolled through a bunch of posts about results for the "What's your Superpower?" quiz. A story flew by, grabbing my attention as hard as a hook in the lip. I scrolled back to see it.

***Please Share!!! Our daughter isn't answering her phone and we're worried about her safety! Her name is Diana Brown, and she attends Mount Sharon High School. Her friends said she left school after third period today. If anyone has heard from her, please tell her to call us and let us know she's safe.***

There was a picture of the girl, a pretty brunette, with her boyfriend, an attractive boy in a Mount Sharon Lacrosse T-shirt. They both looked close to my age.

The post had been shared from Diana's mother, Teresa, with her added comments below.

**We think she might be with her boyfriend Corey Walker, but he's not answering his phone either. Please share this post so we can make sure she's safe!**

There were more comments below speculating on what had happened; some were kind, and others not so much. Some suggested that they'd simply lost service or had a dead phone battery, while others suggested they were off getting high somewhere.

My stomach sank. I'd seen this before. Was this the Runaway Killer? Surely he wouldn't have been so stupid as to start taking girls again from the same place. Yet it echoed Natalie's disappearance, including people saying nothing had happened and that she'd run away. But judging by Diana's mother's comments, it didn't look like she was the type to disappear on her own.

*No.* It was silly. They were teenagers, and they'd probably just skipped school for the afternoon. I mean, I'd done the same thing myself. Although, to be fair, I'd been tracking down a serial killer, so maybe I wasn't the best example.

I hesitated, then clicked on the Share button. Surely they'd turn up tonight.

"What's that?" Annette asked.

"Huh?"

"The glowing thing in your hand," Annette said, taking a tentative step toward me. "It looks like a tiny television. I see people here with them all the time."

"It's a telephone," Lena May said. "People are so attached to them these days."

"That's not a telephone," Annette snapped. Lena May rolled her eyes in response.

"Yeah," Peter said. "Where's the cord?"

I sighed. Explaining wireless technology to decades-dead spirits wasn't my favorite way to spend an evening. As I tried to explain the magical device known as a smartphone to my ghostly companions, my mind still lingered on the missing person post.

If they'd left after third period, they hadn't even been gone twelve hours.

Then again, a lot could happen in twelve hours.

This wasn't my job. Someone else would do something.

*Dammit.*

I sighed. "I'll be back."

# CHAPTER FIVE

I MANAGED TO DODGE both my mom and Donna on the way out of the church. As I stepped out into the night, I pulled my coat tighter around me. With the sun sinking beneath the horizon, it was bitterly cold outside. The overgrown trees cast long, murky shadows over the crowded graveyard.

"Kale?" I said hesitantly. Kale claimed he wasn't an angel, but he was as close to one as I'd ever come. And he had a way of putting things into perspective that always both irritated me and reassured me at the same time.

The night wind picked up, rustling dead leaves over the flat, time-worn stones of the graveyard. I jumped at the whispering sound and took a tentative step back into the hazy yellow light cast by the exterior lights. Even when one saw ghosts on the regular, it was still scary to be in a graveyard at night.

The wind whipped harder around me, but it was strangely warm now. I caught Kale's clean scent a second before I saw him. He smelled alive and fresh, which was a serious improvement over the usual funk of my spirit companions.

His bare feet glowed faintly, which made me envy his immunity to the cold weather. I could already feel the cold leaching into my toes through the mesh of my sneakers.

"You rang?" he said, lips quirking up in a smile.

"I think I might need your help."

"If it's with those costumes, you're out of luck." He waggled his spectral fingers. "I'm not much for fine motor skills."

"Be serious."

He cocked his head, his smile evaporating. "What is it?"

"Missing kids," I said. "Well, maybe." I filled him in on the post I'd seen. Thankfully Kale had been around long enough that I didn't have to explain smartphones or Facebook to him, though he was still confused by the purpose of the selfie. Weren't we all?

"And you think something happened?" he asked when I'd finished.

"No idea," I said. "But it's weird, right?"

"Well, kids take off all the time without telling their parents where they're going," he said. He raised an eyebrow at me. "Present company included."

"It was for a perfectly good reason."

"I'm sure these kids thought the same," Kale replied. He drifted past me and settled onto a concrete contemplation bench. A weathered bronze plaque read *In Memory of Lena May Robertson 1928—2011*. She really had been around a long time, then.

"So you don't think I should do anything?"

"Never said that. You're probably a little trigger-happy after Natalie, but if you want to check it out, then let's do it. Better safe than sorry, right?"

I let out a sigh of relief. "Can you search for her? Like you did for Natalie?"

He nodded. "It'll take me a while. But you got it."

"Okay. I'll be here."

"You should go in," he said. "It's getting cold, and there's a storm blowing in."

"How would you know?"

He laughed. "Well, you're shivering." He put one ghostly hand on my shoulder in an oddly protective gesture. For a second, I felt its weight. "Someone has to have sense out of the two of us."

I was suddenly overcome with the urge to put my hand on his. Would it feel warm under mine? Or would it pass harmlessly through the illusion?

"Go on," he said.

"I'm an independent woman."

"Well, let's not freeze to death in the name of independence, eh?"

I nodded and walked back toward the church. "Let me know as—"

"Soon as I find something," he finished for me. "I hope I don't. You realize if I find something, that's probably bad."

"Well," I said flatly. "Then I hope you come up empty-handed."

He gave a snappy little salute and disappeared in a rush of clean-smelling wind. As he'd asked, I went back inside. Despite my half-hearted protests, I was glad I did. The heat was blasting inside. Instead of returning to the sanctuary, which echoed with the slightly off-key singing of a middle school choir, I followed the back hallway toward the Sunday school classrooms. After testing three of the doors, I found the Pre-Kinders classroom unlocked.

I flipped on the lights and let myself in. The room was decorated with construction paper jungle animals and smelled like crayons and baby wipes. I pulled out a red plastic chair clearly meant for someone half my size and sat down at a low table. My knees jutted up comically over the edge of the table.

The bright-colored room with all its pint-sized furniture reminded me of being little again, back when the world had been simple. And if my life had gotten this complicated by the age of seventeen, I could only imagine what was going to happen by the time I was thirty.

I wasn't sure what I wanted—for Kale to come back right away with information, or for him to come back with nothing. Even after two years of this, I still didn't fully understand how the spirit world worked. But Kale had a way of sensing the newly dead. Back when I'd first heard Natalie was missing, he'd gone out to search for her. He might have found her if she hadn't beaten him to the punch. After I'd found a silver bracelet belonging to her, Natalie had shown up uninvited in my bedroom and scared the hell out of me. I'd banished her temporarily, but she'd harassed me until I acknowledged her and agreed to help her.

As I sat there in the tiny chair, I felt too still, too idle. Maybe something awful was happening to Diana Brown. Maybe she'd been kidnapped, or maybe she'd driven off the road, or maybe she was hurt and crying for help, or—

"Stop it," I told myself. Constantly hanging out with the dead hadn't done much for my worldview. I was as bad as my mother; I assumed the worst all the time. Then again, I spent a lot of time dealing with the walking, talking aftermath of the worst-case scenario.

Still, it felt wrong to just sit and wait on Kale. I'd gotten most of my police and crime education from TV. Mom and I didn't talk much these days, but I sometimes sat on the couch using my laptop while she watched reruns of *Law and Order* or *Criminal Minds*. They both said the same thing—the first twenty-four hours were the most important in a missing persons case. If someone wasn't found by then, the chance that they'd be found alive dropped so much as to be completely depressing.

This was new territory. Until Natalie had come along, all my cases had been…whatever the opposite of time-sensitive was. There had never been lives at stake back then, so I could do my research at my own leisurely pace. I'd had the luxury of working around my school schedule and bumming rides off people. Not anymore.

*Okay, options, Bridget.*

The first person who came to mind was Tara Lynn Bledsoe. She was another "sensitive," as Kale called us, and as an adult who'd dealt with it her whole life, she had a lot more experience than I did. But Kale and I had…well, we'd downright bullied her into helping us with Natalie, after which she'd told me in no uncertain terms that I wasn't welcome on her doorstep. And Tara packed a hell of a spiritual punch. If I had to, I'd call her up, but I wasn't going to antagonize her over nothing.

Then there was Detective Fulbright, who I'd left anonymous tips about Natalie. After it all hit the fan, he'd realized I was his source and left me his number in case I got any more "feelings" about cases. He seemed like the better of my two options.

I scrolled through my contacts until I found Fulbright. I hesitated, then pressed *Call.* My heart thumped as the first ring went through.

What was I going to tell him?

*Hey Detective, I saw something that worried me on Facebook.*

Ring.

*No, I don't actually have anything to tell you. No feelings yet.*

Ring.

The phone clicked, and my stomach leaped up to use my uvula as a punching bag. "You've reached Detective Tom Fulbright. Leave me your name, your number, and a detailed message, and I'll—"

I hung up. Ugh.

Right about now would have been the perfect time for Sal to show up with his police background.

"Sal?" I said tentatively. I closed my eyes and pictured him. Light blue uniform shirt with the neat hole over the breast pocket. Olive complexion, head full of curly dark hair. Slightly crooked smile. Heart of gold. As I pictured his face, I imagined myself reaching a hand out for him.

"Look, I know you're upset because of the holidays, but this is really important," I said quietly. "Please. Sal? I really need you here."

"Bridget?"

My stomach churned. I whipped around in my seat to see my mother standing at the doorway. Her brow was creased, her head tilted in confusion. "What are you doing in here?"

"Uh, I…" *Crap.* "I was just talking to someone."

"Talking to who?"

I held out my phone. "Emily."

"Okay," Mom said. There was something weird in her tone. Had she heard me?

Crap, crap, crap. I cleared my throat and stood up. My knee banged against the low table. Ouch. My cheeks were hot as I tried to avoid her stare. "I was trying not to interrupt rehearsal."

"I see. Come on back," she said. "I didn't see you for a while, and I got worried."

I turned off the lights in the classroom as I walked out the door behind Mom. Great. If she kept this overprotective thing going, it was going to be extremely difficult to help Diana Brown.

The sound of the angel choir got louder as we walked back to the sanctuary. When Mom headed back to the front pew to continue working, I made a beeline for the back stairs. I paused for a moment and watched Mom talking to Donna. She pointed to the hallway we'd just come from, then threw up her hands in frustration and shook her head. The whole exchange made my stomach twist into a strange knot of shame and anger.

There was a part of me that wanted to grab her by the shoulders and tell her everything. I'd tried, a long time ago, back when my sister Valerie was the only ghost I'd seen. Her response was to put me in therapy and pretend it never happened. I could only imagine what she'd say now if I told her I had Bridget's

Bunch of ghosts in the balcony.

But I was so tired of being a disappointment to her. I wasn't as outgoing and beautiful as my dead older sister. Since her death, Valerie had become the Perfect Daughter, and I couldn't measure up unless I died tragically young, too. Then there was my younger brother, who was a star student and never gave Mom even a shred of attitude. He was dealing with things fine, so why couldn't I? As far as Mom was concerned, I was a walking disaster with bad grades and even worse social skills. In other words, an overwhelming disappointment.

When I reached the balcony, Annette and Lena May were still bickering. Peter had bowed out and was sitting at the edge of the balcony with his eyes closed. A floorboard creaked as I sat down on the pew next to him. He opened one dark brown eye and peeked at me.

Back in his day, Peter would have been a handsome guy. With a strong jaw and clean shave, he reminded me of the old black-and-white movie stars. He appeared to be in his forties, and I wondered what exactly happened to him. There was no bullet hole in his sharp-pressed suit, nor telltale marks around his neck.

"You have a problem," he said.

"I have lots," I said. "Be more specific."

His eyebrow arched. "You have moxie."

"I do not."

"It's a compliment," he said, a half-smile pulling at the right side of his mouth. "Anyway, I only meant that you look troubled."

"There are kids missing. And I'm worried."

"You're afraid it might happen to you?"

"No. But I feel like I have to help."

Peter cocked his head. "Why? You're just a child."

I gestured around. "Hello. Not exactly a normal one."

"No, I suppose not. Perhaps we could help."

"How?"

"Well, the three of us aren't in a particular hurry to be anywhere," Peter said wryly. "We could help you search."

"What's this?" Lena May said, turning away from her argument with Annette.

"And another thing—"

"Hush, girl," Lena May interrupted, waving her hand dismissively at Annette. The younger woman's red lips went into a wide O.

"He's right," I said. I remembered how Tara had called Natalie and the killer's other victims. She'd summoned them from all over. Could I do the same thing? "Do you guys communicate with other spirits?"

"As a rule, no," Annette said. "Present company excepted."

"Lucky us," Lena May said, her nostrils flaring in distaste. "But I believe we can. What are you thinking?"

Facebook had its limits. Sure, it was nice to share a post and hope that someone heard from Diana and Corey. But if something had happened to them, then they needed people actively looking for them. And a spirit, unconcerned with things like walls or exhaustion, was the perfect volunteer for a search party.

"I want you to spread out and search. If you meet another spirit on the way, ask them to help. You're looking for a girl and a boy," I said. I pulled up the Facebook post again and showed them the picture. "This is them."

"And if we find them?" Peter said. "We can't exactly help them. We can't even talk to them."

"No, but you can come back and tell me exactly where they are," I said. "And then I can tell the police."

Lena May nodded. "I'm afraid I can't go far. I used to be able to cross town, but over the years, I find myself bound closer and closer to my home. Where I…well, you know."

"Then let's make it a game of Telephone," I said.

Annette stared at me. "What does this have to do with a telephone?"

I rolled my eyes. Pop culture references were so lost on the dead. "If Lena May can go as far as—"

"Highway 2," she said. "More or less."

"Highway 2," I finished. "Then maybe there's another spirit nearby who can go farther. Just keep passing the message. So it spreads out." It would be like one of those math problems we'd done last year in Algebra II. *If Bridget tells three ghosts to hunt for a missing person, and each of those ghosts tells three more ghosts, exactly how many days will she be spending in the loony bin?*

"That's actually rather clever," Peter said. "I like it."

"You sound surprised," I said.

"I am. Pleasantly so. Maybe there's hope for your generation yet."

I rolled my eyes. "Okay, go search. As fast and far as you can."

# CHAPTER SIX

**B**RIDGET, WE REALLY NEED to go," Mom said. "Get your stuff."

I cast a longing stare up at the balcony, which was still empty and had been since I'd sent the spirits on their way. Rehearsal had ended ten minutes ago, with the angel choir shucking off their white robes and returning to the earthly realm of teenagers with questionable pitch. Colin was practically dancing at the door to leave. I never thought I'd be desperate for a bunch of ghosts to show up and start yammering at me. How long did it take the lingering dead to organize a search party? I was guessing Siri wouldn't have an answer for me.

"I left a mess in the balcony," I said. "I should really go clean it up."

Mom waved her hand dismissively and zipped her coat up over her thin pink scrubs. "No one will be back in here until tomorrow. It'll be fine."

"But you always say never to leave a mess. It's rude." Surely she'd have to concede the point, considering how many times she'd nagged me about it over the years.

"Bridget, I'm tired, and—"

"Is there any of that potluck food left? I could go for a—"

"Bridget!" Mom exclaimed. She sighed and combed her hair back. "What has gotten into you? First you disappear for half of rehearsal, and when we're actually ready to leave, you're dragging your feet."

What was I supposed to tell her? *Sorry Mom, I'm waiting to hear back on a spooky search party?* I needed to be here. My heart raced. Surely they'd be back soon. I just had to stall her.

"I know, but I—"

"Enough," Mom said, snapping her fingers. "Look, it's sleeting outside already. We need to get home before it picks up. They're saying we might get snow tonight."

*Kale called it.* All the more reason for me to hang out here and wait.

"Awesome!" Colin said. "No school."

"Tomorrow is Saturday, dork."

Colin's face fell. "Shut up!"

"Be nice to him," Mom said. "We're going, so unless you intend to sleep here tonight, get your stuff and get to the car."

I hesitated. "Can I?" I could always call Emily for a ride after my searching spirits came back.

Mom's eyes went wide. Her nostrils flared like she might start breathing fire at any second. I knew I was pushing her buttons, but she was making my life unnecessarily difficult. Once again, the universe was hammering home the point that I needed to get my license and start driving. Then again, with the way things had gone the last few weeks, she probably would have given me a mandate to be home before dark and had a tracking chip implanted in my forehead for good measure.

"Bridget, get your stuff and go to the car," Mom said slowly.

"But you just said—"

"Jesus, take the wheel."

"Mom—"

"Bridget Leanne Young, if you don't stop arguing with me, you are going to be grounded for your entire Christmas break. So think very carefully about how you proceed," Mom said evenly. When she got good and mad, she didn't yell. She got this scary, eye-of-the-storm calm that meant trouble was brewing.

Colin was watching intently and making no attempt to hide his glee.

"Fine," I said.

"I'm sorry?"

"Yes, ma'am," I corrected. I slung my backpack over my shoulder and stormed out the side door. An icy sting hit my face as I stepped into the sleet. I hurried to the car and grabbed the handle on the passenger side right as Colin did. "No. Get in the back."

"Mom!" he protested. "She got to ride up front on the way here."

"Colin, it's a ten-minute ride home. Stop whining and get in the back," Mom said. "Both of you are about to drive me insane. Just get in the car so we can go home."

Colin looked like she'd smacked him, and I almost felt bad for him. *Welcome to my world, buddy.* At least I was used to her ire directed my way. It was a whole new experience for the Precious Angel.

I sank into the front seat and wedged my backpack between my feet. The seatbelt pressed the edges of my phone into my hip, and I tried to gauge how long I would have to wait to take it out without Mom making a snarky comment about it.

Irritation was practically radiating off my mother as we drove home in uncomfortable silence. I reached over to turn up the radio, but it only managed to squeeze out one line of "Jingle Bell Rock" before Mom turned it down.

"I've been listening to Christmas music for the last two hours," she said. "I'd like some quiet."

"Sorry," I replied.

We rode in silence for the next few minutes. The heated air crawled with tension. I didn't know how to talk to her anymore. It had been bad since Valerie had died, but the whole thing with Natalie had made it even worse. She didn't want to let me out of her sight, but at the same time, it felt like she couldn't stand me. No matter what I did, I got on her nerves. It probably would have been easiest if she could keep me locked in my bedroom, a la Rapunzel, where I couldn't bother her or get myself into trouble. I didn't have the hair for it, but at the rate I was going, I'd have time to grow it out before any princes came calling.

When the clock had crawled forward three uncomfortable minutes, I finally took out my phone to check for updates. Mom was already pissed, so how much worse could it get? I went to Teresa Brown's page again, but there were no updates. Surely if she was asking everyone to share the missing information, she'd make another post if Diana had come home. However, she had posted a link earlier in the evening to one of the local news sites.

*8:01 pm—Local authorities are asking community members to call if they have information about the whereabouts of high school students Diana Brown and Corey Walker. Brown and Walker were last seen at Mount Sharon High School around 10:30 this morning. According to a friend of Brown's, the students had completed their exams early and left campus. They reportedly ate lunch at Joni's American Grille. A waitress at Joni's reports a couple fitting the description ate there and left around 1:00 in the afternoon. If you have any information about these students, please call the number below.*

I glanced at the dashboard clock. It was just after nine, which meant they'd been missing for a little over eight hours by now. We hadn't reached full-blown disaster status yet. It was perfectly possible that they'd snuck off to…do what boyfriends and girlfriends do. For eight hours, though? The only boy to ever be in my bed was a spirit of unknown origin. So I wasn't an expert, but eight hours seemed like an awfully long time to be getting freaky.

As if it had a sense for the worst timing possible, my phone rang.

*"I want a hippopotamus for Christmas!"*

Oh, good Lord. Emily had gotten a hold of my phone during lunch earlier in the week. When I'd asked her what she'd done, she'd just smirked and said, "You'll figure it out." It was sad that it took three days for someone to call so I could catch her.

Mom's eyes rolled clear to the back of her head. I made a mental note to steal Emily's phone for revenge as soon as possible. The caller ID read *Detective Fulbright.* I stole a glance at Mom, then silenced the phone. It would only be a few more minutes until we were home where I could have a proper conversation with him.

"Who was that?" Mom asked.

"Emily. I'll call her back at home."

Mom nodded, but the suspicious lift to her eyebrows said she didn't believe me. There was a lot of that going around lately.

The only sound for the rest of the ride home was the rhythmic *whip-whip* of the windshield wipers and the gentle sizzling sound of sleet falling on the roof of the car. Maybe we really would get snow. Even if it wouldn't get us a day out of school, snow in Georgia was rare enough to be exciting even so.

It didn't happen often, but I could remember the last time we'd gotten enough snow to stick. I was maybe eight or nine, and our family had still been all together. Colin had been barely out of diapers, bundled up in a parka and snow pants so thick he could barely walk. Valerie and I had insisted on building snowmen, although there'd been barely enough snow to pack together. We'd pretty much scraped the yard dry, turning our winter wonderland into a gross brown mess. There was a picture somewhere of all of us in front of the old house, with the increasingly rare sighting of Dad. Those were the kind of pictures that had mysteriously been tucked away in storage when we'd moved to our new house. Walking in our house now, you'd think Dad and Val had never existed.

Mom pulled into the driveway and hit the remote for the garage. She'd barely put on the parking brake before Colin dashed out of the car. He practically dove under the still-rising garage door, like James Bond's dorky kid brother. It was Friday night, which meant he had VIP TV access and permission to stay up as late as he wanted playing video games with his friends. Great. I was in for a night of hearing him yell over a headset and Mom yelling back for him to keep it down. I guess there was eventually a benefit to getting good grades and staying out of trouble.

"Bridget, are you sure you're all right?"

"Fine," I said, freezing with my hand on the door handle. My mouth went dry as I tried to anticipate where this conversation was going. Was it grades again? Or maybe my near-tantrum at the church? When it came to aggravating my mother, the possibilities were endless. "Why?"

"When I came looking for you earlier, you were talking to Val. You said 'I really need you here.'"

For God's sake. "Mom, I didn't...I wasn't..." Crap. What did I say that didn't make me sound crazy? Telling her the truth wasn't an option. "I talk to her sometimes. It makes me feel better."

"Honey..."

"What? You talk to Jesus," I said.

Mom spluttered. "It's not the same thing." She sighed. "I'm just concerned. After losing your sister, and then all this craziness over the Fullmer girl and Emily, I wouldn't be surprised if you were traumatized. If you need to start seeing Dr. Rankin again, I can call him."

"Mom, I don't need therapy or medication or whatever else you're thinking," I said. Well, that was debatable. "But I do wish you would trust me and not freak out if you don't have eyes on me for five minutes."

"Well, all things considered, I wish I could trust you, too. But you're going to have to show me I can. It takes a lifetime to build trust and only one moment to break it."

Heat bloomed in my cheeks, and I had to clamp my jaws together to keep from letting loose a tirade. Instead, I flung the door open. "Well, great. Good talk. Glad to know where I stand. Next time someone's in trouble and texts me for help, I'll make sure to ignore them if it's during school hours." Our cover story had been that the Runaway Killer used Emily's phone to text me, luring me to his hideout where I'd staged my dramatic defense. Not quite accurate, but more believable than the ghost version.

"Bridget—"

I stormed past her and into the house. My heart thumped in time with my footsteps as I thundered up the stairs toward my bedroom.

What the hell was her problem? I wasn't out smoking or drinking or getting high. But I skipped school one time, and suddenly I was Untrustworthy Daughter of the Year. Never mind that I totally saved someone's life. And solved a missing persons case. Maybe this was what it felt like to be Batman. Only with way less money, no cool gadgets, and no butler.

So not at all like Batman, then.

I slung my backpack onto the floor and went to slam my door, but Mom beat me to the punch by slamming the door downstairs. The house shuddered. There was a sudden quiet as Colin's game paused, and I heard muffled voices. I froze with my hand on the doorknob, then stuck my head out into the hallway.

Colin was too quiet to hear from downstairs, but I heard Mom reply, "It's okay, sweetie. Your sister and I are just having trouble communicating. It happens with teenage girls. It's not..." Her voice got quieter and I could no longer make out the words, but I knew she was making sure Colin, in all his angelic perfection, knew that he couldn't possibly have done anything wrong, because his big sister had cornered the market on troublemaking.

I rolled my eyes. Was it too much to ask to deal with one kind of drama exclusively? I could handle the mother-daughter drama, or maybe the ghosts and missing people drama, but both at once was too much.

Instead of a good satisfying slam, I closed the door quietly and took out my phone. Fulbright had left me a voicemail. I put it on speaker and paced on the floral purple rug.

"Hello. This is Tom Fulbright. I had a missed call from this number. If you intended to call and still need to reach me, please call me back. Thank you." The detective's voice was gruff and sounded vaguely irritated.

Rescuing Emily from the Runaway Killer had earned me a nasty concussion and half a dozen stitches in my forehead. I'd woken up in the hospital just in time to meet Fulbright, who I'd been feeding anonymous tips for days. He'd tried to intimidate me into revealing how I'd known everything, but I didn't scare easily. Before leaving, he'd left me a business card in case I ever needed to reach him directly. Unless he'd done some snooping, he wouldn't have any reason to know my number. I hesitated with my finger over the *Call Back* option.

"Good news," a male voice said from behind me, breaking my focus on the phone.

Adrenaline spiked and sent a hot rush down my spine. I jumped and spun around to see Kale leaning against my closed door. Well, doing his ghostly equivalent of leaning, considering he was incorporeal. Like Sal, he was good at faking it, though I wondered whether they did it for my benefit or their own.

"God, you need a bell around your neck," I said.

"You keep saying that." He shook his head. "Wouldn't a bell be every bit as startling?"

"It would— Never mind. What did you find out?"

"Nothing," he said. "Well, not nothing. Car accident downtown with a fatality, a couple of old folks in nursing homes, and a great-grandfather who was pushing ninety-three died at home this evening. All on their way to the great beyond. No teenagers."

"So that's good," I said. "Right?"

"Not for the aforementioned souls. But good for the kids. I assume you wanted to find them while they were still alive, right?"

"Duh, Kale," I said. He stuck out his tongue and disappeared. For a split second, I thought I'd pissed him off. But he reappeared, sitting cross-legged on my desk. "Now the question is where they are."

"What did you find out?"

I filled him on my plan to send the ghosts from the church to start a search party.

He nodded, lips quirking up in a faint smile. "Not bad, Bridget."

"I have my moments," I said. "I tried to call Detective Fulbright, but I don't have anything to give him. I mean, what am I going to say? I saw something on Facebook?"

Kale furrowed his brow and dropped the timbre of his voice. "Well, we'll take it into consideration, Miss Young. Leave the police work to the professionals."

I laughed at his impression. "I also considered Miss Tara, but…"

Kale shook his head a little. Back when we were trying to find who'd killed Natalie, we'd taken the *whatever it took* approach. I'd seen the intense, downright terrifying side of him then. In an instant, he'd transformed from a dreamy, mild-mannered spirit to an angel with lightning in his eyes, shaking Tara's house with his righteous fury. He'd sworn it was only an illusion, but I couldn't shake the memory, and I'd wondered more than a few times since then which one was the real Kale. "I still feel terrible about that. You know, I tried to go back to speak with her."

"You did?"

"I did. But her house is sealed up tight against spirits," he said. "I got the message."

"You know we had to do it. We wouldn't have been able to save Emily otherwise." At Kale's insistence, Tara had taught me how to break down the barrier between myself and the spirits. I'd actually stepped into their world for a moment, giving me the chance to speak to the killer's other victims and find out where he'd taken them.

"Easy to say when you're not the one who had to do it," he replied. "So what now?"

"Now we wait." I peeled off my jacket, still damp from the sleet. After shaking off some of the moisture, I hung it over the back of my desk chair to dry. "I just hope someone can come to me here. I stalled as long as I could at the church, but Mom was being a heinous bi—"

"Bridget."

"Please tell me you're not on her side."

"I'm on the side of you not getting yourself in trouble that I can't dig you out of," he said. "Spirits I can handle. The wrath of your mother, I cannot. If you keep it up, she's going to send you off to boarding school."

"Is boarding school even still a thing? I thought they only did it on TV."

"It's definitely still a thing."

"Maybe it would be like Hogwarts."

Kale wrinkled his nose. "Like…huh? I don't get it."

I sighed. Spirits. "Another time," I said. "I wish she understood."

"Have you ever thought about telling her?"

"Dude, I told her back when I saw Valerie the very first time. She put me in therapy and tried to get me put on medication. Remember that?"

He nodded. "Okay, but to be fair, it was only a couple of months after Val died. It was still fresh. She might surprise you now."

"Yeah," I said. "Getting dropped off at the psych ward would definitely be a surprise. I'm not telling her."

"Okay, okay." He disappeared again, then reappeared on the edge of my bed. His handsome face was oddly sympathetic. He reached out one translucent hand, and for the thousandth time, I wished I could actually touch him. I wanted to lean in and feel the warmth of his skin on mine. His fingers hesitated, then drifted down to hover over my hand. There was a cool sensation, like I was holding my hand in front of the open freezer. "I know this is hard. But I'm proud of you."

"Thanks, Dad."

"I'm serious. Look at me."

My heart froze in my chest. With his gaze locked on me, I saw the way his eyes glowed blue from within. My voice sounded far away. "What?"

"I know this whole thing is difficult. Whatever happens, I have your back," he said. He held up his hand. The low light of my bedside lamp shone through it. His brow furrowed, and the faint glow dissipated. His hand slowly solidified, colors brightening like he was becoming real. I hesitated, then pressed my palm to his. It was cool, but I could feel the physical solidity of it. It wasn't just my mind filling in what I expected and wanted to be there. There was a faint tingle of electricity running up my arm. Without warning, his fingers laced through mine and closed tightly on my hand. "I'm with you. I promise."

I watched his hand grasping mine, unsure of what to do. I wanted him to hang out with me and distract me with silly banter. Or other distractions.

Awestruck, I closed my fingers around his hand. If he could touch my hand, could he kiss me? Could he fold me into his arms and hold me like we were two normal kids? My chest burned, and I suddenly realized I was holding my breath in anticipation. I exhaled a shaky sigh, my heart thumping.

My throat constricted around the words I didn't want to say. I couldn't look at his beautiful eyes when I said it, or I would have lost my resolve. "Then I need you to search."

His hand returned to its spectral state. There was no sense of him pulling away. It felt like cool sand running through my fingers, and I instantly regretted telling him to go. In the blink of an eye, the moment was over. The dream had been real, and then it slipped through my grasp again.

*Wait. Stay with me.* Why did the right thing feel so bad?

"You got it." He flickered, then reappeared at the door. If he felt anything about what had just happened, it didn't show on his face. His blue eyes were solemn, his expression neutral. "What about you?"

"What I do best," I said. "I'm going to sit here being useless and waiting."

# CHAPTER SEVEN

*Friday—11:08 p.m.—Ten Hours Missing*

IT WAS A LITTLE AFTER ELEVEN when Colin finally called a cease-fire on the poor alien planet he'd been bombarding with heavy artillery all night. I heard the faint creak as he came up the stairs, then the gradual crescendo of footsteps toward my door. The hardwood floors in the new house made it hard for any of us to be sneaky, though there was only one of us for whom that was likely to be an issue. Silence fell, but I could see the shadow of his feet under my door. After what seemed like an eternity, he tapped lightly on the door.

I had just refreshed my Facebook for the four thousandth time, looking for updates on Diana Brown. I had it down to a ritual: Diana's page, News Channel 6, Diana's mother, News Channel 21, Parkland Chronicle, wait two minutes, rinse and repeat.

An ugly debate had broken out in the comments section of one of the news reports. This was why Emily's rule for the internet—*never read the comments*—was a good one. Several students from Mount Sharon High had chimed in with their expert opinions, suggesting Corey had done something to Diana. They usually drove separately to school, but Corey had picked Diana up that morning. The next piece of evidence was on Diana's Instagram, where she'd posted a picture after leaving school captioned *Excited for a surprise adventure with my bae!* People were now speculating that Corey had taken her somewhere for a romantic "surprise" that had turned ugly.

People were the worst.

Then again, I had to admit it wasn't an unbelievable story. It actually sounded pretty plausible, at least based on my TV education. And they always said on TV that the first suspect in a disappearance or murder was the spouse or significant other.

Colin tapped on the door again. I sighed. Ignoring him apparently wasn't going to make him go away. I glanced at the Parkland Chronicle's website, only to find that the most recent update was still the Rowdy Reindeer 5K the next morning. I finally got up and opened the door enough to stick my head out. Colin shuffled his feet a little as I looked him up and down. "Yeah?"

"I thought you might want to see," he said. He brushed past me and into my room.

"Colin!" I hurried past him and kicked my backpack under the bed. It was full of ghost supplies like candles, a lighter, and a bag of sage that would look suspicious to my twelve-year-old brother who would waste no time telling Mom about what he thought he saw.

"Look," he said, stopping at the window and spreading the lavender curtains.

"What?" I walked over to him and stood behind him. For a second, I forgot my irritation at him barging into my room. Outside, the damp sleet had given way to a light snowfall. It wasn't sticking yet, but something in me was still excited at the white glittering in the night air.

"Do you think we'll get a lot?"

"Probably not," I said. "It's not cold enough yet."

He sighed heavily, and I couldn't help but feel like I'd told him the truth about Santa. His messy brown hair stuck up in the back. The thin indent on either side of his face from his glasses told me he'd probably fallen asleep on the couch before coming up. He really was a good kid—sweet, even if he was a little on the goody-goody side.

"But you never know," I added, hoping it sounded more convincing than it felt. "The news said there was a cold front coming in."

In the dark reflection of my bedroom window, I saw the corner of his mouth quirk up. Maybe I had the tiniest bit of big sister mojo after all. "Really?"

"That's what I saw," I said. With my obsessive checking for updates, I really had seen some news about the weather. We stood there in the quiet for a few minutes, and then my little brother shocked me.

"I miss how things used to be," he said quietly. "When everyone was still here."

It felt like he'd reached into my throat and grabbed my windpipe. *You and me both, buddy.* We never talked about Val, and we definitely never talked about Dad. When my sister had died, it was the nail in the coffin—bad analogy—on Mom and Dad's already rocky relationship. Within a few months of Val's death, Dad had taken a "contract with open-ended terms" to work across the country. They weren't officially separated, but when he came home to visit, he stayed in a hotel despite the very roomy king bed in the master bedroom downstairs. And those visits had gotten more and more spaced out, to the point that it felt weirder when he was home than when he was away.

"So do I," I said.

Something moved in the reflection of the window. Mom? My gaze followed the movement to the unfamiliar face of an older man. I let out a hiccupping sound of surprise, and Colin whirled to look at me. He frowned. "What was that?"

"I thought I saw a spider," I lied. Considering the old man looked like a fisherman who'd gotten lost and not a stabby serial killer, I was betting he was a spirit. I really had to come up with some kind of alert that didn't send my heart into my throat every time a spirit came to call.

"Excuse me?" the older man said. He stood in the center of my shaggy purple rug, looking around at the room before meeting my eyes again. "Are you the one I'm supposed to talk to?"

"Mom said Dad might not come home for Christmas this year," my brother said, as if the man hadn't spoken. Suspicion confirmed. "Since he just came home after you…you know."

Dad had flown home for all of thirty-six hours after everything went down with Natalie. He'd blamed it on last-minute flights, but we'd seen him for about three awkward hours for dinner and a trip to the mall—no Mom—during which he'd promised to get home more often. He didn't ask too many questions about what had happened. I figured once he'd lost Valerie, he'd decided he was sort of over the whole having-kids thing, like it was a hobby he'd gotten tired of and tossed aside. Honestly, I'd counted it as yet another topping on the double-decker crap sandwich life had handed me two years ago. And if he didn't want to be around us, then I didn't want him around.

"Something about getting ready for an audit or something," Colin continued. "At least that's what Mom said. She was pissed. Uh, I mean, mad." His eyes went wide as he looked over his shoulder, as if Mom was going to burst out of my closet to scold him for his language.

"Colin, really? I'm not going to tell. And that's awfully convenient for him."

"Uh, miss?" the old man said. You'd think that dead people would be a lot more patient. It wasn't like they had anywhere to hurry off to. Wasn't it clear that I was having a sisterly moment?

I tried to give the spirit a *hold on* gesture. Colin caught the movement and frowned. I threw my hands up dramatically to cover for it. "Dad just makes me so mad with all this." That part at least was true.

"They're not going to get back together, are they?" he asked quietly.

*Obviously.* I'd figured it out the first time Dad had "gone on business" to Seattle. "They might," I lied. "But if they don't, we'll still be okay."

"Are you Bianca? Belinda?" the older man said. "Hello? Can you hear me? They told me to come tell you news."

My heart lurched forward. If my uninvited guest had information on Diana and Corey, then the sibling bonding would have to wait until less dire times.

I faked a yawn. "Colin, it's going to be fine. I'm super tired. I really want to go to bed."

He looked crestfallen, and I felt myself drop from *Crappy Sister of the Year* to the *Worst of the Century.* Even though I was technically his big sister by the numbers, Valerie had always been the big sister to both of us. As long as she'd been around, I'd never had to be any kind of role model or mentor to Colin. Considering who got the brunt of Mom's irritation, he could probably give me a few pointers. But I definitely had the leg up on life experience and a view on the world that Val couldn't have come close to. I knew I was supposed to help him get by. I was supposed to say the right words so he wouldn't go shut himself in his room and worry about the axe falling on our parents' marriage. But our house was full of islands, and it would take more than I knew how to do to bring it back together.

"Oh. Okay," he said. "Good night." He walked slowly, like he was waiting for me to change my mind, then closed my door quietly behind himself. All he needed was sad piano music to complete the gut-wrenching effect.

"Miss, am I in the right place?" the older man said.

"Dude, chill," I finally said to him.

"Oh, you can hear me!"

"Yeah, I've been hearing you for the last five minutes," I said. "Did you not notice I was having a private conversation?"

His translucent face pulled into a frown, and the temperature in my room dropped to a sharp chill. I swallowed and took a tentative step back toward my bed. My eyes flicked down to the strap of my backpack hanging out from under the bed. It occurred to me that I was alone with a strange spirit, and the only thing predictable thing about ghosts was their utter unpredictability.

The spirit was an older man in paint-stained cargo shorts and one of those big boating shirts with the inexplicable flap across the back. He wore a floppy khaki fishing hat over close-cropped salt-and-pepper hair. Though the colors were washed out, he had the subtle tan lines of a pair of sunglasses around his eyes.

"Are you Bianca?"

"I'm Bridget," I said hesitantly.

"Oh, thank the Lord." He smiled. If my griping at him had bothered him, it had passed. Tension flowed out of my muscles as I sat down on my bed. Though I relaxed, I knew the backpack full of supplies was right under my feet. "I thought I might have had the wrong place. But you were here like they said."

"Like who said?"

"Sorry, where are my manners? Name's Jerry Corcoran. Used to live about two streets over." He extended a hand, then hesitated as he looked down at it. I gave him a little wave in return and hoped it didn't convey my itching impatience with him. "Nice to meet you."

"Nice to meet you, Jerry," I said. "Do you have something to tell me?"

He nodded. "Well, I met this pretty young lady out by the pond, and she told me she was looking for someone. Well, she'd heard that someone was looking or someone, and she had information, but she couldn't—"

"Excuse me," I said, making a *hurry up* gesture. "Could you skip to the ending?"

"Well, there's no need to be rude. From what I could gather, the people you're looking for are out at Wildwood State Park."

"Alive?" Kale hadn't found them, but a lot could change in a couple of hours.

"They didn't say."

"Because that would be too easy," I said to myself. "Did they give you anything more specific? Wildwood is huge."

Wildwood State Park was miles upon miles of forest surrounding a manmade lake. It was a popular place for locals to hike and camp, with a ton of entrances for boat docks and campgrounds. I could remember several occasions where we'd taken Colin out there for Boy Scout activities, only to find out he'd gotten the location wrong. This was definitely a start, but I needed something specific if there was a chance of getting to Diana and Corey.

"I'm sorry, that's all I got," Jerry said. "Used to fish out there a good bit." He looked wistful. "Can't seem to make it out there anymore."

I knew Jerry had a story of his own and could probably use some help to move on to the big fishing spot in the sky. Everyone had a story with sad chapters, peppered with regrets. But there were real, living people who needed my help tonight. "Thanks, Jerry," I said. He smiled a little, but it didn't erase the sadness from his pale features. I took a deep breath. "Hey, I'm kind of busy tonight, but if you want to come back another time, I can talk to you and maybe try to help you. If you want to."

"That would be nice," he said, the smile widening. The gentle creases in his face reached his eyes, and the sadness evaporated. "It's nice in here with you. You're bright."

"Not really, I'm a pretty solid C student."

"No, I mean…. You're like the sun breaking through on a cloudy day,"

Jerry said. "That's how I found you."

"Well, okay. That's kind of poetic." While I wasn't sure what he meant, it was hard to dislike the comparison. "I appreciate your help. I need to start working on how to find those kids."

"Sure thing. Hope you find them. See you soon."

Once Jerry had disappeared to wherever he called home, I took my phone out again. It was rapidly approaching midnight, but surely Fulbright wouldn't mind me calling if I had good information. I hesitated, then dialed his number. It rang twice, and he answered in a gruff voice. "This is Fulbright. Who is this?"

"Uh, Mr.—I mean, Detective," I stammered. "This is Bridget Young. Do you remember me?"

He cleared his throat, and I heard a muffled voice off to the side. "'Course I remember you. Give me a second." There was a long pause with jostling sounds and a muffled yawn. My heart thumped. What if he didn't take it seriously? He hadn't taken my tips seriously before. I had to hope that I'd established some credibility after what happened with the Runaway Killer. Surely he wouldn't take the risk of ignoring my tips again. Finally, he came back. "I hope there's a good reason you're calling me at…midnight."

"You told me to call you if I ever got any more feelings," I said. "I got one for you."

"Is it about the shootings down on Fourteenth?"

"Uh…no."

"Damn." He yawned and cleared his throat. I heard the rattle of ice into a glass from his end. "Too convenient, I guess. What's on your mind?"

"Have you seen anything about the missing kids?"

"Gotta be more specific."

"A couple of high schoolers from Mount Sharon High went missing this afternoon," I said.

He paused. "Hadn't heard about it. I was working a homicide downtown all day."

I filled him in on the details and finished by reading him the last update from Teresa Brown's Facebook page.

"Well, they're both eighteen, and they haven't been missing for very long."

"Natalie Fullmer was eighteen, and people thought she ran away," I said. "They were wrong. If someone had looked for her, maybe she'd be alive today."

"Christ in heaven. They're not... Do you know if they're alive?"

"I don't know for sure. I think they're out at Wildwood State Park. Can you go out there and look for them?"

As soon as the words crossed my lips, I glanced at the snow and realized that the winter wonderland was going to turn ugly. The expanse of snowy white was beautiful from inside our nice, heated house. If Diana and Corey were stranded outside, they were going to be cold and wet. How long did it take to die of exposure? I mean, Georgia wasn't exactly the Arctic, but—

"Not me personally. But I can pass your tip to the officer in charge of the investigation. I don't guess you want to tell me how you got a hold of this information."

"No, I don't," I said. "But I'm pretty sure it's good."

He sighed. "You're a weird kid."

"I know. Would you rather I didn't call?"

"No. I still think you got freakishly lucky on the Miles case. But I'm not willing to gamble. I'll pass the information on."

"Could I come out and help?" I asked. Maybe Kale and I could tag team it and start searching once we got out there.

"Definitely not. I don't know how, nor do I want, to explain why I've got a middle schooler—"

"High school, excuse you."

"—accompanying me on a case," he continued. "And even if I did have a moment of temporary insanity and let you help me, this isn't my case. I promise I'll pass on the tip. They know what to do from here."

"But—"

"No buts," he said. "Unless you plan to tell me why you know. Otherwise, that's as good as you get, and you can follow the news like everyone else."

The temptation was strong. I had half a mind to spill it all to him. Was the truth any weirder than whatever his theory was? And it would be a lot easier than constantly dancing around the topic. But there was a pretty good chance he wouldn't believe me anyway.

"Whatever," I said. "Thanks a lot."

I wished for an old-school phone that I could slam down and settled for jabbing violently at the End button. Poking the glass wasn't nearly as satisfying.

Well, that was that. Case closed. Missing people found. I'd done my civic duty, hadn't I? More than what most would do.

But what if?

What if they were out there freezing? What if Corey really had turned into an axe murderer? What if the cops just took it "under advisement," set it aside to deal with tomorrow, and missed their window? I wanted them to solve the case, but not by finding two frozen corpses out in the woods. I wouldn't take one bit of pleasure in saying "I told you so" in that case.

*Dammit.*

# Chapter Eight

I MANAGED TO SIT through half an episode of *Pretty Little Liars* on my laptop before the worry started to drive me nuts. I'd kept open a browser tab to check the news, but had spent so much time refreshing it that I had no idea what was happening on my show.

How did people handle this kind of uncertainty? And what were normal people my age doing right now? Sometimes it was hard to remember a time when I wasn't embroiled in the latest episode of the Real Ghosts of Parkland. Allie Williams wasn't spending her Friday night worrying about Diana Brown and Corey Walker's safety, and she certainly wasn't heading up a coalition of the dearly departed to find them.

It wasn't fair, but as soon as the thought crossed my mind, I could hear Valerie's voice as plain as day. She'd lingered here for two years after her death, still managing to keep me from screwing up too badly. When I used to complain about how things sucked, she'd give me this wry look and say, "Really?" And she'd remind me that I could do exactly nothing to change it, so I might as well deal with it. If I ever got a tattoo to remind me of Valerie, it would say, "It is what it is."

I pulled up the shared *Missing!* post from earlier. I didn't want to make a public comment about the park; whether I was right or wrong, it would attract a lot of attention I didn't want. There was a phone number, though. I dialed the number, then hesitated. What if her mom thought I was some creeper?

It rang four times, and I frowned as I pulled the phone away from my ear. I'd expected an immediate pick-up. "The voicemail box of the Verizon customer you are trying to reach is full," a mechanical voice said. "Please try back another time."

Seriously?

Okay, Plan B. I was probably up to Plan D or E by now, but whatever. I tapped on Teresa Brown's name and started to compose a private Facebook message.

**Hi Mrs. Brown—I'm an acquaintance of Diana's, and I heard a rumor at school that she was heading out to Wildwood State Park for the afternoon with Corey. I thought you might want to look into it.**

I stared at it for a long time. God, things were getting complicated. If her mom asked me any questions, my story was going to fall apart like a house of cards in a tornado. Plus, a rumor? I might as well tell her I read it from a crystal ball. I mean, I knew for sure they were out there, but it was weird enough to tell Fulbright that, and I actually had a shred of credibility with him. To Diana's mother, I was going to sound one hundred percent insane.

"Ka—" I stopped myself. Kale was busy searching, and he needed to keep it up. I knew he'd come here in a heartbeat, but he was a lot more useful out there than in here giving me advice on how to lie to Teresa Brown. "Sal?" I closed my eyes and pictured his face—the gentle curve of full cheeks, the curly dark hair. I felt a gentle bumping sensation, like I'd run into him walking down a sidewalk. "I could use your help. I'm at my—"

"What's up?"

I jumped when Sal materialized at the end of my bed, sharp as ever in his neatly pressed police uniform. "Wow, that was fast."

"I was out looking for the missing kids," he said. "You sure stirred something up out there."

"I did?"

He smiled and nodded. "Spirits all over the place talking about it.. Although a lot of them seemed more interested in someone who could talk to them than they were in finding the kids. You just laid down a welcome mat at your door."

"Great." Because I definitely needed more clingy ghosts in my life and in my bedroom. I was going to have to set up office hours at this rate.

"So, what's up?"

I filled him in on my dilemma over the Facebook message.

He shrugged. "I had a Facebook before I…left. You could use mine."

"Sal, we have got to work on your common sense," I said, shaking my head.

"Why? She won't know who I am."

"So you think getting a message from a life-challenged police officer is somehow less weird than a random high schooler across town?"

"If she finds her daughter, she's not gonna think about it any harder," he said. It was a fair point, but if I got a message from a strange person, my first instinct would be to go to their profile and find out who they were. And for Sal, that would spell trouble.

"But if she does…" I didn't want to mention it to Sal, but I'd been on his Facebook page. There were dozens of kind messages and posts in memoriam. While it was all very touching and spoke highly of the kind of person he'd been, and really still was, there was no way Diana's mother would look at it and not have a second thought about it.

"So make a burner account," he said.

"Huh?"

"Like a burner phone. Criminals use them when they don't want their number to be traceable. They buy these cheap prepaid phones from Walmart, load it up with a card, and then trash it when they're done. You can do the same thing with computer accounts," he said with a shrug. "Sign up for a random email, set up the account, and message her from there."

"Sal, that's…that's actually really smart."

"You sound surprised. I'm a little hurt."

"It's not like I'm saying you're dumb," I said quickly. "I just didn't think of you as the technology type."

"I'm not, really. I was an insomniac, so I watched a lot of TV. Amazing what you can learn."

"Hey, whatever works." I hurried to my desk and took out my laptop. The cover was cracked from where Natalie Fullmer had pitched one of her epic death-induced temper tantrums and flung my belongings across the room. Thankfully, we'd worked past her staggering anger issues, but I was still finding my stuff out of place and broken weeks later. I started the process to sign up for a new Google account. "Name?"

"John Smith," Sal said.

I typed in *johnsmith,* which was taken. "No good."

"Duh," he said drily.

"Really? You picked it." I selected one of Google's suggestions—**johnsmith19712**—and went through the confirmation process. I skipped the option to add my cell phone number, and then headed over to Facebook. It took another five minutes to set up the burner account. "I need a picture. This is obviously a fake account." I searched Google Images for a picture.

Sal leaned over my shoulder, giving off a cool aura that sent a chill breaking across my bare arms. "Too good-looking. Too beardy."

"Beardy? I don't think that's a word."

"That one," he said, ignoring my comment. I hovered over an average-looking guy, maybe mid-twenties. "He looks boring."

"That's a good thing?"

"If he's too attractive, you'll look fake. But you don't want to look like a pedophile either."

"Sal! Gross."

"What? I'm just trying to help."

I shook my head and downloaded the picture, then added it to my profile. I quickly searched through some other profiles and clicked *Like* on a dozen different pages. With no posts or friends, it would probably still be obvious that it was a fake account, like the ones that tried to scam people with cheap Nikes or knockoff sunglasses. But it was better than using my own and painting a big fat target on myself for questions.

"You might make a good criminal," Sal said. He frowned immediately. "Not that you should. For the record, I am not encouraging you to be a criminal."

"Dude, seriously?" I muttered. I searched for Diana Brown's mother again and selected her name. "I'm still not sure this looks any less weird than a random girl messaging her."

"But at least she won't know who it is. And when she finds her daughter, I guarantee she won't care. I wouldn't."

"Can the police figure out who I am this way?"

"No." He hesitated. "Well, I guess they technically can. If you commit a crime, they can probably get a warrant to find out who started the account."

My mouth went dry, and I could feel my eyes going wide as I looked up at him. "Seriously?"

"Yeah, but don't worry. It's not a crime to contact someone anonymously."

"Easy for you to say." Then again, it wasn't my first time. When we'd been trying to find out who killed Natalie, I'd hunted down phone numbers for half a dozen other missing girls. I'd even called a few of their families, pretending to be an investigator. No one had come after me, but it occurred to me now that if I made a habit of deception, I might want to learn how to cover my tracks a little better. Why did doing the right thing increasingly look like being a criminal?

I took a deep breath and typed the message.

*Mrs. Brown—*

*I saw your post about your daughter being missing. I have reason to believe that she's at Wildwood State Park, and that she and her boyfriend are both alive. I can't explain how I know, but please take this seriously. I have notified the police, but I hope you'll do whatever you can to help. Thank you.*

"That's as un-creepy as I can make it," I said. "Best I can do."

"I think it works. Good job."

I nodded and sat back and watched the screen for a few minutes. "What if she doesn't look at it? We're not friends, so it's going to get sent to her Other folder. What if she doesn't check there? Or if she's already asleep? Or—"

"Can we skip all of this and go right to the part where you convince me you should go out there yourself?"

My cheeks flushed hot. "How did— I do not— I wasn't going to." I mean, I didn't *want* to, but I couldn't sit still without knowing what was happening.

"The lady doth protest too much."

"You know, that quote is widely misunderstood," I replied. He rolled his eyes. "And it's not the worst idea ever."

"No, going into a serial killer's hideout still outranks it," he said, giving me a pointed look. "But it's getting late, and it's snowing, and you have no vehicle. Explain to me how this is going to work."

"Well, I hadn't gotten that far yet."

"Then let me help you out," Sal said. "Don't."

I took out my phone and started scrolling through my contacts. "Emily. She can drive."

"Are you listening?"

"Nope." It was a little past midnight, so I knew she'd still be awake. I texted her anyway just to be safe.

**You awake?**

The typing animation appeared almost immediately.

**Emily: Totes. What's up?**

**Skype?**

She didn't respond, but a minute later, a beep alerted me to an incoming video call. I answered it to see Emily with her hair pulled up in a messy bun and wearing her glasses. Her face was already scrubbed clean of her usual dramatic makeup, and she was wearing her pink Hello Kitty pajamas. It was weird to see her bare-faced; she looked like a sixth-grader without her makeup and wild hairstyles.

"Hi babe," she said.

"Hi honey," I said automatically.

"Honey?" Sal said quizzically.

I glanced over my shoulder and rolled my eyes at him.

Emily followed the gesture and frowned. "Who's there?"

"No one," I replied.

"Hey," he protested. "I'm right here."

"Well, I mean, Sal is here."

"Oh, just Sal. Don't mind me," he said drily. "Tell her I said hello. And nice pajamas."

"Sal likes your pajamas," I said.

"Bridget! Shit, I don't have any makeup on," she said, and the screen went dark for a minute.

"Did you cover your camera? Seriously?"

"Don't judge me," Emily said.

"So I was wondering if you could do me a favor tonight."

"I'm assuming you don't mean makeup advice."

"I need a ride."

"Bridget, I can't," she said. "My mom will literally hunt me down and lock me up. I'm serious."

"Since when do you care?"

There was a long silence, and then Emily's voice had lost its usual sharp edge. "Since I got kidnapped by a serial killer?"

"Shit," I said. "I didn't mean—"

"I know." She peeled off whatever she'd covered her camera with. In the blackout, she'd taken off her glasses and let her hair down. I would have laughed if not for the solemnity of the conversation. "You tried to tell me not to take off, and you were right. And I hate to say it, but Kari was right all those times she yelled at me about skipping school and lying about where I was going. Bad things can happen." She shook her head. "Where do you need to go this late, anyway?"

"You know the missing girl, Diana Brown? I posted it on Facebook."

"I saw it." Her eyes went wide. "Wait, is she…" She stuck out her tongue and let her head loll to the side, which I guessed was her pantomime for dead.

"Not yet. But I know where she and her boyfriend are."

"Then call the police. Like a normal person," Emily said.

"I did."

"Then why are we even discussing it?" She put up her hands. "Don't get me wrong, I kind of dig your whole 'I see dead people' thing. But you're not a cop. You shouldn't be getting involved in this stuff. I know I'm the last person who should say that, but you could have gotten hurt."

"And if I hadn't, then you—"

"I know!" Emily interrupted, her voice sharp. "I'm just saying. And your mom will kill you if she finds out."

I sighed. Of all the times for her to make this great leap of maturity and start behaving herself, she had to choose now. "I know."

"Bridget…" She shook her head, then let out a heavy sigh. "So where are they?"

"Are you going to help?"

"No, I just want to know."

"They're out at Wildwood State Park. I already called in a tip to the police, and I sent Diana's mom an anonymous message. I'm afraid no one's going to take it seriously." I shook my head. "They didn't take Natalie seriously. And they didn't take me seriously when it was you until it was already too late. If I hadn't gone, then…" I shrugged. I knew it was crappy to lay that on her, but it was completely true.

"I'm really sorry," she said. "I wish I could help more." Ugh. I had to give her props for sticking to her principles, but her newfound conviction was incredibly inconvenient.

I pondered for a minute. "What if I borrowed your car?"

"Mom will hear it start up. I'm sorry. I can't help you this time." She crossed her arms over her chest, then perked up. "What if I called in a tip, too? It would probably sound legit if they kept hearing it."

"No, I—"

"It's actually a good idea," Sal said. "Tell her to do it. Anything to corroborate your story is good."

"Sal says to do it."

Emily smiled. "Okay. So then you won't have to go out there."

I hesitated.

Her smile completely flipped upside down as her face went from satisfied to disapproving in less than a second. "Bridget. You're not going."

"I have to."

"No, you don't. You want to," Emily said. "What if something's out there?"

"I'm not going to get involved. I'm only going to make sure someone's actually looking for them. I think if I go, I might be able to narrow down where they are and call it in."

Emily sighed. "Please don't."

"I have to," I said again. "Thanks anyway, but I need to find a ride." I didn't want to give her another chance to dissuade me, so I ended the call. She called back immediately, but I declined the connection. "Of all the times for her to start caring what her mother thinks," I complained.

"I know, what is she thinking by trying to keep herself out of trouble and not worry her mother to death?" Sal mocked. "Some role model."

"You're not funny," I said, grabbing my phone again. I didn't want to make the next call, but I didn't have many other options.

"I wasn't trying to be," he said. "Maybe you should listen to your friend."

I ignored him and scrolled down to Michael Fullmer's name. If there was someone who'd be sympathetic to the cause, it was him. I hadn't talked to him in a few days, but we'd texted off and on for the last few weeks since he'd found out his sister Natalie wasn't missing, but dead. Neither of us wanted to be in this sad little club, but I understood his strange new world a lot better than most.

*Hey—you awake?*

Michael didn't stay glued to his phone like Emily, and I knew he'd been spending a lot of time playing video games to distract himself and get some time away from his mother. It might be a while before he responded.

As I watched the screen of my phone, I started running through my other options. Walking was definitely out. It was a least a twenty-minute drive to the nearest entrance to the park, and depending on where Diana was, it could be even longer. It would take me all night to walk it, to say nothing of the snow.

I could take a taxi. I'd done it before. But I didn't have much money, and a ride like that would cost way more than I had. A dark idea crossed my mind. I knew exactly where Mom stashed emergency cash. She wouldn't notice anytime soon. And it really was a good cause.

No. If stealing from Mom was the only way I could possibly make it out there, then I might consider it, but I'd exhaust all my other options first. It hadn't taken me long to get good at lying to Mom about where I was going to do my little ghost jobs on the side. I had a feeling stealing money from her would go the same way. Good cause or not, I didn't want to go down that road.

I scrolled through my contacts aimlessly. Despite the recent social media surge, I could count my actual friends on two hands. Emily and Michael at least knew the deal with the spirits. If I called Brady Thomas right now and asked him to drive me out to Wildwood State Park to look for a missing couple, he'd laugh in my face and reconsider his choices of potential dance dates.

My phone buzzed suddenly. I snatched it up to see a new text from Michael.

*Michael: Yep—you ok?*

*Can I call you?*

**Michael: *Sec, gotta go in garage***

A few minutes later, my phone rang. My heart raced as I answered it and said, "Hey! I'm sorry to bother you so late."

"I don't mind. Are you okay?"

"I'm fine," I said. "I wouldn't normally ask this, but I need a ride somewhere."

Long silence. "Tonight? Where?"

"Uh…Wildwood State Park."

Another long silence. "I'm sure you can guess my next question."

"Why," I said. "Which is a great question. Have you seen anything about Diana Brown? She goes to Mount Sharon. She's missing."

"I haven't heard about it. I've been avoiding the news and Facebook since everything happened." There was the slightest hitch in his voice, which I recognized it from my own experience. What he meant was *since my world fell apart, since everything exploded in my face.* "Wait. It's not him, is it? That son of—"

"No," I said quickly. "She's still alive. I want to help her stay that way."

"It'd be a nice change. So what do you need from me?"

"Just a ride. I know it's crazy, but—"

"All right, give me fifteen minutes," he said, cutting off my spiel.

"Wait, really? You'll help me?"

"Yeah. Let's do it. Your house?"

I couldn't help but grin. I knew he would help. "No, I'll meet you at the entrance to the neighborhood. My mom will lose her mind if she hears you pull up to the house."

"I'll see you there," he said and hung up.

"Should have called him first," I said to Sal as I bent down to pull my backpack from under the bed. A can of generic brand salt had rolled out when

I'd hidden it from Colin. I dropped to all fours to reach for it under the bed. My fingers found a handful of dust bunnies, then finally wrapped around the can. When I came up with the salt, Sal was standing right in front of me.

"He's not going to give you good advice," he said evenly. "His sister just died."

"Well, I guess it's a good thing I didn't call him for advice, isn't it?" I replied. My giddiness at Michael agreeing to help me rapidly evaporated. I checked through the bag. I wasn't sure what I'd need, but if I was going to be hanging out with a bunch of unfamiliar spirits, it didn't hurt to go prepared. Salt, holy water, white candles, sage, a lighter.

"Then let me give you some advice," he said. "You should let the police do their job."

I tested the lighter and held it up to the light. Through the clear green plastic, I could barely see the remains of the lighter fluid. It took me a dozen tries to light it, so I threw it in the trash and started digging into the back of my underwear drawer for the multi-pack I'd bought a few months earlier. God help me if Mom found them. She'd trash my room trying to find the non-existent drugs they went with.

"Are you listening to me?" he said.

*Not if you're going to lecture me.*

My fingers finally found the pack, and I grabbed one without looking. I came up with a neon pink lighter, which lit the first time I tried. I dropped it into the front pocket of my purple backpack and zipped it up. "Yes, I heard you, and I respectfully disagree. If I'd taken your advice last time, my best friend would be dead. I called the police, and they didn't take me seriously. I'd be alive and safe, and Emily's mom could go hang out with my mom at the Dead Daughters club."

"You're being overdramatic."

"Over… Seriously? You were there, Sal! Tell me I'm wrong." I could still picture the scene as if it had happened only moments earlier. I woke up in a cold sweat sometimes because I knew that even with my supernatural sight and clever detective work, all it would have taken was a gun in Miles's hand, a traffic jam to hold up the police for two more minutes, anything, and both Emily and I could have been dead. Sure, I'd been bold enough to run in there like a hero, but I didn't have a plan past *find Emily and get her out*. Before breaking into the abandoned restaurant where he'd kept his victims, I'd called the police to report a fake shooting, but I couldn't live with the risk that they'd be too late. Thankfully I'd gotten to her, but after the news broke the story about Emily being missing too soon, Miles had come back early to kill her before the police got to him. In the ensuing chaos, he'd hit me in the head and knocked me unconscious. Luckily for Emily and me, the police had finally taken my tip seriously and scared him off. He'd gotten away, but Emily survived. I knew it had been reckless and dangerous to handle it myself, but I also knew it had been the right thing to do. Because as sure as I could have gotten hurt worse than I did, Emily most definitely would have been dead if I hadn't gotten involved.

"I'm not saying you didn't help her, but—"

"But I should make sure I stay safe and to hell with everyone else, right?" I pointed at him. "That's not what you did."

He froze, his mouth dropped open in shock. "Bridget."

"You helped people all the time. Literally your job."

"And I got shot," he said. "In case you didn't notice it, I died."

I sighed and dug into my closet for a sweatshirt. For a moment, my hand lingered on the wash-worn UGA hoodie, a hand-me-down from Val. I'd worn it constantly after she'd died, but I'd finally managed to put it on a hanger in my closet instead of reaching for it each day like a security blanket. I reluctantly bypassed it for my Fox Lake High School hoodie, which Mom had insisted on buying for me at a PTO meeting last year.

"Sal, trust me, I'd much rather stay home and be a normal kid," I said through the fabric of the hoodie. I yanked the sweatshirt down over my head. It wasn't soft and comfy like Val's, and since I hadn't worn it or washed it much, it hadn't picked up the familiar laundry smell just yet. "I want to sit here and watch Netflix until my eyes bleed."

"Then do it," he said, gesturing emphatically.

"You wouldn't."

"You know what? If it meant I'd get to wake up tomorrow morning to hold my daughter, I would. I'd ignore that wad of cash and send that scumbag on his merry way with a warning."

"No, you wouldn't," I said. According to the news report, Sal and his partner had done a routine traffic stop for a bad taillight. Sal had noticed the driver was carrying a ton of cash and had asked them to step out of the car. The door never opened. Three shots through the window. Sal had died on the scene, and his partner was paralyzed from the waist down.

Sal's eyes narrowed, and I felt the temperature drop sharply with his growing anger. "Bridget, you don't know me as well as you think you do. Look, it's not like you're ignoring the situation. You've already done more than anyone would expect."

"Which will be of exactly zero comfort to anyone if Diana or Corey dies." I pulled my hair into a ponytail and twisted it quickly into a tight bun, wrapping it in an elastic without looking in the mirror. "Besides, this is nothing like what happened with Natalie. All I'm going to do is make sure someone's out there looking and try to narrow down her location. I'm not going in to find her myself."

"You promise?" Sal said. I pretended he hadn't asked the question and shoved my feet into my sneakers. "Bridget. Promise me."

I tied my sneakers tight and didn't look up at him. "I can't promise that," I said. "I don't like to lie."

He laughed, but there was no humor in the sharp sound. "You literally lie all the time."

I looked up at him and frowned. "Not to you. I promise I'll try everything possible to not get myself in trouble. That's the best I can do."

"Well, that's the thing about trouble, Bridget. It finds you the easiest when you're not looking for it."

# CHAPTER NINE

Mom—

Walked down to the Kwik-Stop for a honey bun and cappuccino. I promise I'm fine. Have my phone if you want to call me.

<3 B


I left the scrawled note on my desk. If there was one thing going my way tonight, it was the fact that it was Friday night, which meant tomorrow was officially Sleep-In Saturday. Saturdays meant no alarm clocks and late brunch in the Young house. And Mom had been talking all week about how she was looking forward to taking Saturday off. After a solid week of going straight from work to play rehearsals at the church every night, she was exhausted. Colin would probably sleep in, too. If he didn't, he'd sneak downstairs with his headphones to play Xbox until Mom woke up.

I debated whether to leave the note on my desk or downstairs in the kitchen. It made more sense, if I'd really run out of the house quickly, to leave a note on the counter where she'd see it. But it would take her longer to realize I was out of the house if I left the note on my desk. In keeping with the spirit of Sleep-In Saturday, I'd been known to sleep past noon on a weekend if no one woke me up, so she might leave me alone until then. If she found the note too soon, she'd be suspicious. Considering it would take twenty minutes max to walk down to the convenience store, buy a snack, and walk back, the note wasn't much of a safety net. I was banking on her never actually seeing it.

I eased my door open and walked as lightly as I could down the hallway toward the stairs. My heart thumped as I paused at the top of the stairwell. From downstairs, I could hear the refrigerator's low thrum and the mechanical whir of the heater. I crept down the stairs, wishing we had carpet instead of exposed hardwood. When I hit the fifth stair, the board creaked beneath me.

My mouth went dry as I froze in place. Had anyone heard?

I took the stairs painfully slow, then waited at the bottom as the stillness of the house surrounded me. Down here, I heard the soft ocean sounds of Mom's white noise machine and the faint rumble of snoring through the bedroom door.

There was no way I was getting out the front door silently. The house was still relatively new, and the deadbolt stuck sometimes. Even if it didn't make a loud click, the weather seal was so tight that it made a sound like popping a soda open when you pulled open the front door. The back door onto the porch was sliding glass, which was nice and quiet.

I tiptoed across the living room and pulled up the latch on the sliding door. It made the tiniest clicking sound. A rush of cold air blew through the open door, sending a chill down my spine. The back patio glistened with the damp snow. The cover of brown leaves mingled with pine needles was speckled in white.

"Last chance," Sal said over my shoulder.

My heart crawled up into my throat. I gasped and clapped my hand over my mouth to keep from yelping. I looked at him and put my finger over my lips. No one in the house could hear him, but I couldn't help being startled when my ghostly friends snuck up on me. And Mom could sure hear me if I screamed in surprise. I closed the door behind me and tiptoed onto the patio. The night was eerily silent except for the light patter of the snowflakes landing on dead leaves. It was bitter cold, and I was glad I'd let Mom badger me into getting a heavier coat when she'd dragged me shopping last weekend. I fumbled at the zipper and yanked it up to my chin.

I hurried around the side of the house and down the driveway, then spared a glance back.

"You could still go back in," Sal said.

"I don't need you to be my Jiminy."

"Someone needs to."

"You know, by coming with me, you're basically approving of what I'm doing."

"Your logic is so backward."

"Is it?" I snugged my backpack tight against myself and hurried down the driveway.

Sal chased after me, then floated above the ground facing me so I had to chase him like a greyhound after the rabbit. "Yes. But if you're going to insist on doing this, then I'm going to supervise as long as possible."

"So you're going along with it."

"In silent protest."

"But you're not silent."

"You know, I'm not surprised you don't have more friends," he said.

"That's low." I looked for the slip of his expression that would say he was teasing, but there was none. The disapproval was plastered on his face like stage makeup. There was no question what he thought of the whole situation, or of me.

He shrugged and looked out the window. "The truth can hurt."

I was surprised at how much it stung. What did he know, anyway?

It only took me a few minutes to reach the end of the single street through our small neighborhood. Even in that short time, I was already shivering, and I could feel the cold down into my shoes. The chill went deeper as I realized Diana and Corey might have been out in this for hours. I hoped they'd let their moms pester them into heavy coats.

When I got to the entrance to the neighborhood, Michael's white car was parked in the right-turn lane with the lights dimmed. A translucent cloud of exhaust puffed around the tailpipe. Through the window, I saw his head lowered with the glow of his phone illuminating his pale face.

I approached and tapped on the passenger window. He jumped a little, then reached over to open the door for me.

"Thanks for coming," I said as I sank into the passenger seat. The blasting heat felt amazing. I put my hands up to the vents and wiggled until my feet were baking under the floor vent.

"Thanks for asking nicely this time instead of kicking me in the balls," he said with a smirk.

"You kicked him in the balls?" Sal asked. "Bridget!"

"Sal, not now," I said, flicking my eyes to the rearview mirror.

"Sal?" Michael said quizzically. His eyes went wide as he turned to look at me. His expression said loud and clear, *are you insane?*

"My friend," I replied, gesturing to the backseat where Sal had materialized.

Michael twisted suddenly like he'd seen a massive spider crawling across the seat. "In my car?"

"He's a good spirit," I said. "He's a cop."

"This is so weird," Michael muttered.

"I can hear you," Sal said.

I checked the clock. It was nearly one in the morning. We were losing time fast. "You ready?"

He shook his head. Not him, too. "Before we go, I need you to tell me what we're getting into."

I sighed heavily. "I guess that's fair." I filled him in what had gone down since I saw the Facebook post this evening.

"You've been busy tonight. So you did call the police?"

"Yeah. But I don't know how seriously they took it. Diana and Corey haven't even been gone twelve hours yet."

Michael sneered. "We both know that's plenty of time for bad things to happen. You'd think they would have learned their lesson with Natalie."

"Hey!" Sal said. "That's not fair."

"But he's right," I told Sal.

"Huh?" Michael said.

It turned out that having my friends in on the secret had its drawbacks. Sure, I didn't have to lie nearly as much. But playing the intermediary between them was exhausting.

"You know what? I'm going to prove you wrong," Sal said. He leaned forward so he was between me and Michael. His warm brown eyes narrowed. "I bet they're already looking."

"What are you going to bet me?"

"Bridget," Michael said.

"Hold on," I said to him, then turned my attention back to Sal. "What's your bet?"

"I'm going to the police station," Sal said. "I'll bet you the dispatcher has already sent someone to look into it. I'm going. You call in another tip in five minutes so I can listen in. If they're already on it, you turn yourself around and go back to bed."

"And if they're not?"

His shoulders slumped. "Then I'll be back."

I sighed. "Fine."

Honestly, it didn't really matter if I won or lost the bet. If I lost, then Diana and Corey were someone else's problem. But I'd still be sitting on pins and needles until I found out they were all right. If I won, then they were back to being my problem, and I wasn't much of a rescuer.

The thing I'd realized since this whole ghost-whispering thing started was that I'd lived under an illusion for my whole life. Before Valerie died, I'd believed bad things didn't happen to decent people. I'd foolishly believed that no matter what, things would eventually work out okay. Back then, I'd have seen the post about Diana and Corey, had a moment of concern, and then moved on. I'd have believed that they'd be fine, because the world was inherently fair and just.

Now I knew better.

Two years ago, Valerie had died for no good reason, and the universe had dropped some knowledge on me like an anvil on Wile E. Coyote. Bad things happened to good people all the time, and for no reason other than dumb, wrong-place wrong-time luck. There was no guarantee that Diana and Corey would be okay, no magical spell that would protect them because they were young and had their whole lives ahead of them. A thousand awful things could have happened to them in the twelve hours they'd been out of touch. Knowing all of that, I couldn't relax until I knew what had happened. Regardless of what Sal heard, I lost either way, at least until Diana and Corey came home safely.

Sal disappeared in a rush of cold air, and Michael gaped at me. "What was all that?"

"Sal thinks we shouldn't be going out there," I said. "Apparently I'm reckless."

"And you disagree with him?" Michael said wryly, one eyebrow raised.

"Reckless is a really strong word. I would prefer adventurous. But it's not like I'm going out there so I can get wasted and do the rope swing. This could be someone's life on the line."

Michael held up his hands defensively, and I realized how heated I'd gotten. My cheeks were hot and my heart thumped against my ribs. He nodded. "It's okay, I get it. You know, I wish you'd known about Natalie when she'd first disappeared."

My throat closed up at the sound of her name. When he said it, he flinched then tried to mask it with a fake smile. I knew that look well. It was how Mom had looked when Valerie had first died. Her solution for the pain had been to pretend it hadn't happened. Even now, she rarely said Valerie's name. But every time she did, it was like an electric current ran up her spine.

"Me too," I said. The irony of Natalie's situation was that I'd only come to know her because she was missing. I'd only been useful to her after she was dead. Maybe that was why I'd latched onto Diana and Corey so strongly. "How have you been doing?"

He shrugged. "It sucks. My mom is a mess."

"I know what you mean."

"I get it. She's grieving too, but I don't want to have to take care of her. I'm sure it sounds terrible, but it makes me so mad to see her cry," he said, shaking his head. "Especially because I tried to tell her over and over that something wasn't right. We don't talk much. We just kind of drift around each other, you know? My dad told me I could come live with him, but I can't leave Mom like this right now."

I hesitated, then put my hand out. Without looking, Michael put his hand in mine. His rough fingers folded around mine tightly. The warmth was reassuring. Before he'd known Natalie was dead, there had been the tiniest spark between us. Circumstances had surely put it out, but there was a part of me that still felt connected to him.

"You're a good son for staying with her," I said.

His hand squeezed tighter on mine. His breathing hitched. I kept my eyes forward and pretended not to see the gleam of tears spilling over his cheeks.

"If she'd listened to me, Nat might still be here." He sighed loudly and scrubbed at his face with his free hand. "I'm sorry, I don't mean to dump on you."

"It's completely fine."

"You get it. No one else really does."

"Unfortunately, I do." I glanced at the dashboard clock. It had been five minutes since Sal had left us. "Let me call this in real quick."

As I took my phone out of my pocket, I was careful not to release Michael's hand. I was being comforting. And okay, maybe I was really enjoying a chance to be close to someone with a heartbeat. I dialed the number for the police station.

A familiar female voice picked up. You know, it was a sure sign that life had gotten weird when you recognized the voice answering the phone at the police station. "Fox Lake Police Department," she said. "How can I direct your call?"

"I have a tip regarding Diana Brown, the missing girl."

"You can leave it with me. I'll relay it to the officer in charge of the investigation."

"I can't talk to him personally?"

"No, ma'am," the receptionist said. "We're receiving a high volume of calls tonight, and our officers can't answer them all individually. All tips are immediately passed to the appropriate personnel. What can you tell me?"

"I heard a rumor that Diana and Corey were going out to Wildwood State Park to hang out," I said. "A few of my friends heard the same thing."

There was a brief pause, and I wondered if she was writing it down or just rolling her eyes. If Emily had also called it in, that had to give it some credibility. "Where did you hear this information?"

"I was hanging out with some friends who know Diana and someone said it. I'm not sure where they heard it, but I know they wouldn't make it up."

Michael watched me intently, which made me nervous. I averted my eyes. He'd never gotten to see Bridget in full-blown Pathological Liar mode. To be fair, it was mostly true. I just didn't mention that my friends were ghosts. A simple omission, and not at all relevant to the case.

"Do you have any more specific information? Where at the park, or maybe what time they went out, or what they planned to do?"

"Nothing else." *But give me a few minutes.*

"All right. I'll pass it along to the officer in charge. Thank you."

"Yes, ma'am," I said. She hung up on me, and I shrugged at Michael.

"That was impressive," he said. "You could be a criminal."

"You know, you're the second person to say that tonight. I'm not sure it's a compliment."

He laughed a little. "What about you?"

"Huh? What about me?"

"How are you doing?"

I shrugged. "Same old, same old. Lying to my mom like it's my job, barely passing in school." Math class was pretty much my only solid B. "A lot of people seem to want to hang around me now, which is really weird. I think I'm just the freak flavor of the month."

For a minute, I considered mentioning my invitations to the Christmas dance. I didn't know what I hoped would happen between us. But I knew for a fact if he'd asked, I would have come up with a way to get out of helping Mom.

"Yeah," he said thoughtfully. "I mean, not yeah, you're a freak. I get what you mean, though. That's why I had to get off Facebook for a while. People would act like they were really sympathetic, but then they would always ask about Natalie eventually. Weird stuff. Like how she died, did she suffer, did he…um…" He took a sharp breath and shook his head.

At the sign of his obvious discomfort, I interrupted, "Which is none of their damn business."

He let out a shaky breath. "Exactly." Things none of us wanted to consider, because no one wanted to imagine someone we loved going through what Natalie had. Natalie had showed me the terror and agony of her last moments; I didn't need to see the rest to know it had been horrible.

"It happened to me when Valerie died, too. It'll go away eventually. They get bored and move on to the next exciting thing." Unless you happened to tangle with a serial killer, and then you got round two.

Michael nodded. "The sooner, the better."

I took a deep breath. "So what about your dad? Do you think you'll eventually go live out there? Or up, or…actually, I don't know where he lives."

"Well, right now he goes back and forth between here and Kentucky for work," he said. "Near Louisville. But he's going to be taking a permanent job up there soon. I'd finish high school here, but he's been talking about me coming up there for college in the fall. If I live with him for the first year, he can get me in-state tuition, and my grades are pretty good, so I might be able to get a scholarship."

I felt like I'd been punched in the gut. Kentucky was a long way from Georgia, as in "maybe I'll see you every six months." Not that Michael and I had anything, but it was about as close as I'd gotten in a long time, and with the way my life was going, I wasn't likely to have many other chances. Michael knew who

I was, and it didn't freak him out. Or at least, it didn't freak him out enough to scare him away completely. Being around him was like being in the safety of my room. I didn't have to be scared or worried about anything. If he went away, I might never find that again. "That would be great," I said weakly.

He shrugged. "I guess we'll see. It depends how Mom is doing."

We sat in the quiet for a minute, and I realized he was lightly tracing the back of my hand with his thumb. His hands were warm and dry, and the light contact sent a little tingle up my spine.

"Am I interrupting something?"

*Are you kidding me right now?* I turned to see Sal sitting in the backseat. His somber expression sent a wave of dread rolling across my stomach. The easy comfort of my time with Michael washed away as I reluctantly extricated my hand from his. "Well?"

"They're sending a squad car," Sal said.

"A car? As in one. Singular. *Uno.*"

"*Now* you remember your Spanish," Sal muttered. "But they're doing something. You lose. Go home."

I raised an eyebrow at him. "I don't think one cop—"

"Two."

"Okay, I don't think two cops count as doing something."

"We didn't set specific terms."

"Too bad for you," I told him. "If they were really taking it seriously, they'd send a bunch of people and organize a search party. What are the odds they'll find Diana and Corey with only two people?"

"And what are the odds that *you* will?" he countered, his voice taking on a sharp edge. He laughed, a bitter, unpleasant sound. "But you were going to go either way, weren't you? *Dios mío.*"

93

"No. If you'd come back with news that they'd already been found, I'd be happy to turn around and go home."

Sal muttered something in Spanish. "You are a huge pain in my ass."

"Yes. Well, this shouldn't be a big surprise."

"It's not," Sal said. Again, I waited for the slip of a smile that said he was amused, but there was none. Instead, he sighed heavily. "Well, let's quit beating around the bush and get on with it."

His scathing disapproval made me feel hot and queasy. Why was I catching hell for doing the right thing? It was dangerous, but so what? A distant part of me knew it was because he cared, and he didn't want me in danger. Well, neither did I. But what if they didn't find Diana and Corey in time? What if the morning news tomorrow showed two bodies being rolled out of the woods? What if I had to watch a clip of Teresa Brown weeping for her lost daughter?

*What if?* was enough to override my instinct for self-preservation.

I turned back to Michael. His eyebrows were arched high, teeth pulling at his lower lip. "So?" he said. I had to give him credit. Despite watching me have a one-sided conversation for three straight minutes, he looked more curious than freaked out.

"They dispatched one car. Not enough. We're going out there."

"And you think we'll have better luck than the police?"

"I think we have strength in numbers. And we also have a whole search team of spirits going for us."

"We do?"

"We do," I confirmed. "We'll find them."

Michael's face fell. His eyes creased as the tendons shifted along his jaw. I wasn't psychic, but I knew he was thinking about Natalie. "I really hope so."

# CHAPTER TEN

ICHAEL STOPPED AT THE ALL-NIGHT Kwik-Stop on the edge of town before driving the rest of the way to the park. A sign outside advertised a "breakfast in a cup" that sounded more like a stomachache waiting to happen. As we walked under the jangling bell on the door, the lone clerk shot us a suspicious look. A couple of teenagers in the store after midnight? I couldn't blame him.

Michael picked out two Monster drinks from the cooler, then grabbed a bag of chips. He hesitated at the snack display and added a bag of beef jerky to his stash. "How long do you think we'll be out there?"

I shrugged and grabbed a root beer from the cooler. "Not too long, I hope. But it wouldn't hurt to be prepared."

We gathered an assortment of chips, snack bars, and a couple of candy bars. My mother would have cringed at the sight of the pile of bright wrappers filled with sugar and grease, which made it even more appealing.

The clerk slowly scanned the items and tossed them into a plastic bag. He seemed way more interested in staring us down than in our purchases, like he was trying to memorize our faces. "You two doin' all right tonight?"

"Doing fine," Michael said, taking a debit card out of his wallet. When I reached around him to separate my drink from his pile, he pushed my hand away and smiled over his shoulder at me. The little half-smirk sent a flutter of excitement into my belly. I was going to have start counting my stakeouts with Michael as dates. Maybe it was weird, but I'd take this over a dance with Brady any day.

While I waited, I scanned the display of random items that Mom called the "impulse section." Next to a basket of male enhancement supplements, guaranteed to "boost performance and endurance" —gross—there was a bin full of disposable hand warmer packets. A hand-written sign on orange paper cut into a flame advertised *2 for $3*. I grabbed two packs of them and added them to the pile.

The clerk raised an eyebrow and added it to the bag after scanning them. "Sixteen—"

"Wait, do you have a map of the lake?" I asked him.

"What for?" the clerk asked.

"To navigate? What else do you use a map for?"

The clerk's lip curled up. With eyes narrowed at me, he reached over to the opposite register and took a folded paper map from a plastic stand. He scanned it and dropped it into the bag on top of our junk food stash. "Seventeen ninety-seven."

Michael swiped his card and entered his PIN, then took one of the Monsters out of the bag before handing it to me. "Thanks, man."

The clerk responded by folding his arms over his chest and staring us down. What a jerk. As we walked out the door, I glanced back to see him still watching us. The bells on the door clanked as we stepped back into the icy bite of night. I shivered and turned to Michael. "What crawled up his butt and died?"

Michael pointed to the bag. "He probably thinks we're about to go get high as hell. And then...well. You know." He gestured to the car and gave me a suggestive eyebrow raise.

I could feel my face going red. "But— I— That's just stupid." And I was certainly not going to think about the possibility of hopping into the backseat with Michael to do whatever normal kids did. Not one bit.

"It would probably be a lot more normal than what we're about to do," he said with a nervous laugh. He opened the car door for me. I didn't have to look in the mirror to know I was bright red. My face wasn't cold anymore, thanks to the heat blooming in my cheeks. When he opened the driver door, I tried my best to look normal and settled the bag of snacks on my lap. The engine roared to life, and the heat blasted out of the vents. "So what's the plan? I assume you have one."

I'd spent most of the drive from my neighborhood to the Kwik-Mart trying to figure out the best course of action. If it was only me and Michael searching, it was no good. Sure, we'd doubled the number of people searching, but four people didn't exactly make a dream team. But if I could dispatch the spirits to comb the woods, then we might find them.

"Sal, can you go ahead and start rounding up the spirits?"

"No can do."

"Sal, we've been over this. We didn't even shake on the bet." Not that we could have even if we'd wanted to.

"It's not about the bet."

"Then what? Are you going to pout?"

He was silent, and I turned to see him shaking his head. "Bridget, you ought to be careful how you treat people. Especially the ones who care about you. I can't round them up for you because I can't go much further away from town. Maybe another mile or two, but then I'm gonna hit a wall. I wasn't sure about the distance until we started driving."

"Oh," I said quietly. His tone was quiet and calm, but it sent a hot rush of guilt to my gut. I felt about an inch tall. "Sorry."

If he accepted my apology, his neutral expression didn't show it. I wanted him to say everything was fine, that he understood why I was doing what I did.

But he didn't give at all. His voice was flat and matter-of-fact. "You need to get Kale here soon."

"Okay," I said. I closed my eyes and pictured his artfully messy hair and beautiful eyes. "Kale, I need you."

"Wait, who?" Michael asked.

"Another spirit," I said without opening my eyes. "Kale?"

"So you have dead guys following you around everywhere?"

"How rude," Sal said. "I don't follow her around everywhere."

"He can't hear you," I said.

"Thanks for the reminder." No humor. Just that same flat tone. He'd detached as far as he could without actually leaving. I heard it in my mom's voice all the time, when she'd given up on arguing with me. It said, *I'm done with you right now.*

God, if there was something I didn't need tonight, it was drama with Sal. With a huff, I raised my voice. "Kale, I need—"

"Heard you the first time," he said. I turned to see him sitting in the back seat next to Sal. He tipped his head to the other spirit. "Evening, Luis."

"Kale," Sal said politely. They acted as casual and normal as if they'd bumped into each other at the gym and were catching up on small talk. My life was so weird.

"What's up?" Kale looked around for a moment like he'd just noticed where he was. His eyes narrowed, dark brows furrowing. "Wait, what are you doing out here?"

"Why do you think?" Sal said. "Three guesses."

Oh, good. Now the two of them could lecture me, because it wasn't enough to get it from Sal. Maybe I could get Kale good and mad at me too.

"You most certainly are not going out there," Kale said. "I told you, I'm on it."

"Thank you!" Sal said. "A voice of reason."

"Excuse me," I said. "But I'm a grown—"

"Incorrect," Kale said.

"Mature—"

"Debatable," Sal said.

"Guys!" I snapped. "I can make my own decisions."

"Just because you can make decisions doesn't mean you make good ones. I think we can both agree that you make some objectively terrible decisions," Kale said. "I've been searching all night entirely so you wouldn't have to come out here."

"I don't make terrible decisions," I said.

"Ha," Sal barked. Kale didn't answer, but he gave me a side-eye and pursed his lips in response.

I folded my arms and continued. "Not all the time. Look, it's a trip out to the park. You act like I'm going downtown to a crackhouse or something."

"A huge state park where two kids disappeared twelve hours ago," Sal added. Now his voice was heating up again, like he'd gotten a second wind for the fight. Great. "And you intend to plunge in with no way to protect yourself against whatever happened to them. No, you're right. That's a great decision."

My heart thumped, my cheeks flushing hot again at the anger dripping from his words. "Okay, then what the hell should I—"

"Wait, how do you even know about the park?" Kale interrupted.

"A spirit came to the house and told me someone had found them," I said. "But he couldn't be any more specific than Wildwood State Park."

Kale rolled his eyes and nodded. "Trying to get useful information out of some of those spirits is like talking to cats."

"Wait, you can talk to cats?" My irritation with Sal flew right out of my head as I entertained the idea of Kale staring a fat orange cat in the eyes for an interrogation.

He laughed, a strangely musical sound. "It's just an expression."

"Well, you never know. It could be useful. You should try it."

"I'll get right on that." His smile evaporated, the warm crease around his eyes smoothing into a solemn expression. His tone was all business when he spoke again. "Anyway, I heard the same thing. Someone heard it from someone who heard it from someone else who… You get the idea. I'm still trying to follow it back to the source. I'll let you know when I find it. Just go home where it's safe. I promise I'll keep you posted."

"What if I called the spirits at the park to me? Like I did with Natalie and the others?" I saw Michael flinch again at Natalie's name. "Could I get it from them?"

"You could, but you shouldn't." Kale stopped and sighed. He turned to Sal and threw up his hands. "Is she even listening to me?"

"Nope," Sal said. "Trust me, I already tried."

"Am I wasting my breath by trying to speak reason to you, Bridget?" Kale asked.

"You don't have breath," I said. "So technically, no."

"Well, that's rude. Even if it's true."

"This is so friggin' weird," Michael said to himself. The sound of his voice brought me back to reality. In the heat of the moment, I'd forgotten where I was, and how it looked to Michael. I was twisted around in the passenger seat having a heated argument with the fast food trash in his otherwise empty back seat.

I turned to him and nodded. "Now imagine this all the time. Like in math class or during the SATs. It's pretty not-awesome."

"So how'd you convince him to help? Did you assault him again?" Kale asked.

"No, I asked him nicely, and unlike you two, he isn't trying to talk me out of it." Michael's head was tilted his head slightly, like he was trying to listen in on a quiet conversation. It reminded me of overhearing Mom's phone conversations and trying to piece together what she was saying about me with only one side.

"Right, because the guy whose sister got murdered after going missing is definitely the most rational voice in the room," Kale said.

"Thank you," Sal said. "That's what I said."

"What are they saying?" Michael said.

"Nothing," I said. Judging by the way Sal's eyes had narrowed to slits, I was pretty sure I'd learn some new, impolite words in Spanish if I could hear what he was muttering to himself. I turned to Kale. "So have you found anything else useful?"

"Last I heard, they're out in the woods," Kale said. "All I could pick up was fragments of trees, a lot of leaf cover, damp earth."

"What do you mean, all you could pick up?"

"So, interesting story," Kale said. His eyes lit up, and he started talking with his hands. As much as he scolded me, he was excited. "There's not a lot of spirits out there, which I found surprising. What you do have are a couple of soldiers who died while fleeing from battle in the Revolutionary War, some bootleggers who sank a boat trying to run whiskey down south, and a handful of hunters. But the oldest spirits don't speak anymore."

"Even to me?"

"That remains to be seen. You might be able to get more out of them. All

I could get was a glimpse of what they'd seen. This old, their minds are like cobwebs, shifting and falling apart at the slightest breeze."

"So we should go out and round those guys up," I said. "And I'll talk to them all."

"Oh, that's all?" Kale muttered.

"You're going to let her go?" Sal asked incredulously.

"He's not letting me do anything," I said. "He can't stop me."

"Actually, you're wrong," Kale replied. "But I wouldn't do to you what it would take to stop you." His eyes flared bright for a moment, which turned my stomach to ice. I didn't like what he was implying. He'd been downright terrifying when he'd made Tara Lynn Bledsoe help us. And ever since I'd crossed over the threshold to help Natalie, Kale had been able to touch me if he focused hard, almost like he was human. Only I knew he hadn't changed; I had. I trusted him not to hurt me; I probably trusted him more than anyone else I knew. But one thing we had in common was a shared belief that the end justified the means. I could see him using the classic Mom defense: "I'm your Guardian, not your friend." If he had to, he'd probably be willing to hurt me a little in the short term to prevent something worse from happening.

"So where are we headed?" Michael finally asked. "I'm sorry to interrupt your debate with all your imaginary friends, but it's getting late."

"We're not imaginary," Kale said. His voice had softened, from icy steel to a cool breeze.

"They're not imaginary," I said. "Just invisible."

"To normal people," Kale amended.

"Rude," I said to him.

"You had it coming for that breath remark." Even with Kale's light-hearted teasing, the tension in the car lingered, like ringing in my ears. It felt unfinished, as if I needed to say something to resolve it all and tie it up with a neat bow. But I didn't want to apologize, and they weren't going to cheer me on in my plan, so what was there to say?

I decided on an old Young family tradition: pretending the problem wasn't there and carrying on as normal. "Go to the main entrance. I'll call the spirits there."

Michael shifted into reverse and backed out of the parking spot.

Sal sighed, breaking his silence. The anger held in his clenched jaw had dissipated, leaving a shadow of concern on his face. His voice was gentle, but sounded almost sad. "Obviously I can't talk you out of doing this, so please be careful. You can talk to the dead, but you're not invincible. You have no idea what might be going on out there."

"I'll be careful," I said. "I promise."

He nodded and made the sign of the cross over his chest. "*Vaya con Dios.*"

He disappeared in a cold breeze, leaving Kale alone in the backseat. Despite my persistence in arguing with both of them, a knot of unease had gripped my belly. All I really knew was that as of whenever Jerry had gotten his information, Diana and Corey were alive. I had no idea if they were *still* alive, nor what they were doing out at the lake. Maybe Corey had planned to hurt Diana, and he was about to end it. Maybe she was already dead, and he was disposing of the evidence in the deep, dark woods. Sal was right. I could have been walking into grave danger.

I shook my head as if I could dislodge the troubling thoughts and opened Facebook again. I checked Diana's mother's page again and found a new update. My stomach lurched as I read her newest post, added about an hour ago.

*FB friends and family: this evening I received an anonymous tip from an obviously fake account. This kind of thing is not funny, and I really don't understand why people would try to play practical jokes in a serious situation like this.*

*Unless you hear otherwise, we'll be organizing a search party to begin at 6:00 in the morning tomorrow, starting from the Meridian Gardens amphitheater. Please dress warmly and bring your phones.*

My eyes stung, and I shook my head. It had been a long shot at best, but I'd been hopeful. Well, it was just a reminder that optimism was stupid.

"What's wrong?" Michael asked.

"Nothing. I tried to help out and it didn't work. Again." I switched over to look at the news channel sites. Channel 22 had shared the information about the volunteer search party. Well, if tonight went well, then Diana's mother could call off her search party and have a homecoming party instead. If it didn't, they might be adding Michael and me to their search list.

The glowing streetlights faded into a dark expanse of skeletal trees hanging over the road as Michael drove toward the park. A light blanket of white lined the road, reflecting the headlights in a sparkling veil. I checked the weather on my phone—according to the app, the temperature was down to twenty-two degrees. The snow lost its magical appeal as I contemplated being lost outside in the dark, icy night.

I wanted to punch something. Or somebody. I'd told everyone who had any power to help, and instead of bringing the whole cavalry, they weren't doing anything. What did I have to do for people to listen to me? And why couldn't Sal get this through his see-through head? I couldn't let go of his anger at me. I knew I could be walking into danger. We saw eye-to-eye there. But something was obviously wrong, and if no one else would help, then I had to. Why couldn't he understand that? If something bad happened to Diana and Corey while I was safe and warm in my bed at home, I'd never forgive myself.

I didn't want to do it, but I searched "how long to die in cold" and watched the loading animation with a chill creeping into my bones. As I scrolled through the search results, nausea washed over me in hot, clammy waves. A picture of something dark and streaked popped up. I zoomed in and yelped. Somewhere under a split, black patch of ruined skin was a bone. My stomach lurched, making me glad I hadn't torn into the snacks yet.

"What?" Michael exclaimed.

"Frostbite," I said, jamming the phone back into my pocket. *Holy crap.* I would have been happy to have lived my whole life without knowing what that looked like. "Drive faster."

# CHAPTER ELEVEN

H ARTLEY BEACH WAS THE CLOSEST ENTRANCE to town, so it was as good a place as any to start. When I was younger, we used to go out there for cookouts and boat rides with our old neighbors almost every weekend during the summers. Val and I would fight over who got to sit on the front of the boat, and Colin would happily eat sand on the beach under the umbrella with Mom. It was another one of those memories from before Valerie died, when the whole family had been together. I hadn't been out here for years.

Barely visible in the dark of night, a brown wooden sign with engraved white letters directed us to *Hartley Beach Recreation Area*. We turned right into the park and ended up on a narrow road that curved into the woods. A hundred feet off the main road was a small booth separating the two lanes of traffic. During the day, a park employee would be at the narrow booth accepting payment for a parking hang tag. By night, we were on the honor system.

"Oh, you rebels," Kale said as Michael drove past the parking pass kiosk without stopping.

"There's no one there," I told him.

"There were definitely instructions to leave your payment in the envelope," Kale said primly.

"Did you?"

"I'm an incorporeal being," he replied. "I don't pay for parking."

I laughed at him and shook my head.

"Bridget, I'm not gonna lie," Michael said. "This is super weird. If I didn't know better, I'd think you were batshit crazy."

"Well, don't rule it out yet. I'm still not sure I'm not," I said.

Up ahead was a small parking lot. A squat concrete building with restroom signs sat in the far corner. On the sloped roof, rough patches of black shingle peeked through the accumulating snow. Brown wooden signs pointed toward the picnic pavilions. A narrow paved path cut through the trees for access to the beach.

Michael pulled into the spot closest to the restrooms. The parking lot was empty except for us, which was to be expected at one in the morning in the middle of December. Intelligent people were at home, where it was nice and warm. But I'd hoped to find a car with a Mount Sharon parking tag. If Diana and Corey had driven out to Wildwood, they hadn't started from here.

It was one thirty-three in the morning. Diana and Corey had officially been missing for more than twelve hours, if I used their lunch at Joni's as the beginning of the timeline. A lot could happen in twelve hours.

I grabbed my backpack and got out of the car. It was still cold, but slightly warmer than it had been at home. "It's not as cold out here."

"The lake is still cooling down," Michael said. "It's usually a good ten degrees warmer out here."

"Up here," Kale said, gesturing for me to follow. Not for the first time, I envied his ghostly state. He wore light, casual clothes and no shoes. Though he appeared to walk, every few strides he disappeared and reappeared a dozen yards farther, like he was getting impatient with going through the motions of normal human movement. A few flickering bursts later, he stopped at the first picnic pavilion.

The pavilion was a thick concrete slab covered by a metal roof that had rusted to a streaky orange-brown shade. Splintered picnic tables were bolted to the concrete beneath. A ceramic ashtray filled with cigarette butts sat in the middle of one of the tables. Shards of dark brown glass littered the damp ground around the pavilion, like someone had thrown a beer bottle and missed the trash can.

"I know some guys who come out here to party sometimes," Michael said. "And you?"

"Not my thing. Although my sister probably spent her share of time out here." He chuckled a little, but it was a sharp sound with no humor. "So what do we do? Do you chant or light candles or something?"

I shrugged. "I'm not sure. This is kind of new territory. Kale?" I took one of the thick white candles out of my bag and lit it. The flame danced in the low wind.

"Let me try to bring them to you," he said. "Don't do anything just yet."

"Good, 'cause I'd rather not die this time."

Kale shuddered and shook his head. "You stay put." He disappeared, leaving Michael and me alone under the pavilion.

I sighed in relief. If I'd known the first time that was what it would take, I probably wouldn't have been so insistent on making Miss Tara give me the secret of breaking down the barrier. Then again, it probably should have been more obvious. After all, I wasn't born a total freak. I'd gained my ability after the car accident that had killed my sister. During a surgery to repair catastrophic damage to my leg, I'd flat-lined for a few seconds, which had been plenty to change me. When I finally got off all the funky, mind-numbing medications in the hospital, I'd seen my first spirit. It only made sense that making my ability stronger would require a similar event, though it was a hell of a rite of passage.

The flickering candlelight illuminated Michael's shocked expression. "Did you just say you died? Seriously?"

"Yeah, the last time we did this, apparently my heart stopped for a minute or two," I said. Michael's mouth dropped. "It's okay, Kale woke me up."

"That is not okay!" Michael spluttered.

Well, his sister was the one who was responsible, at least indirectly. "So if I look weird, then you might want to wake me up."

"I was so not prepared for this."

A bitter wind gusted from the center of the pavilion, carrying the faint scent of decay and wet soil. My skin broke out in goosebumps as the temperature plunged. The candle blew out. Michael's eyes went wide. I ignored my racing heart and forced myself to take even breaths as I flicked the lighter and relit the candle. It didn't matter how many times I saw the dead; I never got used to the initial shock.

The spirits had materialized in a tight cluster around me, like a football team in a huddle. Go Team Ghost. Kale hadn't been joking about the ragtag group of spirits. Flanking him were two men in tattered uniforms that belonged in a museum, a bearded man in a flannel shirt with a compass around his neck, and a pretty woman with a men's fedora sitting askance over wild curls. They all appeared dim and hazy, which meant they were losing their hold on this world. If they were as old as Kale indicated, I couldn't believe how long they'd already lingered.

Michael shivered and pulled his jacket tighter around himself. "Are they here?"

"Oh, yeah," I said.

His brown eyes, wide and frightened under raised brows, searched the pavilion. "Where?"

"They're here," I said, sweeping my hand in their general direction. "It's okay. I don't think they'd bother you even if they could."

"Tell him to quit worrying. This isn't about him," Kale said irritably. He blinked out of sight, then reappeared next to me with his arms crossed. I frowned at him. What the heck was his problem?

I ignored him. "Michael, it's fine." I looked back to the gathered spirits, who stared expectantly. They shifted uneasily, like they were ready to leave at the first chance they got. I took a deep breath. "Thank you for coming. I don't know if Kale told you, but I'm Bridget. I'm looking for some missing kids. They're out here somewhere. Uh, their names are Diana and Corey." I took out my phone and opened Facebook. After it tried to load my newsfeed for a few seconds, the screen went gray. A red alert appeared, reading *Network Error—No Internet Connection*. Sure enough, the indicator showed that I had no signal out here. Well, that was going to make things difficult. "Never mind," I said. I jammed the phone back into my jacket pocket. "She's about my age, with dark hair, and—"

The bearded man stepped out of the group. My speech dried up like sand on my tongue, and I instinctively stepped back as he approached me. The backs of my knees hit the bench of the picnic table, and I sat down abruptly. I had no option but to look up at him. My heart thumped.

"You okay?" Michael asked. His voice shook a little.

"Yes," I said, which was probably lie number forty-seven of the night. Time would tell. Seemingly unaware of the other spirits, the man got down on one knee, putting himself on eye level with me. With a bandana around his neck and a canteen on his belt, he looked like a hiker. He was close enough that I could have leaned forward and kissed him if I wanted, which I certainly did not with his crusted, cracked lips protruding from an unkempt beard. Dark, sunken eyes widened as he inspected me like I was some curious new species. He reached out one dirty hand slowly. I froze. Out of the corner of my eye, I saw Kale shift like he was going to intervene.

The hiker's eyes were the same cloudy white that most of the spirits developed over time, but he didn't look angry or dangerous. In fact, his face was hopeful. His thick lips parted slightly, and his brow lifted as he found my eyes.

Though my heart pounded, and a logical part of me screeched *what the hell?*, I put out one hand flat, like I was waiting for a high-five. The spirit lightly brushed his fingers over my palm. His touch was painfully cold to me, but he recoiled and stared in wonder at his fingers. The tips of his fingers were brighter, as if a layer of dust and grime had been scrubbed away to reveal the living, healthy skin beneath. His chapped lips spread into a real smile now. I couldn't help but smile myself. It was almost magical. Suddenly, he put his entire hand into mine, then looked to me expectantly.

*What the hell is this?*

I didn't know what I was doing, but I put my other hand over his and sandwiched his large hand between my small ones. Cold radiated into my hands, but the color shot up his arm like an injection of dye into water. His entire visage brightened.

I glanced up at Kale. "Are you seeing this?"

Kale's blue eyes were narrowed, but his expression was more awed than fearful. His voice was neutral as he said, "Yes. I see it."

"Warm," the hiker said finally. His voice sounded scratchy and rough with disuse. "So bright."

Again with the brightness. First Jerry the fisherman, and now a dead hiker. What did they see that I couldn't? What drew them close to me?

"What's your name?" I finally said. I went to pull my hands away, but his bigger hand clamped around my wrist. The wonder of the moment was diluted by a large dose of fear. My breath quickened, and I tried not to panic. Kale was right here. He wouldn't let anything happen to me.

"Bridget?" Michael said in a shaky voice. "What's happening? Are you doing the heart thing again?"

"Everything's fine," I lied. I forced a smile at the hiker. "Does this help you? My hands?"

"Yes. Bright and warm," he said again.

"Okay." I swallowed hard and tried to even out my voice, like smoothing wrinkles out of fabric. "I can hold your hand, but it would be nice if you would let go. Can you do that?"

The hiker nodded and released my wrist. He hesitated with his hand hovering over mine, then gently laid it on top. He gave me an expectant look. It felt like I'd plunged my hand into an ice chest at a picnic, but I smiled at him anyway. He smiled back, then said, "Isaac. I'm Isaac."

"Okay. It's nice to meet you, Isaac. Do you know where the kids are? Out in the woods."

"In the woods." The gravel slowly disappeared from his voice, and I wondered if it was another side effect of Bright and Warm Bridget.

"Okay, you look like the outdoorsy type, so that probably means more to you than me," I said. "Can you be more specific?"

A cold touch radiated from my shoulder and down my arm. I whipped my head around to see the female spirit with her hand on me. Like the hiker, her form brightened. Color rushed up her arm, beginning at her ragged fingernails and pouring over the sleeve of her long tan overcoat. Her eyes widened, and she smiled down at me.

"I should be charging admission," I muttered. Though the cold bordered on painful, it was almost beautiful to see the way they literally lit up in my presence. It was too bad I couldn't have the same effect on Mom by being near her.

"Careful," Kale said evenly.

"Near a creek," the hiker said.

"That's a little better," I said. "Did you actually see them?"

Isaac nodded. "I can show you."

"Okay."

With his other hand, Isaac touched my cheek. Pressure built all around me, pulling me down.

Suddenly, I was tromping through the woods, leaves crunching underfoot and branches whipping at my face. It was brutally hot even under the dense leaf cover. The strap of my pack had rubbed a raw spot on my left shoulder, and I made a mental note to wrap it when I made camp.

God, I was thirsty. I paused next to a rotted tree stump and propped up my foot. My legs suddenly ached as I gave them a break from all the effort of hiking. I wiped the mask of sweat away from my face, running it over the wiry beard I'd been growing all summer.

The alien sensation of the beard under my hand almost jolted me out of Isaac's memory, but I settled back in. I didn't want to see this; I'd been down this kind of twisted memory lane with Natalie and a girl named Nadia. Even if I wasn't sure of the particulars yet, I knew how this movie was going to end. Spoiler alert: Isaac was going to die. I didn't need or want to know how in order to find Diana and Corey. But this was apparently the price of information.

I reached for the canteen on my belt. A crunch from somewhere behind me broke the afternoon quiet. My body tensed. The involuntary jerk sent my foot plunging through the edge of the rotted stump and down to the ground. As I bent over to brush crumbled bark from my boot, I heard the slow, unmistakable sound of a rattle. Despite the blistering heat, my skin chilled at the sight of the snake coiled inside the hollow stump. The sun gleamed off its diamond-patterned scales. If it was asleep, it would have been beautiful.

It wasn't.

My toe was inches from its head. Tiny black eyes followed me as the forked tongue flicked out of its open mouth. The tail twitched lazily with a *tick-tock* sound. I froze. Was I supposed to run or hold still?

Sweat ran over my lip, and the hint of salt startled me out of my frozen daze. I had to do something. Surely I could move faster than it could. I slowly moved my foot backward, trying to control my movement. *That's a good snake. Just stay there. Good snake.*

Faster than my eyes could follow, the snake darted out and sank its fangs into my bare calf. Sharp pain lanced up my leg. I tried to kick it away, then grabbed its thick body with my right hand. I managed to tear it loose, but the snake twisted and latched onto my wrist instead. I yanked it free and hurled it overhead through the trees with an angry shout. But I never heard it land. I was too busy staring at my wrist. Dread washed over me as I stared at the two oozing punctures.

The sting of pain launched me out of the vision again, like breaking the surface of water while swimming. *I need to see Diana,* I thought, hoping it was polite. I guessed there might be etiquette about this kind of thing, but Isaac was already dead. We weren't going to accomplish anything here by replaying his last minutes. *Please show me Diana. The girl.*

The pressure built again and pulled me under. His memories came in disjointed fragments now—stumbling in the woods, a close-up and way-too-detailed view of a rattlesnake bite after the venom spread, and eventually the sight of Isaac's body under a pile of leaves deep in the woods. The whole thing was tinged with sadness and a hint of shame. Poor guy.

As we lingered over his former body, I felt the insistent pull ease. *Show me the kids,* I tried to think at him. I wasn't sure how the whole psychic thing worked. Even though it was all in my head, or so I thought, I didn't seem to be in control of it.

The scene blurred around me. Now I saw the wet gleam of sleet on piles of dead leaves and a darkening gray sky beyond the skeletal branches. The vision came in fits and starts, like we were getting bad reception. I heard a crashing sound and a rustle of leaves and rushed toward it.

It was a girl. The girl? They'd said a girl and a boy. Her name was...I couldn't remember. Dead leaves hung from her long, tangled hair. She stumbled over a root and went down hard on her hands and knees. Her pale face was streaked in half-dried blood, and her hands were angry pink against the dark ground. She cried in big, heaving sobs.

I wanted to help her, but my hands passed through her like she wasn't there. Like I wasn't there.

Oh, yeah.

That was Diana. I tried to pull myself away from Isaac's vision, but it something held me there in the dim cold of his memories. I tried to think about myself, about my warm hands and Michael and Kale, but I could barely glimpse the world outside his memory. "Kale," I murmured through cold lips. My voice was barely a whisper.

There was a deafening sound like a church bell. Everything went white. Suddenly the world rushed back. Freed from Isaac's cold grasp, my hands and face blazed with heat. I opened my eyes to see Kale standing in front of me, glowing bright enough to hurt my eyes. The other spirits had pulled away from him, cowering in fear. One of the uniformed soldiers had disappeared in terror.

Isaac put his hands up in surrender. His dark eyes were downturned. "Sorry," he murmured. "Didn't mean to hurt."

"It's okay, Isaac," I told him. Well, to be honest, it wasn't okay that he'd nearly pulled me down into…what exactly was that? It reminded me of when I'd connected with Nadia, another victim of the Runaway Killer. That was when my heart had stopped completely. It made me wonder what would have happened if Kale hadn't been around. I thought of myself as tough and independent, but I was swimming in deep waters here. Kale glanced over his shoulder at me, eyes flaring like blue lightning. "He didn't mean to," I told him.

"We're going to have a talk about safety," Kale said.

"Not a bad idea." My chest heaved, and my throat burned with the cold air.

Michael gaped at me. "What the hell just happened?"

"Long story," I said breathlessly. "Isaac, can you point me in the direction you saw Diana?"

"Diana," he said slowly. Then his eyes lit in recognition. He stepped out from under the pavilion. He looked up at the sky, then turned slowly in a quarter circle. He pointed, standing stock still. "This way."

"Which way is that?" I asked Michael.

"Which way is what?"

"This would be much easier if you saw them too," I said to myself. I looked in the direction Isaac was pointing, then stood behind him and mimicked him. "That way."

"Uhh," Michael said to himself. He closed his eyes and did a weird series of pointing in different directions, turning his body slightly with each one.

"Southeast," Kale muttered.

"Southeast," Michael said a few seconds later.

"Showoff," I told Kale. He smiled, looking satisfied with himself. I took out the map we'd bought at the Kwik-Stop and spread it out on the picnic table. I tapped my finger on the blue picnic table icon labeled *Hartley Beach*. "We're here. Isaac says he saw Diana southeast of here."

"Okay, so that rules out…" Michael hunkered in next to me and swept his hand over the map. "Everything from here west and north. You have a pen?"

I dug into my backpack. Under the baggie of sage was a brand-new black Sharpie. I handed it over and watched as he perused the map. It was probably just the contrast after being in close quarters with some needy ghosts, but Michael was warm and smelled really good. Emily insisted there was a universal Hot Guy smell. If there was, then this had to be it. As usual, it was not at all the appropriate time for these kind of thoughts, but I never seemed to have an appropriate time. A girl had to take it where she could get it.

Michael circled the Hartley Beach icon, then started marking off all the entrances and campgrounds to the west and north. We were fairly close to the southeastern tip of the park, so it narrowed our search considerably.

"So we still have all of these," I said, running my finger around the bottom right corner of the map. "Isaac, do you know which of these would be the closest?"

The ghost moved closer. The cold breeze accompanying him brought a hint of dirt and decay. "New map." His voice was going rough again. Most of him was fading back to the muted shades, like shades of gray with the barest hint of color. Except for his hands, where he'd touched me. Weird.

"Ask him where he started from," Michael said.

I shook my head. "He doesn't have to follow all the laws of physics, so his path wouldn't necessarily have to the same as ours. Isaac, if this is where we are now, about where did you see Diana?"

Isaac frowned, then bent over the map. He passed his spectral hand over the paper. For a moment, he traced the curving blue line of a creek, then circled his fingers slowly over a dark green area. "Here."

"He says here," I said, showing Michael where Isaac had pointed. As I put my finger down, Isaac's fingers drifted toward mine. I snapped my eyes to him. "Uh-uh, watch the hands."

"Get back," Kale said sharply. Thunder rolled in his voice. Isaac's eyes went wide as he retreated. He ended up halfway through the picnic table, his upper body standing above the flat surface like we were having a meal of half-rack of hiker. Kale's squared shoulders and glowering expression reminded me of his angel act with Tara. I still didn't know if Scary Kale or Sweet Kale was the real one. Either way, I was glad he was on my side.

Michael nodded and drew a big circle on the map around our search area. "It looks like you could probably get in this area from any of these three entrances," he said, drawing circles on the map.

"Then let's go."

# CHAPTER TWELVE

*Saturday—2:01 a.m.—Thirteen Hours Missing*

OUR NEXT STOP WAS CHATFIELD LANDING, a small campground about half a mile away from Hartley Beach. Like before, we were the only people in the parking lot. The snow was picking up now, forming a sparkling blanket over the dense layer of dead leaves on the ground.

As Michael made a loop around the small parking lot, I checked my phone to see if I had signal here. I had a new message from Emily. Sometime between Hartley and Chatfield, I must have gotten enough of a connection to download the new messages. There was still a single bar in the upper left, but who knew how long it would last?

*Emily: **What r u doing? Tell me u stayed home.***

My heart thumped as I considered my response. I didn't want to fight with her, but there wasn't really anything she could do other than scold me via text. I hesitated, then composed a response.

*You want the truth?*

*Emily: **B! Srsly?***

*Told you I had to help.*

*Emily: **Where r u? And how did u get there***

*Wildwood State Park. Michael drove me*

*Emily: **Fullmer???***

*Yeah*

*Emily: **OMG. Go home!!!***

*No. I'll txt when we get home*

The typing animation came up again, showing me she was working on a reply, but I closed the text window and put the phone away before it came through. When it buzzed in my pocket, I ignored it. She could keep arguing with the blank screen if she wanted, because I was tired of arguing. It was too bad I couldn't shut down an argument with Sal or Kale so easily.

"This isn't it," Michael said.

"Hold on a second. Kale?" I'd sent him ahead of us to start looking for Diana in earnest. I didn't know how to interpret his continued absence. After what seemed like a reasonable waiting period, I moved on to my next option. "Isaac? Do you hear me?" I imagined his bearded face with the cracked lips and dirty bandana around his neck. "Isaac, come speak to me."

I felt a sensation of bumping into someone, and suddenly the hiker's spirit was in front of me, his torso sticking out of the hood of the car. He looked like a flannel-shirted hood ornament. I winced at the sight and said a silent prayer of thanks that Sal and Kale usually tried to appear normal.

"Can you point me toward Diana?" I asked him.

Isaac tilted his head in confusion.

"Is he here?" Michael asked.

I gestured at the hood. "Isaac, the girl you showed me before. Where is she?"

By way of response, he disappeared into the night air.

"Son of a…" I muttered. Kale's assessment had been completely accurate. It was like trying to have an intelligent conversation with a cat.

"What did he do?" Michael asked.

"Disappeared. Just wait."

The clock plodded forward. I tapped my fingers on the window rhythmically as I stared at the glowing green digits. Had they even moved? My fingers drummed quicker.

"Bridget," Michael said. "Stop."

I flushed and gave him an apologetic look. "Sorry. Nervous energy."

Exactly six minutes later, Isaac reappeared between Michael and me. The temperature in the car dropped. All I could see was plaid torso, since his head was effectively cut off by the roof of Michael's car. In a muffled voice, I heard him say, "That way."

"Isaac, take about ten steps back," I said. The car between us didn't seem to affect our communication, because he followed my directions immediately. He backed up and reappeared at the nose of the car. The headlights shone right through him, the beam uninterrupted by his presence. "Show me again." Again, I mimicked his gesture for Michael.

"Still southeast," Michael confirmed.

"Thanks, Isaac." I consulted the map again and drew a checkmark over Chatfield Landing. "We still have Palmer Cove and Southwood Beach to the southeast."

As Michael pulled back onto the road, I tried not to think of Diana crying as she crashed through the woods, which of course only made me think of her more. And courtesy of my expert-level worrying skills, my imagination came in crystal-clear high definition. In my mind, I saw her huddled under a tree trying to hug the warmth back into her stiffening, cold limbs. And what about Corey? Was he chasing her through the woods with a knife, trying to be the star of his own horror movie? Or maybe Corey was dead already, and Diana was running for her life.

My stomach rolled on a stormy sea of nerves. As soon as I told myself to think of something else, anything else, my mind immediately cycled back to Diana, like a puppy stubbornly sniffing at a forbidden plate of people food. I knew that thinking about it and letting my imagination run wild, painting all the worst scenarios I could imagine, wasn't going to help anything. But I couldn't stop. What if we were too late? What if we showed up right as Diana took her last breath? What if—

"How far is it?" I asked Michael, trying to get my mind on anything else.

"Another couple of minutes. Normally I'd punch it, but the roads are really slick."

In the rearview mirror, light reflected from the puddles gathering on the old asphalt. My breath caught in my throat as the wave of anxiety rolled over me. The roads had been icy and wet like this the night my sister had died. I was more than happy for Michael to take his time. "It's cool."

We bypassed another parking kiosk on our way into Palmer Cove. By my calculations, we owed the Georgia State Park Services at least sixteen dollars. Well, we'd just have to add illegal parking to our list of petty crimes. Like our first stop at Hartley Beach, there was a large brown sign pointing us to picnic pavilions, another beach and dock access, and a hiking trail. A chain was stretched across the beach road, with a metal sign hanging from it. In large block letters, it read *Beach Closed*.

Further to our right was the entrance to the hiking trail that sloped up into the woods. Two cars were parked at the curb below the trail entrance, which gave me a spark of hope. One was a white pickup truck with a *Parkland Baptist Church* sticker on the back window. The other was a boxy little red car. I didn't know what kind of car either Corey or Diana drove, but this was light years closer to finding them than we'd gotten so far.

Michael parked on the opposite side of the red car. I peered through my window to look for...for what? Clues? The side windows were tinted, so I didn't see much of anything. When we got out, I'd check it further. Instead, I called for Isaac again.

As soon as his name rolled off my tongue, the hiker appeared right outside the passenger window. And for bonus points, he'd managed to get all of his limbs outside the car. He was getting the hang of it. "Isaac, can you point us toward Diana?"

As before, he disappeared. While we waited, I tried my phone again. I still had a single bar, so I tried to load Facebook to check for updates. My phone gave a valiant effort, but eventually went gray and gave me the *Network Error* message. Great.

I stuck my hands into the fleece-lined pockets of my jacket to keep from driving Michael crazy while we waited. My heart raced as I toyed with the corner seam, worrying at a loose thread in my right pocket.

It was two thirty-nine when Isaac returned and pointed. I mimicked his gesture, and Michael frowned. "North," he said.

"But he's been saying south and east all this time." My heart sank. Had Isaac been confused all along? We'd been following him for over an hour now, which was time Diana didn't have.

"No, look," Michael said, smoothing out the map on the console between us. He touched the green-shaded area around Palmer Cove on the map. "From where we're sitting, it's north into the woods."

"So you think this is it?"

He shrugged. "I think this is the best we've got."

"So now we can call the police and tell them she's out here," I said. "Isaac, was she still alive?"

"Show you," he said, holding his hands out toward me.

I recoiled from him. "No, you don't have to—" I gasped as he touched my face. It felt like plunging my head into ice water, and my entire body became one gigantic goosebump.

I saw Diana again, but she was barely moving. She was in a crumpled heap against a tree trunk, arms curled tight around her legs. Through dry, blue-tinged lips, she made hoarse sounds that had probably stopped being sobs hours before. Her long-sleeved pink shirt was damp in spots. As I watched, she got up, walked in a wobbly circle, then stumbled again in the wet underbrush. What was going on?

I tore away from Isaac's grasp and held up my hands in a *stop* gesture. He frowned. "I know, bright and warm," I said. The heat of the car was almost uncomfortably warm after the cold chill of the vision. "But we have to help her. Can you show me the way to her?"

Isaac nodded. "Not far."

I wasn't sure he was going to be the best judge of distance, but I also didn't think he was going to lie to me. "Okay, we need a plan," I said to Michael.

"They're definitely here?"

"Diana is. I don't know about Corey." I looked at Isaac again. "Did you see a boy?"

He shook his head. "Pretty girl. Like you."

"Well, thanks. But no boy?"

"No boy."

"No Corey," I told Michael.

"That doesn't bode well," he said. "Do you think he did something to her?"

"Or someone did something to him and is still chasing her. Anything is possible, and none of it's good. Okay. I promised Emily and Sal I would do this as smart as I could."

"Which is an improvement."

"You too, really?" I gave him a mock irritated look, but he was smiling. His eyes crinkled in a warm gaze that made my stomach flutter. I smiled back, then closed my eyes. "Kale, I need you." As I said his name, I pictured his face—beautiful blue eyes, ageless features that made the pop stars my friends followed on Instagram look like gawky sixth graders. I turned around, expecting to see him in the backseat. I frowned. There was nothing but the same takeout garbage that had been there before. "Kale?"

"Nothing?" Michael said.

"Weird. Kale?"

"Isn't that a vegetable?"

"It can be a name too," I said hotly. "When he shows up, he can confirm Diana's out here. If she's here, then this is probably Corey's car. That should be enough to get the police to take it seriously enough to drive out here for them."

"And we take off."

"We definitely take off. I don't know about you, but the last thing I want is to be on the news."

"Again."

"Again."

After Natalie's death, the case of David Miles, AKA the Runaway Killer, had been all over the news. My mom and Emily's mom, Kari, had shielded us, refusing to give any kind of interviews or other information. They'd directed all questions to the police, which was fine with me. I'd never wanted to be famous at all, but if it happened by accident, I certainly didn't want it to be in association with something like that. Michael hadn't been so lucky. His mother had been all over the news, crying for Natalie when days before she'd been dismissing her daughter as a runaway delinquent like everyone else.

"I want to check something," I said suddenly. I opened the car door and was immediately buffeted by a gust of cold air. For a moment, I expected to see a new spirit, but it was only the winter wind. I bent over to peer into the dark-tinted windows of the red car. I still couldn't see anything. I walked around to the front, but even the windshield was tinted dark. Damn.

I shoved my hands into my pockets and made a circle around the car. There were no stickers or decals that gave away anything about the car's owner. I'd hoped to see a tag or sticker for Mount Sharon High. Isaac's vision was enough to convince me that they were out here, but it would have been nice to have a confirmation of the license plate to give the cops. Well, I could give them the tags for both vehicles and hope for the best.

I slid back into the heat of the car and rubbed my hands together.

"Did you see anything?" Michael asked.

"Nothing. But Isaac is sure." I checked my phone again. Patience was a virtue, but not one I could afford right now. "Kale, please hurry. I really need—"

"What?" he snapped. Cold air filled the car, and I saw Michael shiver. Instead of his usual cool green smell, there was an electric scent.

"Jeez, what's wrong with you?" I asked. His brow was furrowed, his upper lip curled in what had to be anger. Was he angry at *me*? That was something I'd never seen, and it made me feel strangely guilty. After all, I was trying to do this right at his request.

"It's Diana," he said. "And Corey."

A chill broke across my skin. "What about them?"

"They're in really bad shape."

"What do you mean? Are they alive?"

"For now. He might make it a few more hours, but she's struggling." He clenched his fists, which was probably a lot more satisfying when you were made of flesh and blood. A low rumble like distant thunder filled the car.

Michael's gaze flicked toward the back. Had he heard it too? "Is everything okay?"

"He says Diana's struggling," I said. "Are we talking minutes, hours?"

Kale shook his head. "I don't know. And I can't do anything to help her. Unless she dies." His lips twisted into a bitter smile that didn't belong on his face. "Then I'm a huge help."

"You've helped me before," I said.

"You're different." Gee, thanks. "Look, until now, I was with everyone else on Team Stay Out of It, but this may be the only way Diana gets out alive."

"Then let's go." I grabbed my backpack and got out of the car. I shivered and tugged the zipper of my jacket all the way up to my chin.

"Fill me in," Michael said as he got out and walked around the front of the car to join me.

"We need to go find Diana. Kale says he doesn't know how long she has. If we wait—"

"We won't wait, then," Michael said. "Let's go ahead and call 911, and then we can go find her."

Kale nodded vigorously, then turned away, his gaze far away as he looked toward the woods. Could he sense Diana still? "Okay, can you call?"

Michael took out his phone and frowned. "I don't have a signal at all." He held the phone up and dialed 911. He placed it to his ear, then shook his head. "Not going through. You try."

I took out my phone, but the graphic read *No Service*, not even an empty circle to indicate the signal I didn't have. "I've got nothing." I held it up in the air and walked slowly toward the center of the parking lot. I tried dialing 911 anyway and held the phone to my ear. There was no sound at all, just the slightly fuzzy sound of an open line. "Nada."

"We're probably pretty far from a tower," Michael said. "Plus all the trees."

I tried the call again and still got nothing. I shoved it back into my pocket. "Okay. Then you should drive back toward town? I was getting texts from Emily at Chatfield Landing. Maybe you should go back there."

"Are you insane? I'm not leaving you out here by yourself," Michael said. He folded his arms across his chest.

"I'm not by myself. Kale's here."

"Fine. I'm not leaving you out here with no one but your ghost BFF to protect you."

"I am not a ghost," Kale muttered.

"Look, I don't want you to leave me alone either," I said. Actually, the protective guy thing was pretty nice, and a marked improvement from my last rescue mission. Unfortunately, it was also entirely unhelpful. "But you staying here with me because it makes you feel better doesn't do anything to help Diana and Corey."

"So what are you going to do to help?" Michael asked.

Considering my track record, I resented his implication that there wasn't much I could do. With Kale's help and a whole slew of spirits to speak to, I could do a lot more than he could. But I held my tongue and said, "Whatever I can."

"And what if you get lost, too?"

"Then I have my ghost BFF," I said. "Now go."

# CHAPTER THIRTEEN

*Saturday—3:01 a.m.—Fourteen Hours Missing*

A S I WATCHED MICHAEL'S TAILLIGHTS recede and eventually disappear into the dark of night, I regretted telling him to leave. Kale might have been there for moral support, but he didn't have heat.

My breath puffed in a plume of fog as I sighed and turned to him. "Guess it's me and you."

Kale smiled. "Then we're both in good company. You better than me, of course."

"Hey now."

His grin made me feel warm and fluttery. "This way."

Kale moved quickly toward the dense wall of trees at the edge of the small parking lot. A brown-painted wooden sign with blocky yellow letters read *Hiking Trail.* Wooden planks laid into the ground provided the first few steps up to the trail, but beyond that it was all nature.

A chill ran over my skin that wasn't entirely from the winter weather, although it was miserably cold outside. This wasn't the half-dark of city life, where there were streetlights and lit windows, and everything simply seemed muted by night. This was shades of black, where I could barely make out the sharp outlines of leaves and the tall, columnar silhouettes of the barren trees. My heart thumped as I stared into the darkness, hoping for a miraculous three-hour advance on daylight.

"You know, I really need to put a flashlight in this bag," I told Kale.

"I'll make a note," he replied.

Instead, I took out my phone and switched it to airplane mode to preserve its battery. Michael wouldn't be able to contact me out here even if he tried, so there was no point in wasting all the battery life searching for a signal. I turned on the phone flashlight and held it out in front of me, casting a pale blue glow on the damp asphalt in front of my feet.

"Technology really is amazing," he said.

"So what did they have when you were alive?"

"Certainly not that."

"So you *were* alive at one point?"

"What is it, really, to be alive?"

I groaned. "Why are you so sly?"

"Why are you so nosy?" he replied. "Come on."

"Someday," I said to myself. One of these days I was going to trick him into revealing more about himself. "Lead the way."

He hurried ahead, drifting above the ground. Though he glowed faintly, he didn't cast light on the ground beneath him. I tried to keep up with his pace, swinging my phone in wide arcs to illuminate the way ahead of me. A narrow path of damp earth and water-logged pine needles had been worn into the ground, curving gently between the trees as it rose slightly. The ground was wet, but it hadn't yet been covered in snow. I pointed as much out to Kale.

"It's still warmer here than in town," he said. "That's one thing in our favor."

"It's something. How far are they?"

"I'm really not sure. Distance doesn't feel the same to me as it does to you."

"Corey! Diana!" I called. My voice died out immediately, like it was swallowed up by the night. My heart thumped, blood roaring in my ears as I stood there, waiting for an answer. Something crashed through the brush nearby, and I yelped as my heart leaped into my throat. A rapid-fire slideshow ran through my mind: *psycho killer, tiger, bear, zombie.*

"It's just an owl," Kale said.

"Some of us can't see in the dark." It had to be a mutant owl, because it sounded like a three-thousand pound bear on steroids. With an axe.

"I don't see like you do," he replied. He put out one hand. "Do you want to see?"

I narrowed my eyes. "I'm not entirely sure. Are you going to show me like Isaac showed me?"

"I have much better control than that. I won't hurt you."

A thrill of fear struck me. With Kale, I felt the hint of danger restrained behind a powerful calm and control. Yet again, he said he wouldn't hurt me, not that he couldn't. Whatever he was, I was glad he was on my side.

I offered my hand, and he moved to take it. For a moment, it felt like I'd passed my hand through a cold slush. A cool sensation ran up my arm, but it wasn't the biting, burning cold I'd felt in Isaac's memories. It was the pleasant cool of a summertime swim.

The night changed suddenly, with the deep black exploding into a gleaming expanse. Glittering blue dust speckled the nightscape like snow. I looked down to see my own hand covered in it, glowing brightly. Along the trunk of a tree in front of me, tiny clusters of blue moved in a neat line. A few feet away, a quick moving blur of light soared overhead, then landed in a tree. As it settled, I could see the outline of an owl's squat body and tufted head. It was brighter in the center, like looking at the heart of a flame. Awe and wonder struck me speechless. The tiny clusters had to be ants, each with their own little spark of life. I stared up into the sky. Here and there were small blue lights in the branches of the trees. Birds, bats, who knew?

"It's beautiful," I said in a dazed voice. I turned to look at Kale but I couldn't even make out his shape. He was just an unrelenting brightness that hurt my eyes. Blood roared in my ears, and it was so loud I thought I would go deaf. I tore my hand away from his cool grasp and pressed my hand to my forehead. "You're so bright."

He hesitated, then smiled. "That's how they see you. The other spirits, I mean. That's why Isaac couldn't keep his hands off you."

"I thought it was a guy thing," I joked weakly. The thought that I looked like Kale, a blazing star confined to a human shape? It was about half cool and half terrifying. "Is that what all living people look like? To you, I mean?"

"No." He kept moving ahead on the trail, gesturing for me to follow. "Most people look no brighter than the animals. Life is life, regardless of the size. But you're different. Special."

"I'm special all right," I muttered. Why did I look more like Kale—a spirit of questionable origin—than a person?

"You are," he said. "You're not all there."

"Gee, thanks." Even my mother could have told him that. As we reached a signpost that indicated *Slippery Path Ahead,* I realized I'd been busy talking to Kale and not doing what we were here to do. I paused and peered at the path before us. The dirt had been worn away to expose huge flat rocks that were slick with standing water and moss. "Corey! Diana!"

He waited silently while I listened for a response. There was nothing but the gentle whisper of the wind. Kale said, "You're not entirely in this world, I meant. You're alive, but you're different."

I paused and turned to him. "Really?"

"Really. First your surgery, and then what you did for Natalie. You've crossed into the other side twice now. So you kind of have a foot on each side."

"What does that even mean?"

He sighed. "I don't know how to explain it." He pondered, arms folded across his chest. Finally, his eyes lit up. "You know how you've been practicing your Spanish with Sal?"

"Yeah, I still suck at it."

He laughed. "*¿Hace frío, sí?*"

"Kale."

"Sorry. Think of this like becoming bilingual. But the only way you can even learn the first hint of the language is an experience like you had. Imagine you were standing in a room of people who only spoke Spanish, and you couldn't see them to even try to guess at what they meant. You'd never learn a word without knowing a few to get you started."

"So when my heart stopped in my surgery, I got a crash course."

"Something like that," Kale said.

"But that still doesn't explain why I look more like you than a normal person," I said. "That freaks me out."

His brow wrinkled in confusion. "I don't understand the issue. You're *not* normal."

I sighed. "No joke."

"It's not a bad thing." He pondered, then held his hands about an inch apart like he was pantomiming a sandwich. He shook his lower hand. "This is the living." He moved his upper hand. "And this is the spirit world." He moved his fingers. "They're right here together. When your heart stopped, it wasn't the spirit world that changed. It was you. You simply became aware of something that had always been there." He moved his hands and pressed them around my hand. I could feel the cool sensation pouring off him. "This is you. You're touching both. You speak both languages now."

"And it changed again when I used Tara's ritual," I said, more a question than a statement.

He nodded. "When you brush with death, you pass into the spirit world. If you're revived, it yanks you back into your body. But it's like you crammed in an advanced course in Spanish in that time."

"Oh! Like the Matrix." I did a karate pose. "I know kung fu."

He stared at me. "I don't understand that reference."

"You and I are going to have a movie night when this is over."

He smiled. "It's a date."

My gaze found his as my heart thumped hard enough to shake my whole body. For a split second, I allowed myself to entertain the idea of me and Kale curled up on the couch under a blanket. In my little dream, he was warm and real and didn't glow, which was perfectly fine. My cheeks flushed.

"We have to focus," I said, taking a tentative step on to the slippery path. I hoped the sudden flush didn't register as extra-hot spots in Kale's Life-O-Vision. "Corey! Diana!" I shouted. My foot slipped, and for a moment I felt the stomach-churning sense of losing my balance. I steadied myself, then swung my flashlight around and gasped. Off to my right, the path seemed to drop away. There was a plunging drop; in the dark I couldn't guess how far down it went. "Shit."

"We're close. Look."

He pointed down. At my feet lay a folded paper map. It still looked crisp and new, though it had gotten wet lying on the ground. There was also a black piece of plastic a few feet away. I picked it up to examine it. It was a circle with two spring-loaded latches, with *Canon* on it in white letters.

"Lens cap?" I said. Kale shrugged. I yelled again. "Corey! Diana!"

Only the night answered, with a rustle of wind in the trees and the mournful call of a faraway owl. I called again and closed my eyes to concentrate. As I stood there in the quiet dark, I heard the faintest groan. I gasped. Had I actually heard it, or was it just my own breath? "Did you hear that? Corey! Diana!"

There was another groan, then a croaking male voice. "He-hello? Down here."

"It's him!" I crowed. "Corey, hold on! Help is coming!" I whirled to look at Kale. "Which way is it?"

Kale hovered near the edge of the path. "Certainly not this way. I'm guessing that's how Corey went. Probably didn't go well. Hold on."

Then he disappeared, leaving me in the darkness with only the light of my phone flashlight. My heart raced as I turned to look behind me. The woods were dark and massive. I felt tiny and alone there between the hulking trees, with the slick path ahead and a plunging drop to my right.

What would I do if I fell over the edge and got hurt? There would be no keeping the secret, and Mom would probably put me under lock and key until I was twenty-one. And that was assuming I survived the fall and somehow got help.

No. Kale was here, and he would make sure I was safe. I was certain of it.

Mostly.

But the thought of going over the edge made me dizzy. I crouched down and placed my hands on the ground. The rough rocks were coated in a layer of cold, slimy moss. The slimy moss on the rocks made me feel rooted to the ground instead of the untethered sensation of teetering over a precipice.

"What are you doing?"

I screamed and nearly jumped out of my skin. "Holy crap, you scared me."

"I was gone for all of thirty seconds," Kale said.

"You said before you have a poor sense of distance." I stood carefully and

135

flung bits of moss off my fingers. "Clearly you can't tell time either."

"Okay, a minute, tops. Whatever. Come on. We have to go the long way down, but I found a safe way for you."

I hurried after him, passing the phone flashlight in wide arcs to make sure I wasn't going to trip. The light caught off the wet surface of the rocks, like little mirrors laid into the ground. Gradually, the path shifted downward. My feet rustled in the dark layers of decaying leaves. My heart drummed, though I wasn't sure if it was excitement at finding Corey or apprehension at what kind of condition he was in. What the heck was I supposed to do if I got down the hill to find him beat up and slashed by some psycho?

Something slashed at my face. I threw my hands up to fend it off, yelping wildly. With my arms crossed over my face, I launched myself backward. "Help!" I shrieked. I pistoned my feet out to kick away whatever had attacked me.

"Bridget, what the heck?"

My breath came in short, shallow pants. My throat burned. I looked up to see Kale standing over me. He looked baffled. "Something got me," I said.

"There's nothing here." He frowned and leaned closer. "But you are bleeding."

After touching my cheek gingerly, I came back with wet fingers. I shone the flashlight on them to see blood mixed with the soggy moss clinging to my hands. "Ouch." My cheeks went hot, as much from the cut as embarrassment. With a groan, I got to my feet and brushed my jeans off. My butt was wet and cold from the ground. As I raised the flashlight, I saw my malicious attacker: a wet tree branch. "I hate this so much."

"I'd like to remind you who insisted on coming out here," Kale said.

"Shut up. And you wanted me to."

"Only after the fact. Come on. As much as I enjoy arguing with you, we have bigger priorities tonight." He disappeared, then reappeared a few yards down the path.

As the path grew steeper, my balance started to shift so I was jogging down the hill after him. My feet skidded in the wet leaves, and I felt the nauseating jolt of the almost-fall. I slowed down, taking more careful steps.

"Here," Kale said. As I walked to his side, the sloping path evened out. My feet found the comfort of flat, even ground. I breathed a sigh of relief.

Near the bottom of the path was a cluster of trees. A bluish glow illuminated a vaguely human-shaped shadow. I held up my phone flashlight. "Corey?"

He gasped and looked up. The object in his hand cast a harsh light from below, throwing deep shadows over his features. "Who—who's 'ere? Diana?"

"No. But we're here to help."

"We…" he said blankly. "Who?"

I held the phone up to light the ground. The trees' gnarled roots were exposed, rising from the ground like twisted scars. Corey sat between two thick roots, one leg out at an awkward angle. A few feet away, my phone light reflected off something glass. A backpack lay open near him with a thick red strap hanging out. I turned the light to Corey. He cringed, covering his eyes. "Sorry," I said quickly.

Corey was wearing a bright pink jacket, and while I wasn't the type to judge someone's fashion choices, it obviously wasn't his, considering he couldn't zip it up. My guess was that it was Diana's since Isaac's vision had shown her with no jacket. But why would Corey take his girlfriend's jacket? Something didn't add up. Suddenly, my mouth went dry, and I felt the shaky, tense feeling of anxiety creeping over me.

"Corey, why are you sitting down here? Did you get lost?" I wanted to ask, *why are you sitting down here while your girlfriend is wandering alone and scared?*

"Diana," he said again. His voice was weak, like he was drifting off to sleep. What was going on?

"No, I'm not Diana," I said irritably. I crouched next to him, and my foot caught on something solid. Corey let out a shout, then clamped his lips together as he groaned. What the hell?

"His leg," Kale said quietly.

I moved the flashlight to look closer at him. His right leg was twisted, with his knee turned inward and his foot twisted outward. His hips were cocked at what had to be an incredibly uncomfortable angle to let him sit that way. I shone the light up the hill, then over to the glass I had seen. "Did you fall over the edge?"

He nodded slowly. "M-leg."

"Do you think you broke it?"

His face contorted, and I saw the liquid sheen of tears springing to his eyes as he nodded. The sight of his tears made me feel like a complete turd for suspecting him of hurting Diana. I almost wanted to apologize for suspecting the worst, even though he'd never know. My heart sank.

"Did someone push you? Is there anyone else out here?"

He stared at me. "Diana?"

"Just Diana? No one else?"

"Yeah," he murmured.

"Where is she?"

He shook his head.

"Did you try to call for help?"

"Naberry," he said.

"I'm sorry?"

"No berry," he said emphatically. He took a deep breath. "No battery."

"Your battery died," I said. Upon closer examination, I realized it wasn't a phone in his hand, but the body of a fancy digital camera. "So you used your camera for light."

Corey nodded. It gave him less light than my phone flashlight, but anything was better than sitting here in complete darkness. Poor guy.

"Does Diana have her phone?"

"Think so."

"Do you know her number by heart?"

He squinted his eyes like he was trying to keep tears from falling, then shook his head.

"It's okay. We don't have a signal so I don't think I could get her anyway."

"I'm not sure that's comforting," Kale said.

I shot him a glare, then looked back to Corey. Careful not to jostle him again, I shifted my position and held out my phone. "Can you hold this so I can see?"

Corey took the phone, but a violent shiver tipped it right out of his hand. He clenched his fingers. A grimace twisted his face. "Sorry."

In the harsh light, I saw the tremble in his hands. "Oh, your hands," I murmured. "I'm sorry."

I turned the phone over and put it on the ground between us with the light shining up. I held out my hands and closed them around Corey's fingers. His hand felt like a block of ice, and the skin on his palm was pale white. Was this frostbite? It didn't have the grotesque black and red I'd seen in the picture, but I hadn't looked at anything else.

"You're warm," Corey said.

"I get that a lot lately," I said to myself. I rubbed his hand vigorously, hoping I wasn't hurting more than I helped. I didn't know what the hell I was doing, which made me wish my mom was here. She was sure to lecture me until I died of old age, but she was also a registered nurse and would know what to do. "Am I hurting you?"

"No. Feels good."

"Okay." I took the other one and rubbed warmth into it while I contemplated what to do. What would Barbara Young do? After a blistering tirade about dangerous and risky behavior, of course. "First thing, you need to zip up."

"Can't," Corey said.

"If I can squeeze into a pair of yoga pants, then you can fit in this jacket," I told him. After fumbling the tiny zipper pull, I forced the zipper up. The bright pink fabric around the zipper strained and rippled, but I got it zipped all the way to his chin. Next, I leaned over him and pulled the hood up over his bare head. Mom was always lecturing us about wearing warm clothes, especially covering our heads when it was cold. She said we lost fifty percent of our body heat through our head, reciting it word for word each time like she'd just heard it. Once, Colin had called her on the fact that it was an old wives' tale, but she'd shut him down with, "Well it certainly won't kill you, will it?"

I pawed through my backpack. "Can you eat?" Unless they'd brought snacks, he might not have eaten since their lunch at one. I knew I'd be starving.

He nodded, and I pulled out a Snickers bar and a bag of chips. I opened the candy bar for him and watched him as he wolfed it down. I was afraid he'd choke, but he managed to get it down with a few coughs and a string of caramel on his chin. Once he was done, I opened one of Michael's Monster drinks and held it for him to take a sip.

"Sorry I don't have anything hot," I said. "We didn't really plan very well."

But fate, or maybe a kindly spirit I hadn't yet met, had the right idea when we went to the Kwik-Stop. I tore open one of the packets of handwarmers. They looked like tea bags without strings. The heat radiating from them was heavenly.

"Here," I said, depositing one in Corey's right hand and gently closing his fingers around it. "Now stick it in your pocket."

His face smoothed out in visible relief as he jammed his hand into his pocket. After I gave him the other one, I examined the packets. We'd bought a total of eight, so if I gave him four, I'd still have enough for Diana.

"Diana," he murmured.

"Been through this," I said as I opened two more packets.

"Sick."

I narrowed my eyes. "She's sick?"

"Merging."

"Emergency," Kale said.

My icy fingers were stiff and clumsy, but I managed to untie Corey's left shoe. After loosening the laces, I wedged one of the warmers down the inside of his foot. His foot was damp and cold, and I wished I had extra socks for him in my bag of tricks. He winced as I laced his shoe back up and adjusted his pants leg. I regarded the other foot warily. "Do you want me to try to warm it up?" He nodded. I swallowed hard as I eyeballed the twisted joint. "Please remember it's totally not my fault that your leg is broken."

"You should work on your bedside manner," Kale said.

"You wanna do this?" I asked him.

"Huh?" Corey said.

"Not you. Never mind." I hesitated, staring at his other sneaker like it was a ticking bomb. It was hard to tell where the actual break in his leg was. If I touched his foot and he started screaming, I was going to scream right back in

141

fright and then wallow in guilt for the next week. Finally, I took a deep breath and started picking at the shoelaces. By some miracle, I managed to get them untied without jostling him, but the time came to loosen it up. My stomach twisted as I pulled the front of the shoe open and slid my fingers down to his instep. As my fingers touched his damp sock, he sucked a sharp breath through his nose. "I'm so sorry."

"It'll help him more than it hurts," Kale said.

I swallowed the lump in my throat. "That's easy for you to say." I pushed the warming packet into his shoe and left the laces loose. "Is he going to be all right?" I asked Kale.

Corey looked at me quizzically. "Who?"

"I'm not a doctor," Kale said. "But you probably kept him from getting frostbite. If we can get an ambulance here soon, he might be okay."

"Might?"

"Bridget, you know me. I'm not going to make empty promises. Hopefully Michael got in touch with them."

I sighed. "You know, you've lied to me before. This would be an acceptable time for it."

"That was for your own good." He pulled his face into an obviously fake smile. "Everything is going to be perfect, and there's no chance that anything bad will ever happen. Better?"

I gave him the finger. "Smartass."

"Better than the alternative." His mocking expression softened into a real smile. "On a positive note, he thinks you're a raving lunatic."

I looked back to Corey, who was staring at me like I was crazy. Which was a fair assessment, since as far as he was concerned, I was talking to thin air. Well, if fate was kind, he wouldn't remember any of this, or I could blame it on the cold messing with his head.

"Corey, you said Diana was sick. Were you trying to say there's an emergency?" I asked.

"Diana," he said again. He shivered violently. "Dice bed it."

"Okay, that probably sounded way different in your head," I said. "I don't understand."

He grunted in frustration. Maybe it was the cold sinking in and making it hard for him to think straight. His voice was thick and slurred as he tried again. "Dice bet it." He looked around, then took one hand out of his pocket. He held up his fist with the thumb sticking out, then pressed it down to the thigh of his good leg. Then he pressed his thumb deliberately down to his fist. "Insin."

I stared at him. *Dice bet it. Insin.* I rolled it over in my mouth. "Oh my God," I said. "Is she diabetic? She needs insulin?" I desperately hoped I'd translated wrong.

He nodded and stuck his hand back in his pocket. "No food. Went help."

Dammit. "Is she in trouble?"

Tears pricked at his eyes again. "Find Diana."

# CHAPTER FOURTEEN

COREY, I'M GOING TO FIND Diana, okay?" I told him, hoping it wasn't a colossal lie. Brewing in my stomach was a huge dose of panic mixed with grim determination, and a dash of exhilaration.

I pawed through my backpack and checked through the bag of snacks. We hadn't even been thinking about feeding someone else. We'd just grabbed junk food to keep ourselves fed and awake. I'd have gotten something a little more substantial, like some protein bars or a couple of those greasy microwave burritos, if I'd been thinking more logically. *Stupid,* I chided myself as I ripped open a Hershey's bar for him. I also took the Monster drink and put it on the ground close enough for him to reach without moving. "Okay, Corey, there's something to drink here. You've already been really tough, so I need you to hold on for a little while longer. My friend went to call 911 before I found you."

Corey nodded. "Diana."

"I know, I got it," I said. He had a one-track mind, but it was hard to fault him for that kind of devotion. "Does she have insulin or something?" I silently prayed there was a kit in his backpack with a syringe and step-by-step instructions on what to do.

"No shot," he said. "Shooter."

"Shoot her?"

"Sugar," Kale said, giving me a pained look.

"I should give her sugar?" I asked. "Are you sure? I thought diabetics weren't supposed to have sugar."

He shook his head violently and yanked his hand out of his pocket.

"Needsteet."

I squinted at him. "Needs to eat?" Corey nodded again. I was getting good at this after all. I checked the snack bag again. We still had a bag of Hot Cheetos—Michael's choice—a couple more candy bars, and a Coke. "Anything else?"

"Help Diana," he said again.

"Got it. You'll be home soon, okay? Hang in there."

"Thank you," Corey said.

"All right. Let's go," I told Kale.

"She's this way," he said, turning away to head into the shadows of the trees.

Beyond the clearing beneath the steep path, the ground sloped gently downward into the deep woods. The path wasn't as clear here. Bare patches of earth emerged from the leaf cover like bald spots. Thick roots snaked out of the ground and curled across the path. All it needed was a *Keep Out* sign to really complete the ominous look. Maybe some long-forgotten bread crumbs and a few stray bones. I shivered at the sight of it and wondered if it was too late to reconsider my daring rescue plan.

Unbothered by the foreboding gloom of the forest, Kale darted through the trees. As far as I was concerned, the world was a tiny globe around me lit only by the glow of my phone flashlight. Anything beyond a few feet was dark and formless. Moving the light back and forth from the ground up to eye level made me dizzy. My foot caught on a root, and I stumbled headlong to the ground. The impact jolted my cold joints. My phone went flying and landed light down, plunging me into darkness.

"Kale, wait!" I called. I swept my hands over the damp, cold ground. My heart raced. I was seventeen years old, and I was not afraid of the dark. I rested back on my heels and looked around. I could see him zipping ahead through the trees like a giant firefly. Then he disappeared from sight.

Okay, I was a little afraid of the dark.

My fingers finally found the smooth, round edges of my phone. As I snatched it up, I let out a heavy sigh of relief. I waved it around to light the ground at my feet, like I needed to make sure the earth hadn't fallen away in the few seconds of darkness. When I got to my feet, a spark of aching heat ignited in the frozen soles of my feet and burned all the way up my shins and into my thighs. My feet were wet and cold inside my sneakers, and now my knees were damp from falling. I was flat-out miserable.

"Kale?" I said tentatively. There was no answer. Dizzy panic swelled up like a wave to pull me under. My chest trembled as I took a deep breath.

*Don't panic. He's not going to abandon you out here.*

"Okay," I said aloud. I took a deep breath and checked my phone. It was nearly four in the morning, and I'd been awake since five-thirty. School, play rehearsal, even riding out here with Michael seemed like another lifetime. Deep in the woods, I was in another world.

I looked up at the sky. The dark blue-gray of the night sky was cut into irregular panels of stained glass by bare tree branches. Between the jagged shadows, snow swirled through the air in a sparkling blur. The wind whispered in the trees. For a moment, the world was beautiful. My breathing slowed, and the tension slowly dissipated.

Now I could think rationally. At least I knew I wasn't dealing with a psycho killer stalking Corey and Diana through the woods. So things could definitely be worse. Still, I was worried about Diana. It was bad enough that she was lost in the frigid weather, but with a sugar crash, there was no telling what condition she would be in when I found her.

Everything I knew about first aid or medicine in general came from either Mom's lectures or watching TV. I knew diabetics had to give themselves insulin shots, but not much more. No service on my phone meant I couldn't resort to my trusty friend Google for help. And I'd always thought diabetics weren't supposed to eat sugar, but Corey seemed certain that was she needed. Hopefully Diana would be fine. Maybe it wasn't an emergency.

And maybe pigs would fly. I'd gotten lucky with the whole no-axe-murderer thing. Good luck didn't run in the Young family, so I probably wasn't going to be that fortunate again with Diana.

I held up the phone to eye level and tried to focus on the distant shadows. "Are you out there?" I asked. I had to be patient. He was probably going ahead to find the safest way to Diana. He was pulling double duty, and I was strong enough to handle being by myself for a few minutes.

I thought I'd seen something on TV where a diabetic had passed out. Crap. If Diana was unconscious, I didn't know what I'd do. Even if she was the tiny, top-of-the-pyramid cheerleader type, I couldn't carry her all the way back to the parking lot. I wasn't sure how much ground I'd covered already, but it was more than I could handle with an unconscious girl.

A cold gust whipped around me, snapping me out of my worry about the future and back into the present. I gasped and spun around to see Isaac. Though his bright color from touching me had faded, he still looked brighter and more solid than he had when we'd first seen him at the picnic pavilion. He gestured to me with one dirty hand, then pointed away into the trees behind him. "This way."

I took a tentative step toward him, then hesitated. A split second of relief at a familiar face was replaced with a lingering sense of unease. The realization that I wasn't really alone out here was much less comforting than I would have expected, especially considering Isaac had already dragged me down into the broken memories of his death once. Still, I tried to be polite. It seemed smarter to not antagonize a spirit if at all possible. "Is Diana that way?"

He just stared at me and pointed the same way. "This way."

My heart thumped. Isaac pointed at a sharp angle away from the path Kale had taken. Then again, Kale was searching. Maybe he'd ended up going the same way. I wanted to believe Isaac was still helping us.

My cooler, rational side finally kicked in. *Trust your instincts,* I thought. If Isaac was really on Team Save the Girl, then he'd wait patiently for Kale to come back.

"I'll wait," I told Isaac, tightening my grip on the phone. "Kale will be back soon, and we can all find her together."

"This way," he said again, his voice more insistent. My gaze followed his pointing gesture more closely this time. His forearm was bruise-purple and bloated beyond recognition. The underside of his wrist had the color and texture of raw hamburger. My gaze flicked down to his leg, which looked just as bad. His calf was so swollen that it was bigger than his thickly muscled thigh. My stomach heaved at the sight. I tasted burning acid at the back of my throat.

On instinct, my hand started to inch back toward my backpack for the holy water. This was rapidly becoming a Bad Situation. He was showing very clear signs of his death, which meant the emotions of death—anger, despair, grief— were starting to override his personality. The longer he lingered, the more dangerous he'd be. I tried to help spirits move on before that happened; it had barely begun when I'd finally said goodbye to Val.

Isaac's clouded eyes caught the movement and narrowed slightly. He lumbered toward me, sending a hot shot of adrenaline through my system. Wobbling slightly, I stepped back onto a thick branch and stumbled backward.

Eyes still on Isaac, I managed to get my hand all the way inside the backpack, but all I could find was the wet, cold surface of the Coke we'd bought at the gas station.

Dammit.

I broke my gaze for a split second to get the water out of my backpack. When I turned back, I screamed in surprise. Isaac was inches away, bathing me in a reeking cloud of decay. A spark glinted through the milky haze in his eyes. His snake-bitten hand swiped at me, leaving a trail of ice down the side of my face. I recoiled and flung the holy water at him in a spraying arc. The water spattered on him, dissolving him away like smoke. He stared down in horror, then threw his head back and disappeared.

"Bridget?"

I screamed in surprise at the sound of Kale's voice. I looked up to see him standing between two trees. "Where the hell were you?" I tried to catch my breath. "And by that I mean I'm really glad to see you."

He frowned. "What were you doing with him? It was like a wall around you."

"He was trying to pull a strangers-with-candy act," I said, panting heavily. "What do you mean, a wall?"

"It was just like with Natalie," he said. "I couldn't even get close."

When I'd first encountered Natalie's spirit, it had driven Kale away. He'd been fine around other spirits in the past and since, but Natalie had been different. She wasn't the first murder victim I'd encountered, but the brutal violence of her death had certainly shaped her personality as a spirit. Once I'd finally figured out where her killer had been taking his victims, Kale hadn't been able to get anywhere close. It had been inconvenient, to say the least. "What is it that makes them so different?"

"It's the emotion." He shook his head. "So much pain. When I get close to it, it feels like something is tearing me to pieces."

I raised an eyebrow. "Well it didn't exactly feel great when Isaac was sucking the life out of me for a little body heat."

Kale flared brighter. "I'm not talking about a little discomfort." He shook his head, and I swear he actually rolled his eyes like he was a human teenager instead of a mysterious being of indeterminate age. "You're still rooted to your body, so you can't understand. It feels as though it's going to undo me entirely."

"But you stood right there with me when we talked to him earlier." I pushed down my irritation. It wasn't like Kale to be overdramatic, so I had to believe that he would help if he could. Still, he wasn't much of a protector if the angry spirits—you know, the dangerous ones—scared him off. I didn't need protection from the nice ones like Sal and Lena May.

"Then something's changed."

"Well, yeah," I said. "The signs are showing. Maybe my little turbocharge did it for him." I frowned and pointed in the direction Isaac had directed me. "He was trying to get me to go this way."

Kale shook his head and pointed the opposite way. "Diana's this way. I'm having a harder time finding her now, but she's definitely this way."

"What do you mean, you're having a harder time finding her?"

His mouth set in a grim line. "It means we need to hurry." I didn't have to read his mind to know what he wasn't saying aloud.

I spared a look back to where Isaac was trying to go. "What do you think is back there?"

"I think it's unimportant right now."

"Kale, he's going to come back," I said. "And if you can't protect me…"

He flinched slightly.

My temper flared again. I didn't have the luxury of nursing hurt Guardian egos right now. I took an even breath. "I don't mean to insult you," I said, carefully measuring each word so my temper didn't leak out. "But if he's turning like Natalie did before I helped her, then he's going to get set on whatever he wants me to see. He'll find a way."

"I know." He sighed. "You don't know how frustrating this is. It's my job to watch out for you. But I'm useless when an actual threat rises."

"It's okay," I said. Though I shared his frustration, it seemed nicer to put him at ease.

"Not really." He shook his head and gave me a half smile. "I'm sorry. Self-pity is a waste of time. Do you have salt in your backpack?"

"Of course." There was my Kale—quick to be rational and think about the big picture. I twisted around so I could dig in my bag and came up with the dark blue can of salt.

"Just like before." He gestured a circle with one finger. "On the ground around yourself if you have to. Use the water to scare him off. Once we're out of the woods tonight, it won't matter."

I nodded and jammed the salt into the pocket of my jacket. "For the record, I would prefer a shotgun."

"You watch too much TV. A shotgun's not going to hurt an incorporeal spirit."

"But it would sure make me feel like a badass," I said.

"I've seen you drive. I definitely wouldn't trust you with firearms."

"That's offensive."

"And accurate." He shook his head. "Come on."

The flashlight bounced in dizzying arcs as I hurried after him. The ground flattened beneath my feet, and I moved as quickly as I could over the tangles of roots and under low-hanging branches. My heart thumped with exertion and apprehension. I kept finding myself looking back for the bearded specter.

Soon I proved to myself that it really was wiser to quit looking back. While my head was turned, my foot clipped a hard edge on the ground. I stumbled and took a few clumsy steps to regain my balance. As I caught my breath, I shone the flashlight on the ground in front of me. There was a shallow stream just ahead with a few wooden planks laid across it. Nerves twisted my guts into a tight knot as I carefully put my foot on one of the planks. The water wasn't deep, but I didn't want to get even my toes wet in this cold. And I was sure a couple of warped planks barely qualified as a bridge, and definitely hadn't passed safety inspections.

A bright light materialized in front of me. "Are you okay?"

I gasped and took a quick step back. I teetered precariously, then caught my balance. "I was," I said. Despite my fright, I was relieved to see Kale at the other side of the plank bridge. "I need you to slow down. Some of us have a harder time navigating."

"Her light is fading fast. I can't slow down, or I'll lose it."

I scowled at him. "If you want me to make it to her in one piece, then you have to."

His face slipped into an irritated expression for a moment before he caught himself. I bit back on my own irritation. It was cold, I was tired, and the last thing I needed was an argument with my only companion in the middle of a dark forest.

I used the flashlight to light the night in either direction. The stream went as far as I could see. "Can I go around?"

"This is the fastest way."

"As the angel flies," I murmured.

"Not an angel," he replied. He disappeared and reappeared on the other side.

So unfair.

I let out a deep breath and walked cautiously onto the planks. They sagged a little under my weight, but held as I took a careful step across the stream, then another. One of the planks dipped low under my foot and gave a warning creak. I tried to move to the other side of the makeshift bridge, but my foot found a gap in the planks. Instead of giving me stability, it sent me reeling.

"Bridget!"

I fell sideways into the water and landed hard on my wrist. Pain lanced up my arm, and ice surrounded me as I went into the water. I gasped in shock at the cold. My foot was twisted awkwardly, and when I tried to pull it to me, the plank came with it.

I couldn't help myself. I burst into tears.

"Are you okay?" Kale asked. He crouched in front of me, buffeting me with cold air. I wanted him to go away, but I also wanted to magically teleport back to my nice, warm house.

"No," I said between hiccupping sobs. The tears ran down my cheeks in burning trails. The fact that I was crying made me even angrier.

"What's wrong? Did you break something?"

"No." I braced my free foot on the plank and yanked my other foot clear. My shoe came loose with splinters of wood clinging to the loop of shoelace. I kicked the plank away, then looked around for my phone. I saw it just in time to see the flashlight flicker, then go dark under the shallow water. I cursed and grabbed it, getting a handful of slimy creek dirt with it.

"Talk to me," he said.

"I'm fine." I wanted him to leave me alone. I was embarrassed for falling, and on top of it, I was freezing. Literally. I stood up and instantly felt the bite of the cold air on my wet jeans. I jammed my dead phone into my back pocket and scooped up my backpack. Water ran off it, and I hoped it hadn't ruined everything inside.

"Bridget, I know you. I know you're not fine."

I scrubbed angrily at my face and wished I could smack him. "Fine! I told you to slow down. You keep forgetting that I'm human. I can't magically float over the water and rocks and roots like you can. And it's dark and cold and I can barely see and you keep disappearing." The words spilled out in a whining, frustrated jumble.

"It's not my fault you—" He caught himself and closed his eyes. After taking a moment to compose himself, he said in an even tone, "You're right. I'm sorry."

"Yeah, well…" I hesitated. "Dammit, Kale. You were supposed to keep arguing."

His mouth quirked up, and my anger dissipated like releasing an inflated balloon. "Would that make you feel better?"

"Yes."

"Well, I'm right and you're wrong. And you're a terrible driver."

I sighed. "Nope. Moment's gone. You ruined it."

"I know, what was I thinking by apologizing for doing wrong?"

"Your apology isn't doing anything for my wet ass." I lifted each foot in turn and tested it, then flexed the fingers on each hand. My right wrist felt tender, but it wasn't enough to keep me from going on. "Let's go."

"You sure you're okay?"

I angrily scrubbed my hands clean on my jeans and stomped through the shallow creek. I was soaked from the waist down, and my feet squelched as I walked. My phone was dead. I wasn't okay at all, but I wasn't giving up. I wasn't going to be defeated by a stupid piece of wood and a foot of water. "I'm sure," I said. "We have work to do."

# CHAPTER FIFTEEN

WITHOUT MY PHONE TO GUIDE ME, I had no idea what time it was or how long I'd been walking. My feet were so cold that every step made them hurt, and I'd started shivering uncontrollably. I wanted to rip open the rest of the heat packets, but I just kept picturing Diana, stumbling through the woods sobbing. I couldn't do it.

With no bright light, my eyes were forced to adjust to the darkness. Soon enough, the rough lines of trees emerged from the sea of black. Roots and rocks were hard edges underfoot.

"We're close to her," Kale said.

"I'm cold," I said for the hundredth time.

"I know." He sounded a lot more patient than I would have been to hear myself complaining about the cold for so long. "I wish I could do something about it, but I can't."

I had the candles and a lighter in my backpack, but unless I planned to give up my search for Diana and start a bonfire, the only way that was going to help was by lighting myself on fire. Which didn't sound like a terrible option at this point.

I wondered if Michael had managed to call the police. Maybe they were already here and ready to help Corey. Oh, what a thought. Maybe they'd followed my trail somehow, and they had big, warm jackets and blankets and hot chocolate. And one of them would give me a piggy-back ride all the way home. A girl could dream.

My teeth clacked together in a noisy rhythm. I clenched my jaws and hugged my arms tight across my chest to stop shivering. "I need to upgrade my ghost bag."

"Oh, yeah?"

"Yes. Flashlights. Lots of them."

"What else?"

"A phone with a better signal," I added.

"Wait." He zipped back to stand in front of me. "Duck your head, then take a big step over the log."

I raised one hand over my head until I felt the rough knobs of a low-hanging branch. After ducking under it, I stuck my foot out to feel for the offending log. My toes scraped over the log's bark and into the gap below. I would have done a full-on faceplant if he hadn't warned me. I hitched up one leg, then swung the other over the log. "Clear?"

"You're good," he said. Something crashed through the brush ahead of us. The unexpected sound sent a shock down my spine. My feet were rooted to the ground as I searched frantically for the source of the sound. Kale glanced back. "Just a minute."

"Kale?" He disappeared, and I was left in the dark. "Oh, you suck."

Maybe it was the cold, but my patience was virtually nonexistent by then. I knew he had to go, but I equally knew I wanted him to stay within arm's reach at all times.

Had I made a mistake coming out here? Sal and Emily had been adamant about me staying home, but I'd been so sure it was the right thing to do. Maybe they'd been right. I didn't know the first thing about staging dramatic rescues. Maybe this was the hubris Mrs. McDaniel had taught us about in lit class. It never worked out well in stories.

And my mother was going to kill me for destroying another phone after she'd just replaced it. To be fair, the first time had been Natalie's fault, but I couldn't very well tell Mom that a pissed-off dead girl had broken my phone while having an epic temper tantrum. And I definitely couldn't tell her I'd ruined my new one after I'd snuck out to traipse through the woods in the middle of the night.

I shivered and tugged at the strings of my hood to cinch it tight around my head. It didn't do much, but it made me feel better, like I was being proactive and fixing things somehow.

Soon, Kale reappeared a few yards ahead of me, his eyes wide. He was glowing painfully bright, which meant he was agitated or excited. "Come on!" In a rush of cool air, he zipped toward me and held out one hand. Staring down at it, his eyes narrowed. The pearly translucence of his palm brightened to a healthy-looking solidity. He extended his hand to me, trembling with the effort. I slowly put mine in it, and his cool, dry fingers closed around my hand.

For a moment, his comment about me not being all here hung in front of me. Before Natalie, he'd never been able to touch me, nor I him. Most spirits, except the angry and desperate like Natalie, couldn't affect me physically. But things had changed. Now it was like we met in the middle, with him reaching toward the living and me reaching toward the dead. Assuming I didn't get myself killed, how much more would this power change me?

A gentle tug pulled me forward. The trees were dense and so dark I couldn't see a thing, but I ran after Kale, clamping down on the cool, solid feel of him. I trusted him to get me there in one piece. A faint vibration ran up my arm like an electrical current. Twigs snapped underfoot. Branches whipped against my face, but he never slowed, and neither did I.

"Step down," he said. I took a big step down. There was a disconcerting jolt as my other foot skidded down a slope. After a bit of a stumble, I righted myself. "Good?"

"Good," I said in a breathless whisper. I heard a ragged sigh ahead. It wasn't Kale. My heart leaped.

"She's here," he said.

"Diana?" I said. "Diana!"

She answered with a sharp gasp, followed by the rustle of leaves underfoot. Then she was still, though I still heard the rapid, shallow sound of her breathing.

"I'm here to help you," I said to the dark spot where I thought she was hiding. I bent down to dig out the lighter from the front pocket of my backpack. I flicked the switch and cast a tiny globe of light around it. In the dim light, I made out the outline of her body, leaning against a tree. Suddenly, she lurched toward me and knocked the flame out of my hand. "Whoa!"

"No!" Diana said. Her hand struck my face, and I reeled backward in surprise.

"Diana, it's okay," I said. I bent to pick up the lighter and relit it. When I reached out to her with my other hand, she slapped it away. It wasn't a hard blow, but the contact was enough to send a shock of pain through my ice-cold hand, up my arm, and straight into the mean streak I usually managed to contain. My temper flared. "Oh, I did not come all the way out here for you to be a total—"

"Bridget," Kale warned.

"Say way!" Diana said, holding up her hands defensively. Her hair was tangled and knotted around her face, which was criss-crossed in angry red scratches. She looked like a wild woman who'd been living in the woods all her life.

"Say way," I said. "Stay away?" I was getting good at Lost in the Woods speak, apparently.

"Say way!" Her words were barely understandable; it sounded like she was talking around a mouthful of food. If she'd been out here all night, then her tongue was probably about half frozen. I'd only been here a few hours, and I was a walking popsicle. The hard shell of anger dissolved. She had to be terrified and ten times as miserable as I was.

"Diana, you need help," I said, easing toward her. She went to slap at my hand again, but her legs buckled and she crumpled to the ground. I rushed toward her staying at arm's length.

"Say way," she said weakly, waving one hand in a half-hearted attempt to threaten me.

"Tell her about Corey," Kale said.

"Diana, we found Corey," I said. She froze. "He's okay. Help is coming." She didn't respond. "He said you might be sick. You're diabetic, right?"

She looked up at me. Her tangled hair hung in heavy locks around her face. Her dark eyes were so wide I could see the white all the way around.

"And you haven't eaten in a while?"

She shook her head, swinging her long hair through the dead brush below.

Even in the dim light cast by the lighter, I could see she was corpse-pale. If I didn't know better, I'd have thought she was already dead and appearing in spirit form. Her eyes were sunken in shadow, and her lips were bluish.

"I don't want to hurt you," I said. "I came to help you." I held out the lighter to her, but when she put one hand out, it was as stiff and unmoving as a mannequin limb. She tried to bend her fingers around it but barely managed to twitch the small joints. Her eyes crinkled up in discomfort.

Now it was time for the battle of my better nature and my selfishness. Diana was wearing only a thin long-sleeved shirt and jeans. If I had to put it all together, I'd guess that Corey fell down the slope when they were walking, and she went off to get help after giving him her jacket to keep warm. But she'd gotten turned around and gone in the wrong direction, probably panicking over what to do.

After stowing the lighter in my jeans pocket, I unzipped my puffy jacket and peeled it off reluctantly. Instantly, the cold bit through the fabric of my cotton hoodie. It was better than a T-shirt, but it did nothing to cut the icy wind.

With a longing sigh, I held the heavy purple jacket out. The sight of her stiff fingers made my stomach clench up in sympathy, and I shuffled over to get behind her. "Arms," I said. She put her arms out straight like a little kid letting Mommy dress her. I maneuvered one arm into the coat, and then the other. As I pulled her hand through the cuff, I noticed a ponytail elastic on her wrist. I pulled it over her ice-cold hand. "Can I fix your hair?"

"Yes."

I sat back on my heels and combed my fingers through her matted hair as best I could. Some of the tangles were far beyond my capabilities, but I managed to get most of it pulled back into a ponytail. I pulled the hood over her head. "Better?"

"Mm-hmm," she murmured. I scooted around again in front of her and zipped the jacket up. Once she was bundled into the jacket, I opened my backpack and felt around for the plastic bag of snacks.

"Corey said you might be sick. I don't know anything about diabetics and I really don't want to kill you by accident. Do you understand what I'm saying?"

She squeezed her eyes shut, then opened them comically wide like she was trying to shake off a post-nap daze. She said each word slowly and deliberately. "Yes. Need to eat."

"Okay," I said. My hand closed around a damp plastic bottle. I pulled it out, then went back in for a snack. Serrated paper brushed over my fingers, and I turned them to pull out the thin chocolate bar. "Corey said you needed sugar. Is that right?"

"Yes."

I set the Coke down and opened the Crunch bar I'd pulled out. As soon as I handed it to her, she grabbed it and took a huge bite. I ignored the crumbs of chocolate falling from her dry lips. As she chewed, I opened the Coke, which was even colder than when we'd gotten it from the cooler. Once she'd finished her bite of the candy bar, she gestured for the drink, and I let her take it. She took a long drink, her face relaxing in relief. She coughed then, spraying Coke all over. I grabbed it back before she spilled the rest, then capped it. "I'll hold on to it, okay?"

"Okay." She took another big bite of the candy bar. I didn't know how long it would take for her to feel better, but I hoped it was sooner rather than later.

While she finished the candy, I took out the remaining heat packs and tore them open. For a second, I clutched them in my icy hands and let out an honest-to-goodness moan. They felt so good, like wrapping my hands around a cup of hot chocolate. Surely if I was giving her my jacket, I could justify...

*No,* I told myself. I was a big girl. I'd be fine.

"Hand," I said before I lost my resolve. She finished off the candy bar in another big bite and offered me her chocolate-stained hand. I put one heat pack in each hand and stuffed them deep into the fleece-lined pockets, then kneeled between her feet and wedged the others in her shoes like I had Corey's. As I retied her shoelaces, I mentally kicked myself for not buying more handwarmers, and added them to my future shopping list. Next time I did something stupid, I'd at least be prepared.

I pulled my hood around my face and got my backpack situated on my shoulders. "Are you ready to go?"

"Yeah."

I held out my hand to help her up, and I had to use all my strength to get her on her feet. Dread knotted in my stomach as I tried to calculate how far we had to go. Michael had driven away right around three. The last time I'd been able to check my phone, it had been close to four. I knew from school I could run a mile in about nine minutes, and I wasn't anywhere close to running through these woods. So I could have gone maybe two or three miles in an hour. Considering all the stops and delays, it was probably closer to two. I hoped it wouldn't take as long to get back, but with Diana in tow, it might be a tough road. And I wasn't feeling great myself.

Diana leaned heavily on me, and I looped my right arm around her waist. Her body shook violently against me. It felt like one of those massage chairs on display at Brookstone, although with exactly none of the comfort or benefits. With my free hand, I flicked the lighter to give us the tiniest bit of light. Between holding the lighter and supporting Diana, both my hands were exposed to the cold, and they didn't care for it.

"Okay, we're going to be okay," I told her, as much for her as for myself. A wave of shivers rolled over me from head to toe. I curled my toes against the cold, wet soles of my shoes. It sent a sharp, burning sensation through my feet.

*Think warm thoughts.* I thought about how nice it was going to be to get back into Michael's car with the heat blasting, and then to get home and sink into my bed. Those were real things, no matter how cold and miserable it was right now.

"Kale, how far is it?" I asked.

"You've got a while," he said. "Just keep moving."

# CHAPTER SIXTEEN

*Saturday*

**M**Y CHEST HURT. My legs were wobbly and heavy. My eyes were wind-burned and crusted half-shut with dried tears from the cold breeze. Everything from the waist down was cold and wet. More than once, the thought had crossed my mind that if I peed my pants, it would at least be warm for a few minutes, which was a sure sign of how bad things had gotten.

This completely sucked.

"Can we sit down?" Diana said. She pulled back, reminding me of when I'd helped Emily walk her dog and the dog had refused to quit sniffing a tree, apparently a local canine hotspot. Too bad I couldn't use Emily's solution, which was to scoop up the stubborn Dachshund and carry him home. As it was, Diana was dead weight in a puffy jacket.

"No, we can't sit down," I said. "We have to get warm."

"So tired," she complained.

"Keep her moving," Kale said. Well, that was easy to say when you were an incorporeal being who wasn't literally freezing to death.

"She thinks she's tired," I muttered. I planted my feet and pulled her along. She stumbled a little, but she kept shuffling along with me.

"Fallen log," Kale said. "Big step up."

"Step up," I told Diana, flicking my lighter to illuminate the ground ahead of us. Her foot barely cleared it. As we stepped over the log, she let out a heavy sigh and sagged against me. Those lovely downhill slopes that had led me deeper into the woods weren't nearly as nice coming back. My legs were burning with exertion.

I wondered how Michael had fared. I tried to shut down the worrying part of my brain—which was the majority of my mental real estate—and think positive thoughts. Even if he'd had to drive all the way back into town to call, he should be back by now. Assuming he didn't run into trouble, or get a flat tire, or...

They had to be there.

"Stream," Kale said.

I lit the lighter again and held it up to light the path ahead. The stream was a darker streak in the ground. Only one plank remained. The other lay across it at an angle, half in the dark water after I'd dragged it with my shoe. *Stupid planks.*

"I fell in," Diana said mournfully.

"Join the club," I told her. "There's no way I'm getting her across."

"At this point, cut your losses and walk through," he said.

"It's cold," Diana said.

"You're already cold," Kale said.

"We're already cold and wet," I told Diana. "Really not gonna matter that much."

She resisted, but I pulled her along and splashed into the stream. I might have talked a big game, but I gasped involuntarily when the cold water filled my shoes. We came out the other side with wet pants plastered to our legs.

Standing on the other bank, Diana shivered and planted her feet "Can we rest?"

"No!" I snapped. I knew it wasn't fair to get irritated with her, but I couldn't help it. "We're not stopping till we're out of these damn woods."

She started to sink down to the ground, and I couldn't keep her on her feet without falling down with her. *I will not backhand her,* I told myself as I let her slip out of my grasp and flop to the ground. Instead, I took the half-drunk Coke from the mesh pocket on the side of my backpack and offered it to her. Maybe if I kept jolting her with sugar, she'd keep moving.

"Not thirsty."

"I don't give a damn if you're not thirsty. Drink it or I'm leaving you here."

"I don't care."

"Kale, I'm gonna put my hands on her."

"Be nice," he said mildly. "She's exhausted and sick. It's not her fault."

I sucked in a long breath through my nose and held it until it was uncomfortable. The way she was acting reminded me of when Valerie had gotten her wisdom teeth pulled the summer before her senior year. She'd been loopy and had acted like a five-year-old, suddenly deciding she'd wanted a chocolate milkshake at three in the morning and pouting when she hadn't gotten it.

"Diana, please," I said, softening my voice the best I could. I kneeled down and held out the drink to her. "You've been out here a really long time. I'm not an expert, but I'm pretty sure if you lay down and go to sleep, it's not going to end well. And I can't carry you. I'm not that strong."

Arguing aside, it really did feel good to settle down on the ground in front of Diana. It was warmer there, like the ground was squirreling away some heat for us. Anything was an improvement after the cold water, and my legs and feet were instantly relieved with the weight off them. *Don't get too comfortable,* I told myself. It was like tempting fate by hitting snooze after the alarm, even though you knew there was no coming back from that nest of warm blankets.

"Plus, we're going to get Corey," I told her. "But if we don't keep moving, we won't see him, and they won't know where to find us in here."

She sighed and finally accepted the drink. She took a tentative sip and coughed. "I'm tired."

"Me too, but we're really close now," I said. I knew full well we weren't close, but she didn't.

"Not really," Kale said.

I glared at him. "Remember when I said it was okay to lie about certain things?"

"Sorry."

"Who are you talking to?" Diana asked.

My stomach sank as I turned to see her staring at me. "Imaginary friend," I replied. "We need to go."

"But—"

"Nope," I said. "Now come on."

I brushed off my knees. Part of me wanted to stay there on the ground with her. But the smarter part of me was still winning out. That part knew that if we didn't move, Diana was in trouble, and it might be a while before anyone was able to find us.

I felt like I'd gained a thousand pounds while sitting down, but I hauled myself up and extended my hand to Diana. I planted my feet and pulled her up, then started moving immediately before she reconsidered and plopped back down.

There beneath the dark shade of dead branches and a cloudy sky, time stretched out. We could have been walking for minutes or days, and I wouldn't have known the difference. I focused on my feet. One foot, then the other. Tug on Diana. One foot. The other. Pull. Flick the lighter. One foot.

"How much further?" I asked. My eyes were focused on the ground in front of me, watching the rhythmic plodding of my dirty sneakers through the decaying layer of leaves.

No answer.

"Don't know," Diana murmured.

*Not you,* I thought. I looked up to see nothing but dark woods around us. I looked back over my shoulder. No Kale. Only shadows. Fear came over me, like a cloud covering the sun. This wasn't right.

No, he'd just gone ahead to find a path. "Kale?" I said. But he still didn't respond. *Count to ten before you freak out,* I told myself.

"What?" Diana said. "Who are you talking to?"

I ignored her.

One.

Two.

I reached ten, and there was still no sign of him. A chill ran down my spine. A sudden wind surrounded me with the smell of damp soil and something rotten. My eyes widened as a familiar spirit materialized between the trees ahead.

"Isaac?" I said.

"Who?" Diana asked, her voice more insistent as she pulled away from me and stared. She obviously thought I was crazy, but I had a bigger problem standing in front of me.

The bearded spirit looked as bright and vivid as ever. Swollen beyond recognition below the knee, his leg was discolored in shades of angry red and purple. His distended lips were chapped and crusted over, framed by gaunt cheeks. "This way," he said. His voice had strengthened. The deep resonance of it rattled my bones and set my stomach rolling with dread.

My breathing quickened as I patted my pocket for the can of salt. "Kale?" I said quietly. My hand found only soft wash-worn cotton. Crap. I reached over and patted Diana's pockets, earning another incredulous look from her. On my way into the woods, the salt had been in the pocket of my heavy jacket. But there was nothing in hers. It had to have fallen out somewhere. "Oh, no."

Isaac rushed toward me, and I did the only think I could think to do. I shoved Diana away. She squawked in surprise as she stumbled over a thick root. "Hey!"

I reached my back to my backpack for the holy water, but Isaac gripped my shoulders tight and sent a shot of pure ice down my arms. An inexorable gravity pulled me down into myself like an undertow.

Everything went white.

Color leached back into the world, but everything was hazy and blurred, like looking through chlorine-stung eyes. My ears were filled with the sound of rushing water and faraway pounding drums. Autumn leaves rushed past in a fiery swirl. The bright blue afternoon sky spun in a manic merry-go-round with the earthy brown of soil and tree trunks. I stumbled through the woods with the midday sun beating down on my bare skin. Sweat poured off me.

My body was on fire. Fierce cramps wracked my guts. My right arm and leg were slabs of molten metal, all fire and pain that was somehow attached to my body by aching bones and sizzling tendons. The limbs didn't feel like mine; there was no sensation except pain there. My leg had turned purple already. How long had it been? Minutes? Hours?

My left hand shook as I fumbled for my canteen. I splashed lukewarm water on my face. *Focus.* I just had to get back to the path. It was here somewhere. The trail, then home, then Laura. Home. Safe.

I jolted suddenly and realized I couldn't breathe. A cold band tightened around my chest, filling my lungs with ice. *Isaac,* I thought desperately. *Please let go of me.*

I was dying. I'd seen it before, an outdoorsman's nightmare. My head pounded. My stomach churned. A sharp branch scraped my leg. My vision went white as I fell to the ground. Lightning bolts of pain stabbed through my body.

I vomited up the half-digested lunch I'd packed. I sat back on my hands in the dry brush and looked again at my leg. The bites were turning purple. My flesh had melted away from the punctures, leaving angry red muscle below. I vomited again and again until I saw spots and couldn't keep my head upright.

Then it was dark, and I was lying on my back between two pine trees. My vision was blurred, and all I saw was the white of the moon through the fine needles like a veil. How long had I been gone from home? Laura was waiting on me. Was she worried about me? She would never know how I felt.

My mouth was a desert. There was no water left in my canteen. I was burning up and freezing at the same time. My body shook with uncontrollable tremors.

*Isaac, please!*

Then it was bright again. Something crawled across my face. My hand wouldn't respond to wipe it away. Breathing was agony. Sandpaper scraped down my raw throat. "Mama," I croaked. "Laura." *Someone. Anyone.*

Then in a heartbeat, the pain was gone. One moment, I was in my poison-ravaged shell, and the next, I was standing over it looking down. "Come on, get up," I told the lost hiker. He looked like hell. Wait a minute. I knew him.

Day turned to night turned to day, again and again. The body returned to the earth. I didn't go anywhere. What was supposed to happen here?

A new pain, hot and sharp, struck me. My world rattled and shook. I opened my eyes to a pair of wide, dark eyes and wordless shouting. Another hot sting hit my face. I sucked down a breath of cold air and coughed violently. The real world slammed back into focus. Diana was screaming in my face and shaking me by the front of my sweatshirt.

"Okay! I'm awake!" I croaked. I gasped for air, then lay flat on my back for a moment.

"What the hell was that?" Diana said.

"Long story." Suddenly, I realized that the cause of my troubles wasn't going to be scared away by a girl screaming at him. I bolted upright. The world spun beneath me, but I struggled to my feet.

Isaac stood a few feet away, and to his credit, he looked horrified. Well, at least he felt guilty about it. His whole body was bright and vivid. He stared at his tanned hands in wonder, then closed them. "I don't want to hurt anyone."

"Well, you might want to reconsider your approach," I said, still catching my breath.

I wanted to banish him or exorcise him or whatever they did in the movies. What if I hadn't been alone? Without Diana to shake me awake, things might have ended with another spirit for the gang out here at Wildwood. The thought made me shiver even more than the cold.

But despite myself, I couldn't muster up any real anger. I'd been there with him in his memories. I'd felt the agony of his death and the desperate loneliness as he'd lingered here. And like so many before, I knew what I had to do.

I took a tentative step toward Isaac, while my instincts screamed at me to stay away. The movement took a tremendous effort, like I was walking through a pool of Jell-O.

"Isaac, what do you want me to see?" I asked him quietly.

His shoulders drooped as he bowed his head. "Sorry." His voice sounded small and distant.

The unkinder part of me thought, *you should be*, but I knew it was petty and mean. I took a deep breath. *Better Nature Bridget, take the wheel.* "I know you didn't mean to hurt me," I said. "Did you?"

He looked up at me and shook his head violently. "No!"

My face felt frozen, but I forced my dry lips into a smile anyway. "I didn't think so. Do you want me to see something?"

"Yes."

I looked back to see Diana staring at me in disbelief. "I need you to sit right here. I promise you'll be safe. I have to do something really quickly."

"No!" she said. "Don't leave!"

I shook my head. She was going to think I was such an asshole. I turned to Isaac. "I need you to do something. My other friend, Kale, can't come to me when you're close. So you've got to go away for a few minutes so I can talk to him. You can come back shortly, and I promise I'll come see what you want me to see."

Eying me warily, he nodded. "Okay." He closed his eyes and disappeared.

Diana spluttered, "Have you lost your mind? Who are you talking to? What happened?"

This was so much harder with someone who didn't know. I wasn't sure if it would help or hurt to tell the truth. "Don't worry about it."

"How do I know you're not a psycho?"

"Why would I come all the way out here and rescue you if I was a psycho?"

Diana paused, staring intently at me. "You're crazy."

"Probably," I said. "Look. I don't have the time or energy to explain it to you. So let's make a deal. You accept that I'm talking to my imaginary friends, and I'll get you out of these woods. Cool?"

Kale appeared between us before she could respond, his blue eyes wide and frightened. "What happened to you? Did he hurt you? You look awful."

"I don't think he meant to," I said. "And thanks." I ran my hands over my hair. My fingers found the crispy texture of dead leaves clinging to the underside of the tight bun. I picked one out. "Better?"

Kale huffed. "I'm not talking about your hair. You're so dim."

"I would agree."

"Bridget, enough with the jokes. You look as bad as she does now." The somber tone stopped my humor. I didn't feel particularly light-hearted myself, but it helped distract me from thinking about how epically bad things almost went. "Why didn't you use the salt?"

I put my hands on my hips. "I lost it somewhere between falling in the cold-ass water and helping stubborn-ass here."

"Hey," Diana protested.

He shook his head. "Bridget." He pressed his hand to his forehead in a painfully human gesture. "We need to go."

"Well, you might as well stay mad," I said, steeling myself for his inevitable argument. "I need you to wait here and keep an eye on her. I'm going to follow Isaac and see what he needs."

"No!" Kale exclaimed. "I forbid it."

"Forbid away," I said. His eyes flared bright as Roman candles. For a moment, I thought about his chilling comment earlier. He could stop me, but he chose not to. What did that mean? And where would he finally draw the line? Maybe this was it, and maybe it wasn't, but I knew I had to try to help. "He can't rest, Kale. Isn't this what I'm supposed to do?"

"She's alive," Kale said, pointing to Diana. "He's not."

"It'll only take a few minutes. I may not get out here again once we leave."

"You're assuming you make it out of here in the first place." He folded his arms across his chest. "And just so we're perfectly clear. You're about to leave the living girl all alone while you go check on the guy who's already dead. If she falls unconscious or goes into shock, I can't do anything to help. And I can't even come tell you about it."

My argument dried up on my tongue as I spared a look at Diana. She was

173

watching me with wide, confused eyes. We'd come so far. And Isaac was already dead, which wasn't going to change any time soon.

But Isaac had also helped me and Diana. And he hadn't hurt me intentionally; he was like an injured animal lashing out in pain. I took a deep breath.

"Kale, if that happens, I can't do anything either. So we just have to hope it doesn't. I know it's not logical, but it's the right thing to do. Please."

He looked to Diana, then back to me. "I disapprove. Do what you think is right, but I hope we aren't about to add to the spirit population out here."

I swallowed hard. "Let's hope."

# CHAPTER SEVENTEEN

*Saturday*

KALE DISAPPEARED, LEAVING ME questioning myself as much as ever. I tried to bolster myself. I didn't need his approval. At some point, you had to stand for something. And while I knew his logic made sense, I couldn't leave Isaac alone without giving him some kind of hope.

"You're weird," Diana said finally.

"Very," I said. I crouched in front of her. "I know you won't like this. But I have to go off the path for a few minutes. You'll—"

"No, no, no," Diana said, her voice rising on each word.

I held up my finger in front of her. "You'll be fine. Just sit here and rest for a minute. I'll go as fast as I can. But I have to do this."

Her face creased, and she looked like a toddler deciding whether to start bawling or not. But she finally set her jaw and wrapped her arms around her knees for warmth.

A few moments later, Isaac returned. He was still bright, though the color had already started to drain out of him, his lifelike color fading back to gray. He looked hopeful as I walked toward him, away from the path I knew would take us home to safety and warmth. I prayed this wasn't as stupid as it sounded.

"Let's get this straight," I said. "No more bright and warm. I'm pretty sure if you do that again, I'm going to die. And then I can't help you. Got it?"

His eyes went to the ground as he nodded.

"Look at me and promise," I said. Ghosts probably didn't have to honor the pinky swear, but at least I could whine *he promised* if I ended up on the other side with Kale saying, "I told you so."

His head slowly came up, and his cloudy eyes met mine. "Promise."

"Okay. I'm going to do what I can for you, but I don't have long. You understand you're dead already, and I can't bring you back. But that girl over there is still breathing. I might be able to save her. So you have to understand."

He nodded again. "Understand."

"Okay, lead the way."

He perked up and rushed backward through a tree. He started down a winding trail that led off at an angle from the way we'd gone across the stream. I kept my hand cupped around the tiny lighter flame as I followed him. My legs were heavy and achy, and I hoped it wasn't far.

I heard the tinkling rush of water and realized our path was following the stream. In theory, it wouldn't be hard to get back even if Isaac proved to be less than trustworthy.

As we walked, I thought for the thousandth time how nice it would be to be somewhere dry and warm. If I'd been doing normal teenager things tonight, I'd most definitely be in bed with all of my blankets and central heating. Yet as much as I wished I had those things right now, I didn't want to be anywhere else. Call it fate or destiny or whatever, but I knew I was where I was supposed to be.

Isaac stopped suddenly and stared down at the ground. The spectral image of his hiking boots and snake-bitten leg disappeared into the solid, tattered remains of a hiking backpack. A sense of foreboding squeezed my chest as I stepped closer. Dead leaves and debris had partially covered the water-logged tatters of a bedroll attached to the pack. Lying next to it was a skull that had long been picked clean. It was buried to the upper jaw in pine needles and leaves. My breath caught in my throat. I didn't want to see this, but it was exactly what he needed me to see.

"Is this…" I looked up to Isaac. "What can I do?"

This close to his remains, where he'd finally died from the poison in his blood, he was more solid than ever. His pale face was sad but calm as he regarded the skull. He looked over to me. "Laura. And then rest."

I cocked my head. "Who's Laura? Your wife?"

A sad smile curved his cracked lips. "I never asked." He bent over as if he was going to open the pack, but his hands passed through it. His eyes creased in pain.

"Let me," I said. I crouched next to the pack. Exposure and age had discolored it, but it looked like it had been red at one point. I pulled at the zipper, which was crusted over by rust and mud. The movement shook the bag. Something black and many-legged crawled out of the water-logged bedroll. I shuddered and yanked my hands away. Ghosts didn't scare me much, but bugs were another story. Ugh. I gingerly unzipped the bag, then peered at the inside. It was a dark mass that was the perfect home for all things creepy and crawly.

"Inside pocket," he said.

I let out a quiet groan of disgust and then held my lighter over the pack. In the low light, the dark shadows resolved into the lines of recognizable objects at the top of the pack: a couple of plastic bags that were surprisingly untouched by the years and exposure and a hunting knife in a leather sheath. I took a deep breath and slid my hand down the inside. It was wet, but nothing took a bite out of me. My fingers found the texture of a zipper and traced it to its pull. Inside the pocket I found a curved velvet surface. I grabbed it and pulled it out.

In my hand was a red velvet ring box. The soft fabric was spotted with water and rotted away in a few patches, but there was no mistaking what it was. "Can I look?" He nodded. The hinges were rusted over, but with a little effort, I managed to get it open to reveal a diamond ring inside. The stone sparkled in the dim flame as I tilted it back and forth. "It's beautiful."

He smiled. "I came out here for a hike to clear my head. She was supposed to meet me for dinner that night. I was going to ask her over dessert. Get down on one knee and everything."

"But you never made it back," I said quietly. I took out the ring. Inside the gleaming gold band was engraved *La-La—My Forever Girl.* Tears pricked at my eyes as I thought about Laura, wondering where her date was. How long had she wondered? "When was it?"

"Ninety-seven. I tried to go see her, but I could never get out of the woods."

Wow. Almost twenty years gone. I nodded. "You're bound to the place where you died," I said. "Some spirits can travel a lot farther than others, but everyone has a limit."

"I just want to know if she's okay. And my mom. She always worried when I went off camping alone. I used to tell her I'd be fine, but I guess she was right."

"What do you want me to do?"

He looked down at his remains again. "Will you tell them what happened to me?"

"I will. What was your last name?"

"Watkins," he said. "Isaac James Watkins."

"Okay." I carefully put the ring back into its box and snapped it shut. "What about this?"

He regarded it warily. "Part of me wants to tell her. But she probably has another life now." He bowed his head. The color was nearly gone from him. "Can you come back and tell me about her?" He paused, then looked up at me. "I'd like to know that she's happy. She deserves it. I always thought I was so lucky because she could have done better than me, but out of all the guys in the world, she loved me."

I kept my poker face. Assuming I ever got out, I didn't want to see the woods ever again. But the thought of him lingering here for twenty years, unable to see anyone? It was awful. Spirits like Sal and Lena May could see the ones they loved, and even if it made them sad to see, they knew their world had gone on. Isaac was out here with no one but the other restless spirits, who probably weren't any better company than he was, and his own dried bones to remind him again and again of what had happened to him. "I'll find out and I'll come back," I promised. I didn't know how I'd make it happen, but I would somehow.

Relief washed the tension away from his face. "Thank you."

I tucked the ring back into the pack, then shoved my hands into the warm pocket of my hoodie. "I have to get back to Diana."

The peaceful expression faltered. He looked suspicious. "You won't forget?"

"I won't forget," I said. "Can you help me get back to her?"

He nodded eagerly and flickered away. I hurried after him. How long had we been gone? My heart thumped. My body was heavy and sluggish. I moved as quickly as my exhausted legs would carry me. When it felt like we'd been walking for a reasonable amount of time, I paused. "Okay, Isaac. I need to meet up with my other friend, so I have to leave you now. But I will come back. You kept your promise, and I'll keep mine."

When he disappeared, I was alone in the dark of the woods. I kept walking in the same direction, trying to ignore the growing sense of fear. One of these days, I'd have to learn how to fake a sense of optimism. I'd been a little more optimistic before the whole ghost thing. Now I knew that things went bad, and there wasn't a damn thing I could do. Positive thinking wouldn't stop the chemicals in Diana's body from going haywire, and it sure wouldn't warm either of us up. However, what I lacked in positive thinking, I made up for in stubbornness, which I was pretty sure Kale would confirm.

The wind picked up. Out of sheer instinct, I whipped my head around, looking for the newly arrived spirit, but there was none. Just run of the mill ice-cold wind cutting right through my damp clothes. Excellent.

Soon, I saw the hazy blue-white glow of Kale hovering near Diana. I raised my hand and called out. "Kale!" I was surprised at how rough my voice sounded. I tried to pick up my pace, but my legs wouldn't cooperate.

Kale disappeared and reappeared in front of me. "Are you all right?"

"I'm exhausted. But he behaved."

He nodded grimly. "Diana's fading. You need to get her up."

I sighed. "Can't you do some angel mojo on her?"

"Not—"

"I know, I know. But it would make me feel better if you made something up."

Diana was still sitting on the ground with her arms wrapped tightly around her legs. Her head rested on her knees, and she was visibly shivering.

I stopped next to her. "Diana?"

She didn't respond.

I touched her shoulders lightly. She startled, but not with the violent reaction I might have expected. She looked up at me sleepily, eyes heavy. "Hrm?"

"We have to keep moving," I said to her. She sighed heavily and put her head back down on her knees. "Nope." I pried her arm, planted my feet, and pulled with all my strength. It felt like trying to lift a five-hundred-pound weight. "Diana, come on."

She whined. "No."

My exhaustion exploded into frustration. "Then I'm gonna leave you here.

Come on."

"Fine," she said.

"Kale."

"This is all yours. That frustration you're feeling right now? I understand it well."

"Shut up." I sucked a sharp, dry breath through my nose. Even my nostrils felt frozen. I crouched and hooked my arms under her armpits. She whined in protest as I launched us both upward. My legs burned with the effort. She was wobbly and threw me off balance, but I managed to keep her upright. When her legs started to buckle, I planted my feet and kept her up. "We have to keep moving," I said. "We're almost to Corey. And then we can go home."

"Home," she murmured.

Between the cold and Isaac's sneak attack, I felt like I was running on the slightest of fumes. Fighting the dizzying exhaustion, I put one foot out, then the other. The thought of the car, of the parking lot, seemed a million miles away. I focused on the next step. One more step. Another. Another. Every few yards, Diana sagged, like she was falling asleep on her feet. Each time, I planted my feet and hauled her back up. Each time, it took a huge burst of stubbornness and willpower to move my feet again. One more step. One more.

My gaze stayed on the ground, watching my soaked, muddy sneakers scuffing through the decayed carpet of leaves and pine needles. Time didn't exist. The ticking of seconds was replaced by the plodding steps of my frozen feet. I breathed hard, like I was sprinting the whole way.

"You okay?" Kale asked.

"I hate this."

"I know."

"Huh?" Diana said.

"Imaginary friend," I told her. "Remember the compromise."

"Hmph."

"You're close," Kale said.

"Am I really, or are you trying to make me feel better?"

"You really are. The drop is up here. Just keep walking."

It seemed like days had passed, but soon I saw the bluish glow of Corey's camera cradled in his lap. The can of Monster was tipped over by his leg, and his head lolled to one side. "Shit," I said as I let go of Diana and rushed toward him.

She wobbled on her feet but stayed upright. "Corey?" she said blankly.

Right when I got to him, she perked up and walked faster than she had the entire time since I'd found her. Oh, *now* she could move.

I couldn't tell if he was breathing. "Corey?" I said loudly. I nudged his shoulder. "Corey!"

"Hit his leg," Kale said. "That should wake him up."

"Meanie," I said. I licked the back of my hand and put it under his nose. "I saw this on TV once." The damp spot cooled quickly, but I couldn't tell if it was the cold air or his breath.

"Is he okay?" Diana asked, more alert than ever. "Corey? Corey!"

"Calm down," I told her. I unzipped the top of the pink jacket and stuck my hand inside. Mom had tried again and again to show the three of us how to find our pulse. I ran my fingers down his jawline, probing for the fat artery on his throat. His skin was cold and dry under my fingers. Something bumped against my fingertips, and I froze. Was that it?

"Kale, is he…"

Kale drifted toward me. "He's alive. Weak, but alive."

I leaned back and let out a sigh of relief. "Okay." I looked up the hill and groaned. The fact that Michael wasn't here yet could have meant two things. The ambulance hadn't arrived, and he was still waiting. Or they had arrived, and they didn't know where to go. Either scenario meant I needed to get up there so I could show them the way.

But what did I do with Diana? I knew I couldn't get Corey to safety on my own. It would be easiest if I left Diana here with him while I went for help. But what if Diana got a wild idea to take off for help on her own five minutes after I left? If I had duct tape, I'd tape her stubborn ass to a tree. Kale wouldn't like it, but I was a firm believer in "the ends justify the means."

And then there was the issue of her diabetes. I wasn't a medical expert, but I knew dosing her with sugar wasn't a long-term fix. The candy bar was a Band-Aid, not a cure. I didn't know what would happen when she crashed, but I knew it wasn't good.

I looked up at the hill behind us. It was a steep climb to get back up to the main trail. When I'd been hurrying down, it hadn't occurred to me that I'd have to climb back up at some point. And it certainly hadn't occurred to me that I'd be dragging a resistant Diana behind me.

I closed my eyes to ponder, and they had barely closed when firm hands grabbed my shoulders and shook me. Cool air washed over me, and Kale appeared, kneeling on the ground in front of me. "You cannot go to sleep right now." His eyes were creased with the effort of keeping his grasp on me.

"I didn't. I closed my eyes for two seconds."

"You were asleep," he said. His grip dissolved, hands passing through my arms. "If you stay still, you're going to crash, and you can't. Not yet." He closed his hands around my wrists. "Now get up."

I let myself sag as dead weight for just a moment, and he flared bright in response. The current from his touch intensified and jolted me painfully as he pulled me to my feet.

"Don't make this difficult," he said.

"I'm not that heavy," I said, trying to inject some humor into my voice. It fell flat.

He shook his head. "It takes a lot of effort for me to touch you. Way more to pick you up off the ground. And I need every bit of energy to make sure I can get you back out of here." He looked remorseful. "I'm getting tired."

Oh. "Diana, we gotta go."

She groaned, and I hauled her up by her arms again. "I wanna stay with Corey," she said.

"And I want a hot bath, but we don't always get what we want," I said. "Let's go."

# CHAPTER EIGHTEEN

*Saturday*

SO YOU GET TIRED TOO?" I asked Kale as we slowly climbed the steep trail Corey had fallen from. Anything to take my mind off the painful cramping in my legs and the prickly sensation in my feet. At least I could still feel them. That was a good sign, right?

If Diana was a real team player, she'd be walking on her own, but as it was, I was practically dragging her forward, like making a life-sized doll walk. I'd considered having her climb on my back, but I wasn't strong enough to carry her more than a few steps before collapsing.

"I do," he said. "All spirits do."

"So what do you do after this? Take a nice, long nap?"

"Something like that."

"You know, you could stop being vague for once."

Kale sighed. He sounded terribly put-upon. "You know, they didn't warn me you would be so sassy."

"Who? Wait, let me guess…you can't tell me." I knew I was verging on irritating, if I wasn't already there. But the curiosity had gotten a hold of me, and I couldn't resist the intrigue. Besides, the banter took my mind off the fact that all my limbs were turning to ice. "Does that mean there's more of you? More Guardians?"

"Yes."

"Oh my God," I said. "Is there, like, a club?"

"Bridget," he complained.

"Seriously, I'm not joking. Do you get together and complain about your disobedient humans?"

He laughed despite himself. "You're not 'my human.' That makes you sound like my pet."

"That's for darn sure. You have to tell me."

"Yes, there are many of us," he said. "There's a hierarchy. We don't often convene. There's little reason to. I occasionally have contact with a superior."

"Tell me more." As we talked, the burning exhaustion in my legs faded away, and my imagination ran wild. I pictured Kale around a great wood conference table surrounded by spirits in white, all of them acting very serious as they discussed the antics of the people they watched over. "Do you talk about me?"

"Sometimes," Kale said.

"Really?"

"Really. They were very concerned about what you did to help Natalie."

"Did I break the rules?"

He laughed again. "Would you care if you did?"

"Well, I can't really be blamed. 'Cause I didn't know there even were rules to break. Because someone doesn't tell me anything."

"Nice try. I was instructed to keep a closer eye on you and to ensure your safety." He sighed. "They felt I should have stopped you from going in after Emily."

"They'd rather she died?"

"They think bigger picture," Kale said. "There's work for you to do. And you have to be alive to do it."

I paused as the gravity of the statement settled over me. "Work? Like…a destiny?"

"Yes." He shrugged. "There are important things you need to do."

"Like what?"

"They don't tell me."

I made a frustrated sound. "You can't just drop that on me and not tell me more."

"Sure I can." He zipped ahead out of sight, then came back. "You're close to the top."

"I don't believe you, but it's nice of you to say." I shook my head. "And this conversation is so not over. What kind of work is there to do?"

Kale was saved from responding. My balance shifted suddenly. Diana was falling, and taking me with her. I twisted awkwardly and fell back on my butt to keep from going sideways and joining Corey in the Broken Leg club. I skidded in the wet leaves and dug my heels into the ground. When I'd caught myself, I immediately scrambled back up on my hands and knees. "What's wrong?"

"Tired," Diana said. Her pale face glistened with sweat, and she went to unzip the jacket. I pulled her hands away, and she slapped my hand hard. It stung against my ice-cold skin. "No! I'm hot."

I clenched my jaw and slapped her hand back. She stared at me, eyes wide and mouth open in shock. "How do you like it?" I said. "You're not hot."

"I'm so hot," she complained, moving her hands toward the zipper again. What the hell?

"You are not hot," I told her. "You are straight-up cuckoo for Cocoa Puffs right now." I got up and grabbed her arm. "Now get up."

She tried to pull away, but I clamped down on her thin arm hard enough to make her yelp and hauled her to her feet. "You're mean."

"Yeah, I know." I was too cold and tired to feel guilty about it anymore. "You can cry about it later."

"She's sick," Kale said. "Be nice."

"We've established that. What do you want me to do about it?"

"Hurry," he said.

*I'm going as fast as I can,* I thought irritably, but was I? I had to reach deep down. The idea of it sucked, but if someone put a gun to my head right now, I knew I'd find some shred of energy to take off running. I could do more.

"Come on," I told her. I looped my arm around her waist again like she was my drunk prom date and started hurrying up the hill. *You're not tired,* I told myself. *Not even you, legs.*

"Just keep climbing," I murmured. "Just keep climbing." I said it over and over, anything to take my mind off how cold and tired I was.

Soon, our balance shifted, and I realized we were on flat ground again. Diana bumped into a wooden sign and grunted. I used the lighter to illuminate the *Steep Path Ahead—Use Caution* sign. We were close. So close.

"Can we rest?" Diana asked.

"Nope." I tightened my grip on her waist and pushed forward. Every other step, she stumbled, pulling me all over like a shopping cart with a bad wheel. I kept pushing ahead, until I was practically dragging her over the ground.

"You're so close," Kale said. He materialized next to me, and I felt the firm push of a hand on my back. A shiver ran up my spine. "I've got you."

"Just keep moving," I told myself, whispering in tiny plumes of fog. "Go. Go. Go."

I was so busy chanting to myself that I almost missed the sound of movement in the trees. There was a breaking, crashing sound ahead of me, punctuated by male voices. I froze.

"Natalie! Are you there?"

Natalie? I couldn't have heard right.

"Diana Brown? Corey Walker?"

I didn't recognize the voice, but I didn't care. "Here!" I said. My voice came out rough and cracked. I cleared my throat painfully. "Here!"

Flashlights bobbed, casting bright beams and cutting a path through the dark. After traveling by the tiny flame of a lighter for so long, they looked like spotlights. A male voice shouted, "Over here!"

A light shone right in my face, blinding me. I squeezed my eyes shut and covered my face with my free hand.

The voice said, "Diana?"

I shook my head, still covering my eyes. "This is Diana."

"Okay. Then you must be Natalie," the man said.

I uncovered my eyes and squinted at him. He was barely more than a silhouette in my unadjusted eyes. "No, I'm—"

"Go with it," Kale said mildly.

"Natalie," I said. "Sorry, I thought you said Valerie."

"Okay, Natalie, you're gonna be okay. My name is Derrick, and you're gonna be fine," the man said. He wore a heavy black parka and a hat that said *Volunteer Fire Dept,* and he was the most beautiful thing I'd ever seen. "Come on, let's get you out of here."

Nothing had ever sounded so good. But I shook my head. "Corey is still out here. Her boyfriend. He fell down the path and broke his leg."

"We'll come back for him."

"Bridget, let him do his job," Kale said.

"No," I said. "I'll show you."

"Or you could ignore me," Kale muttered. "I'm used to it."

Cry me a river.

Derrick sighed. "Okay." He unclipped a radio from inside his jacket and said, "I've got two females here. One is the missing girl. The other says the boy

189

is down in the woods with a broken leg." He paused. "Copy that."

Another man came up and shone his flashlight on us.

Derrick turned to him. "Yo, Paul. This is Diana. Get her down to the truck ASAP." He gestured to Diana, and without a breath, the other man swept her off her feet as if she weighed nothing.

"Hey Diana, my name's Paul," he said. "You're gonna be okay."

Diana's head lolled against his chest.

"Um, excuse me," I said as he started to turn away. "I don't know if they told you, but she's diabetic. I think she's sick. She said she needed food, so I gave her a candy bar, but it's been a while and she hasn't had insulin."

Paul nodded. "Thanks for letting me know. We'll make sure she's okay." He turned away and hurried back down the trail. Diana's ponytail swung over his arm. As I watched, I slightly regretted not taking Derrick's offer for help. For one, he might have picked me up. No more walking sounded like a win to me.

No. I promised Corey he'd be all right. I turned back to Derrick. "Corey's down here."

A pair of EMTs came through carrying big blue duffel bags and a metal frame with a stretcher. I didn't know how they were going to get Corey up the hill, but I was ready to let them figure it out without me. My part was about to be done. "This the one?" one asked.

Derrick shook his head. "She said he's down here."

I turned to Kale and gave him a subtle nod. He moved ahead, guiding the way through the trees. In the bright glow of the EMT's flashlights, the woods seemed way less imposing. I had to invest in a good flashlight. When we got to the *Steep Path Ahead* sign, I held up my hand. "I think he fell over this edge. If you follow it down and around, he's sitting by a tree."

The EMTs nodded and headed down for him. I started to go after them, but Derrick blocked my path. "All right, sweetheart. You've done enough. You need to get checked out."

"I don't need it."

"At least let me get you out of these damn woods." He took off his heavy black jacket and put it around me. The heavy down made me feel instantly warmer, and I snugged it tight around me. As we walked through the woods, he asked, "What the hell were you guys doing out here?"

"Uh…"

"Your friend said you came out to hang out and happened to see the car," Derrick said. "Why would you come out here in the middle of the night when it's snowing?"

"Poor judgment."

"Finally, the truth," Kale said.

"When we get out, we'll get your full name so we can call your parents and let them know you're safe," Derrick said.

That would definitely *not* be happening, but I wasn't going to argue with Derrick. Soon, we saw the most beautiful thing I'd ever seen. The wall of trees split apart like curtains as we crested a small hill, and I saw the paved path that ended at the curb of the parking lot. Michael was pacing at the end, blocked by a police officer with a thick knit hat on. When he saw me, his face lit up.

"Natalie," he said loudly, eyes going wide. His slow, emphatic nod said *follow my lead.* He held his arms out, and I let him hug me. Oh, God, he was so warm. His breath was hot against my ear as he whispered, "You're Natalie, and I'm Steven."

"Got it."

"You two, I need you to make a statement," the police officer said.

Derrick waved him off. "It can wait. We need to check her out and maybe

191

transport her with the others."

The parking lot was a flurry of activity, and my stomach twisted into a knot at the sight of all the flashing lights. There were two police cars and an ambulance with the Fire Department logo on the side. Michael's car was parked on the opposite end of the lot, closest to the exit. Smart boy.

"Let me go get my phone out of the car so we can let our parents know what's going on," I told Derrick. I reluctantly shrugged off Derrick's coat and handed it back. He frowned. "I have one in the car."

He shrugged and walked back to the ambulance, where they'd wrapped Diana in a heavy blanket. Someone was in her face, shining a light into her eyes. Another EMT was asking her questions, but she was too dazed to answer. Still, she was alive. To heck with modesty. She was alive because of me. And it felt good.

My moment of pride was short-lived. I saw the police officers talking and gesturing at Michael and me. I shoved my cold hands into my pockets and hurried toward Michael's car.

"What are you doing?" Michael said.

"We need to go," I replied. "If he calls my mother, I'm dead."

"Bridget, you look like a ghost. You might actually be dead if you don't go to the hospital."

"I'll be okay." I waited for him to unlock the doors, and I immediately plopped into the seat with my backpack between my feet. As I sank into the cushion, my entire body felt like it turned to stone. The adrenaline drained out of me, and I was more exhausted than I'd ever been. My chest heaved, and suddenly tears spilled out of my eyes, almost painfully hot against my cheeks.

Michael hurried around and dropped into the driver's seat. He looked at me in shock. "What's wrong?"

I couldn't help the tears. I wasn't sad or angry or anything. I was so tired and overwhelmed that I didn't know what else to do. "I'm...so...tired," I sobbed.

"Oh my gosh," he murmured. He started the car and cranked up the heat. It was just cool air at first, but the knowledge that heat was incoming was enough to make me cry harder. He reached over to hug me. I was too tired to even return the hug, so I just sat there with my wet face pressed into his shoulder, leaking like a faucet. "I really think you should go let them check you out."

"I'll be fine," I said. The hiccupping sobs turned to violent shivers.

"You're freezing," he said into my hair.

"I can't. My mom will kill me."

He sighed and pulled away from me, holding my face gently in his warm hands. "You're officially the most stubborn person I know."

"Thank you," I said through chattering lips. I could feel my nose running over my frozen upper lip, and I knew I had to have reached new lows for unattractiveness. When I'd pictured Michael holding my face lovingly, this had not been at all what I looked like. Less snot. More glamour.

"It's not a compliment," he said, though he smiled anyway.

I glanced at the dashboard clock. It was almost five thirty in the morning. "I promise I'll be fine. Can you please take me home?"

Michael sighed. "Fine." Suddenly he frowned. "Where's your jacket?"

"Shit." I peered through the fogged-up window. Through the blur of condensation, I could see the first ambulance pulling away, and with it, Diana and my jacket. "My mom is gonna kill me."

Michael laughed. "You're a mess."

"I agree. Let's go."

He backed out of the lot. I watched the fogged rearview mirror as the flashing emergency lights receded behind us. When the warm air started to blow finally, I put my hands up to the vent. They were painfully stiff and cold, and I had to try extra hard to bend the frozen digits. When they finally felt like they were thawing slightly, I shoved them into the pocket of my hoodie and leaned my head back.

It felt like I'd just closed my eyes when someone shook me. I opened my eyes to see the warm yellow glow of golden arches overhead. We were at the twenty-four-hour McDonalds near school. It was five fifty-seven in the morning. "Do you want something to eat?"

The thought of eating sounded awfully difficult. "No, but I would kill for something hot."

"Come on. Just for a minute."

As we walked into the heated building, I felt like I'd gone to fry-grease-scented heaven. It was hot enough to be stuffy, and it was glorious. Michael ordered pancakes and a coffee, and I ordered a huge hot chocolate. We were the only customers, so they had our order ready by the time I'd yanked out a handful of napkins from the drink station. I examined the excessive pile of napkins in my hand. No question about it. I was my mother's daughter.

We took a booth in the corner. The first greedy sip of hot chocolate burned my tongue and burned like molten lava going down. I coughed and peeled off the lid to blow on it. While I waited for it to cool, I satisfied myself by wrapping my hands around the hot cup.

"So that was kind of insane," Michael said.

"Tell me what happened."

"I drove back to Hartley Beach, but my signal was too weak to get a call through. I kept calling and it would drop the call every time. So I drove back toward town and kept trying to call. I finally got them, but then they were asking me for specific locations and how I knew someone was out there. They actually sounded really suspicious."

"Did you tell them—"

"I told them I'd seen the car," he said with a smile. "And that I was sure of it."

"And?"

"They asked what their condition was, but I didn't know. They told me it might be a while, because the closest ambulance was coming from the fire department in Greenridge." Greenridge was a tiny blip of a town out past the park. He took a big bite of pancake, then offered me one. I shook my head. "Then I waited for you. I tried to call you, but I didn't have enough signal."

"It wouldn't have mattered," I said forlornly. I took my phone out of my pocket and showed him. There was still murky stream water dripping out of the headphone jack. Oh, God. What if Mom had woken up early and realized I was gone? If she'd been calling or texting, I'd never know. I might have just jumped from the freezer into the fire. Well, nothing to be done about it now. I stuck it back in my pocket and gave Michael a smile that hurt my frozen cheeks. "Thank you for doing all of that. It was really smart to give them different names."

He smiled. "Thank you. I didn't really do much. So what happened with you? Your version is probably a lot more exciting."

I shrugged. "I'm still not sure exactly what happened with them. They were both so disoriented, it was hard to get anything clear out of them besides 'cold' and 'tired.' There was this really steep path, and I think they were hiking when Corey fell over the edge and broke his leg. Then I think Diana went to find help but got turned around and went the wrong direction."

Michael shook his head. "And you found them all with help from the ghosts?"

"Just Kale. He's better than GPS."

"Why, thank you," Kale said, materializing next to me on the bench. I glanced over at him. He seemed paler than usual, and more translucent. I could see right through his body to the plastic red bench, which rendered him a lovely rosy pink instead of his usual classic white. I'd never seen him that way. His words about using up his energy and needing rest just like I did echoed in my mind then. Until now, I'd always thought of Kale as some kind of Energizer Bunny, a force of nature that never waned. Even though he'd been against it, he'd sacrificed his own well-being for me. I felt oddly guilty, especially considering he'd never complained about what it would do to him to help.

"This is crazy," Michael said. "Do you do this often?"

"Is that a pickup line?"

He laughed. "You know what I mean."

"This is my first daring midnight rescue." I finally took a drink of the hot chocolate. I winced in preparation, but it had cooled enough to be tolerable.

"It's kind of awesome," Michael said.

"He's a bad influence on you," Kale said primly.

"It's nice to know you helped someone," I admitted. "Hey, can you pull up Facebook on your phone?"

He nodded and took the phone out. Then he frowned. "Damn. My battery died. It was probably searching for the network while I was waiting on you."

"It's okay." I glanced up at the clock on the wall. It was past six. "Crap, I really need to get home."

I fell asleep again on the way home, and Michael shook me gently to the sight of my neighborhood. The brick signs were decorated with Christmas wreaths and glowing yellow lights, and I felt like I'd returned home to the real world after a strange dream. "Are you sure you don't want me to take you all the way to your house?"

I shook my head. "My mom will hear you pull up." I hesitated with my backpack in my lap. I didn't want to get out of the car—mostly because it was so nice and warm, but also because in some weird way, I didn't want to leave Michael. He and I had yet to go on a normal-person outing. Before, we'd been searching for clues to his dead sister's disappearance, and this obviously had been par for the course in terms of normality. "Thanks for helping tonight. I really couldn't have done this alone. It means a lot that you believe in me."

He smiled. "I don't think that's entirely true."

"Oh?"

He reached out and took my hand. "Somehow, I think you would have worked it out even without me. I don't know you that well yet, but one thing is pretty clear. You don't let go easily."

I smiled. "You're not wrong. But still. It's nice to talk to someone about this who has a heartbeat."

He smiled. "Well, if you ever need help again, you have my number. You can call anytime."

"Thanks." I reluctantly extricated my hand from his. There was a silly little girl inside me who wanted one of those romantic movie moments when he'd surprise me with a kiss. Maybe that was the exhaustion talking.

The cold air outside the car seemed doubly cold after the near-stifling heat inside the car. As I bundled the hood of my sweatshirt back over my head and started walking toward the house, Kale reappeared next to me. "Gonna make it?"

"I'll be fine," I said. I sighed. It was Kale. No point in acting tough. "To be honest, I'm exhausted, and I probably should have gone to the hospital with Diana. But Mom would kill me."

He smiled, a little sad. "She would rather have you alive."

"I know. But she doesn't trust me."

"Can't imagine why."

"How do people usually deal with this?"

"How do you mean?"

"What does your Guardian Club have to say about leading a double life?" I said.

He laughed. "Well, most sensitives don't get it this young."

I sighed. "So there's no manual specifically with directions on how to stay out of trouble with your overprotective mother?"

Kale laughed. "Afraid not." He blinked out of sight, then stopped in my path. With the snow still falling gently around us, he looked even more angelic than usual. "No matter what, I'll always be here to protect you."

"Yeah, you can say that. Don't think I forgot about our conversation. One day you have to tell me the whole story."

"I will someday."

I tilted my head. Kale had been giving me coy, evasive answers as long as I'd known him. "Really?"

"When you're ready." That was more like it. He gestured to the house. "You should get inside and get warm."

"Will you go check on Diana and Corey?"

He sighed. "Yes. And then we both need to rest."

"Okay. Hey, I'm sorry."

His brow furrowed, his gaze locked on mine. "For what?"

"You look exhausted," I said. "I know it's because of me. I'm sorry to cause you so much trouble."

He smiled, an expression that made him glow even in his tired state. "Can

I quote you on that for next time you get a crazy idea?"

"Um…"

"I'll be all right soon. I'm just glad we could help them. Though we are due for a serious talk about safety."

"Okay, Mom," I said. "I'll see you soon?"

"Of course," he said. Then he simply faded away like a plume of smoke into the night.

I hurried up the driveway and around the back of the house. The snow was a thin white carpet over the driveway and yard. If Mom had woken up to find me missing, she hadn't left the house to find me, which mean she probably hadn't woken up at all. At least something was going my way tonight.

I tiptoed up the back deck and slid the glass open. The house was pleasantly warm, though I could have stood for it to be a sauna. I carefully closed the door behind me, then turned to see the second-to-last thing I would have wanted to see. Mom was at the top of the list, but this was close behind her.

My little brother stood in the middle of the kitchen with a glass of water in his hand. "What are you doing?"

# CHAPTER NINETEEN

MY MOUTH WENT DRY, and I had to think quick. "I was outside looking at the snow."

He just raised an eyebrow. "I'm not stupid. I saw you walk around from the front. You've been gone for a while."

"No I haven't." My heart raced. All of this, and it was going to be ruined by a stupid seventh grader. Well, a very perceptive seventh grader who apparently couldn't go a whole night without a glass of water. Ugh.

"Tell me where you really were," he said. "Or I'm telling Mom."

I grabbed his arm and hustled him upstairs. "Shh," I hissed when he protested. After pushing him into his bedroom, I eased the door shut behind us. Where my room was light and airy, his was dark and subterranean. The walls were plastered in grim-looking video game posters. Along one wall he had bookshelves from floor to ceiling, overflowing with books, manga, and action figures. The windows were covered with blackout curtains, and the only light was from a blue-shaded lamp by his bed. "You're not telling Mom anything." I folded my arms and stood in front of the door so he couldn't run out to wake her.

"Then tell me what you were doing." He scowled at me. "Are you smoking drugs?"

"Good lord." I laughed at the absurdity of it. That would have been a lot more normal than what I was actually doing. "No, I'm not doing drugs."

"I know you left the house. A long time ago."

"How do you know that?"

"Your stupid computer kept going off. So I went in your room to tell you to turn it down."

"What do you mean, going off? And wait, you went in my room without permission?"

"Well, if you'd been there, you could have given me permission. It's not my fault you snuck out," he said. "You should have been there to tell me not to."

"Your logic is breathtaking." Though he had a point.

He ignored me. "Emily was calling you on Skype, and it was ringing and waking me up. So I went in there to tell you to turn it off, but you were gone. I answered and told her you weren't here, and she told me to text you."

"You answered my call?" I spluttered. "What else did Emily tell you?"

"She said to check on you later. So I tried to text you, but you never responded."

I sighed and took out my phone. "I was ignoring her messages, and then it got wet. I probably missed yours in there. You didn't tell Mom, did you?"

"Emily said she'd heard from you, so not to tell Mom unless you weren't home by morning."

"And you didn't?"

"I was going to. You can't just sneak out in the middle of the night."

"It was really important, Colin."

"What was it?"

"I can't tell you," I said.

He let out a growling sound. "Maybe I should tell Mom."

My temper flared, and I resisted the urge to say, *maybe I should punch your face in.* "Colin, I'm begging you. Mom already doesn't trust me."

"This is why!" He threw up his hands in frustration.

"And I can't tell you why, but I promise it was for a good reason. Believe me, I don't want to get in any more trouble."

He looked forlorn, eyes downcast as he hesitated before speaking. "I was worried. I thought something bad might happen to you. Like Valerie. Then it would just be me and Mom."

It was suddenly hard to breathe. "You were worried about me?"

He rolled his eyes, then gave the tiniest nod.

"I'm sorry. I didn't think anyone would wake up."

He shrugged. "Give me your phone."

"No," I said automatically.

"Do you want it fixed or not?" He held out his hand toward me.

After eyeballing him, I placed the wet phone in his hand. He brushed past me and headed for the stairs. I followed him down to the kitchen, where he took a Tupperware container out of the cabinet and set it on the counter. He pawed through the pantry until he found a big plastic container filled with white rice. After pouring a small layer of rice into the bowl, he tore off a paper towel. He dabbed my phone with it, then carefully wrapped it like he was wrapping a snack for later. Scooping out a little nest for the phone-burrito, he pushed the phone in the bowl, then poured in rice until the whole thing was covered.

"Sometimes it works," he said. "If it doesn't, I still have mine from before the upgrade. I know how to switch the cards so you don't have to tell Mom you ruined it."

People could sure surprise you. I'd have expected him to rat me out to Mom within thirty seconds of realizing I was gone. "Thanks, monkey. It was really cool of you not to tell on me."

"Don't forget fixing your phone," he added. His lips curved faintly. "You're welcome. And don't call me monkey. Turkey."

I smiled. "I'm going to bed. You should too."

We walked up the stairs quietly, and I let myself into my room. I started my laptop and peeled off my damp, cold clothes while I waited for the computer to start. I layered on clothes—a pair of tights, sweatpants, a tanktop, a couple of long-sleeved shirts, and Valerie's hand-me-down sweatshirt. Bad habits be damned. I'd take all the layers I could get. I pulled the laptop into bed with me.

As I got snuggled into the covers, Kale reappeared at the foot of my bed. "They're at the hospital now. Both alive."

"Thank you," I said. "I know you need to rest."

He smiled at me. There was something about his smile that made the rest of the night seem like a minor inconvenience. "It was worth it. You should have seen their parents' faces," he said. "I wish I could have brought you a picture."

I grinned and gestured for him to come around. He sat cross-legged on the bed next to me, looking over my shoulder at the screen. Diana's mother had posted an update about forty-five minutes earlier. With him hovering nearby, I realized his presence brought with it a biting chill he didn't normally have. Maybe that came with being tired. I sneaked a look at him. I half expected to see some telltale sign of death like with the other spirits I'd encountered, but he was just paler and more translucent than usual. Relief washed over me.

> **FB Friends and family—I just got word from the BCPD that they found Diana and Corey and are transporting them to the hospital. Pls pray for my baby! Thank you!**

A quick circuit around the news sites brought no further updates. They probably wouldn't post a story until the morning, if they said anything at all. I was a little worried about what Diana and Corey would have to say about me; I definitely didn't want a Spider-Man-style news story about a mysterious rescuer. It was cool in theory, but the whole secret-vigilante thing didn't turn out well for Spider-Man or Batman. Maybe I'd be different, but I didn't want to test my historically terrible luck.

I closed the laptop and put it on the floor by the bed, then burrowed deep under the covers. "Don't you need to get some rest?" I asked Kale. "You look really tired."

"Soon." There was a heavy quilt at the end of my bed. He raised his hands, his whole body glowing brighter. The quilt rose from the bed and fell open as it hovered over me. He made a little gesture, and the quilt dropped on me, giving me another layer of warmth.

"Showoff," I said.

"I live to please." He tipped an imaginary hat to me.

"Uh, so I might have a slight problem."

"You have lots of problems."

"Kale."

"What is it?"

I told him about my run-in with Colin. "What if he tells Mom? Oh! Can you scare him like you did Tara?"

Kale laughed. "Not exactly. I could probably stage a respectable haunting. But I don't think you'll need me to."

"No?"

"People love keeping secrets."

"But what if—"

Light fingers brushed across my forehead, leaving a light tingle in their wake. "You worry too much. If he does, we'll deal with it. Just rest for now. I'm sure you're going to have a busy day tomorrow thinking of new ways to give me a heart attack."

"You don't—"

"Figuratively speaking," Kale said. "Get some sleep. You've earned it."

# CHAPTER TWENTY

*Saturday—11:49 a.m.—Six Hours Found*

THE KNOCK AT THE DOOR first awoke me, but the smell of bacon downstairs got my eyes open. "Sleep-in Saturday," I groaned. I scrubbed at one eye and peered at the alarm clock. Eleven forty-nine. Damn. I'd only been asleep for about five hours. I could have done with another twelve.

"Mom said come downstairs or she's eating the rest of the bacon," Colin said through a tiny crack.

"I'm coming down," I yelled.

I sat up and threw off my blankets. The room was spinning a little, but I couldn't resist the call of bacon. Sometime during the night, my body must have warmed back up, because I was sweating like I'd run a marathon on the equator. I peeled off the layers and put on a clean pair of pajamas. My feet ached as I walked over my shaggy rug. They were a little red, but they felt normal to the touch. Surely I'd know if I had frostbite. After another look at my bright pink piggies, I added a thick pair of socks just to be safe.

I opened the door and jumped a little to see Colin still standing there. After a surreptitious look over his shoulder, he took my phone out of his pocket and held it out. "I got to it before Mom woke up," he whispered. "There's still some water under the glass."

"Does it work?"

"Yeah. Well, I guess. I got it to turn on, but you have the password on there."

I took the phone and typed in the password, then swiped through the menus. There was a wet spot in the upper right corner, which gave a rainbow effect with the light shining through it. But it seemed to be fine otherwise. Oh, thank God. Even with Colin's card-switching idea, Mom would eventually notice that I wasn't carrying the new phone, especially since she'd been so adamant about getting the shatter-proof case after I irresponsibly destroyed the last one. "Thanks again, Colin."

He nodded, then hurried back downstairs.

I followed him into the kitchen, where Mom had a half-eaten pan of cinnamon rolls, scrambled eggs, and bacon sizzling on the stove. "Good morning, sleepy-head."

I looked at the clock. Eleven fifty-three. "Almost afternoon."

Mom looked over her shoulder. "You must have slept good, huh?"

*I earned it.* "I guess so." I got a plate down from the cabinet and scooped eggs onto it. "Did you already eat?"

Mom nodded. "You can finish it up."

I scraped the remains of the eggs onto my plate, then pulled two of the sticky cinnamon rolls off the pan. Finally, I added enough bacon to feed the entire school football team. I was ravenous.

"Are you feeling all right?" Mom asked.

I glanced at my plate. "I'm hungry."

"Not that. Eat up. You look really pale. I hope you're not getting sick." She got closer and pressed the back of her hand to my forehead, then to each cheek in turn. Her hands felt blazing hot against my cheeks, which were still cool from last night. "You don't have a fever. But what did you do to your face?"

"What?" I said innocently.

My heart thumped as she examined my cheek closer. Her brow furrowed. "Bridget, your cheek. What did you do?"

"I don't know what you mean. Must have done it in my sleep." Or maybe a wild tree branch had attacked me while on a covert daring rescue.

"Lord have mercy. Make sure you come down here and let me clean it before it gets infected."

"Okay." I plopped down at the kitchen table to eat. I tore into one of the cinnamon rolls and nearly swooned. A glass appeared next to me. I looked back to see Mom pouring orange juice with one hand while she pointed the remote at the TV with the other. "Thanks."

She nodded and gestured to the TV. "Did you hear anything about this yesterday?"

The news report showed a side-by-side picture of Diana and Corey. A caption along the bottom read *Missing Teens Recovering In Local Hospital.*

"I think I saw it on Facebook."

A pretty reporter stood in front of the hospital. "I'm here at Parkland Regional Hospital, where two local teenagers are recovering from a harrowing night in the woods. Diana Brown and Corey Walker were reported missing yesterday afternoon after leaving school. Police received a tip that the teens might be out at Wildwood State Park and dispatched officers to search for them throughout the night."

I didn't want the credit, but I still felt a little irritated at her version of the story. The police *wouldn't* go search in any kind of numbers, which was why I froze my happy butt off to find them.

"But the story took a strange turn," the reporter said.

I froze with a strip of bacon hanging out of my mouth. *Oh, crap.* Derrick, who had given me his puffy jacket, appeared on screen with a fire station in the background. The nameplate read Derrick Adams, First Responder.

"Yeah, we got a tip around three-thirty in the morning that their car had been spotted," he said. "When we got out to the state park, a young man was waiting for us. He was the one who called. About half an hour later, a teenage girl brought Diana out of the woods, and then she walked us right to Corey."

*No, no, no.* The cinnamon roll suddenly felt like a lump of sludge in my mouth. I gulped down orange juice and watched the TV with a growing sense of dread. I hadn't told them my name at any point, had I?

The camera switched to Diana, who was sitting up in bed. She looked tired and pale, but alive. Her dark hair was brushed and braided neatly over her shoulder, which was a vast improvement over her Wild Woman look. "Me and Corey went out to the park to get some pictures for my senior project. We were only supposed to be out there for a few hours. Anyway, I slipped and dropped one of my lenses off the trail. Corey tried to get it, but he fell over the edge and broke his leg. I went down after him and tried to go back for help, but then I got lost."

"What about the girl who helped you? Do you know who she was?"

Diana smiled a little. "She never even told me her name." *Phew.* "She kinda came out of nowhere and said she was there to help. She gave me her jacket so I could get warm." Her eyes welled up. She wiped at them and smiled sheepishly. There was an IV in the back of her hand and a heart monitor attached to her finger. "Somehow, she knew I was diabetic, so she made me eat, and then no matter what, she wouldn't let me stop walking. I was so tired, but she told me she was going to get me out of the woods."

Her mother dabbed at her eyes and patted Diana's hand. "I know God was watching out for my baby," she said. "If Diana hadn't gotten something to eat when she did, she could have gone into a coma and..." Her voice hitched. "Died."

The camera cut back to Derrick. "The girl said her name was Natalie. She told me she was going to get her phone from her car, but when I went back to find her, both her and her friend were gone." He shook his head. "I don't know, man, it's weird, right?"

I looked back to see Colin staring at me, eyes narrowed. He knew, no question about it. As casually as I could manage, I bit another piece of bacon in half and took a sip of juice. "I'm glad they found them."

"Bridget, don't talk with food in your mouth," Mom said automatically. She reached over me and took a sip of my orange juice, then returned it.

"Mom."

"Oh, whatever. I gave birth to you. You can share," she said. "Those kids were lucky."

"Very lucky," Colin said evenly. "I wonder who found them?"

"It was probably just a lucky coincidence. Some kids went out there to get high," I said. "Or have sex."

"Bridget!" Mom said. "Not in front of your brother."

"What? Kids do it all the time. Not me, I mean."

"I know about sex, Mom," Colin said.

"Jesus, no you don't," she said, rolling her eyes. "Whatever it was, they're safe now. The Lord works in mysterious ways."

And so did I. Trying to avoid Colin's laser stare, I wolfed down my breakfast, then ran back upstairs to check my laptop. I searched for Teresa Brown again and found that she'd posted several updates since last night. The most recent read:

*Thank you for all your prayers and concern. Diana and Corey are both safe and making a good recovery. Both of them had hypothermia, and Diana suffered from a severe diabetic episode. Many of you have seen the news and heard about our guardian angels. The only information I could get was that the boy went by Steven, and the girl said her name was Natalie. Diana said the girl had on a Fox Lake High School shirt. If you know who these two people might be, please contact me. I'd like to thank them in person. They saved my daughter's life last night. If you're reading this, thank you from the bottom of my heart. You answered my prayers.*

There were half a dozen comments already about angels and Christmas miracles. That was new. I'd never been accused of being an angel. I briefly considered showing Mom so I could remind her the next time she started scolding me about my latest disappointment.

I looked up to see Colin standing in my door. "What?"

"Was it you?"

"I left at least three pieces of bacon for you."

"Cut the crap," Colin said sharply. He walked in and closed the door behind him. He had his tablet in one hand, and I could see the familiar blue navigation bar of Facebook reflecting onto his glasses. "Did you go find those kids last night?"

This was by far the weirdest dilemma I'd ever found myself in. Which would be better for my little brother to believe? The truth? Or should I tell him I'd snuck out with a cute senior boy and we'd just happened to go to the park?

"What do you think?" I cocked my head. "Do you think I'm going to go stomping through the woods in the snow to find some girl I don't know?"

He folded his arms over his skinny chest. I could practically see his brain ticking. My brother was too smart for his own good, and he couldn't stand secrets when he was on the outside. "Where's your jacket?"

My heart skipped a beat. I tried to look surprised and hoped it didn't come off as a guilty expression. "Huh?"

"Your new winter jacket. Where is it?"

"I don't know." That wasn't a lie. I'd left it with Diana, so I had no idea where it was now.

"Because you weren't wearing it when you came in last night," he said. "But you had it when we left the church."

"What are you, Sherlock Holmes?" I was going to have to watch him. He was a lot sharper than I had ever given him credit for.

"Answer me," Colin said.

I sighed heavily. "I don't have it."

"Interesting. Because you know what else I noticed? You were wearing your Fox Lake sweatshirt last night."

"There are two thousand students at Fox Lake. And they sell those sweatshirts every year."

"Yeah, and how many Fox Lake students came in at six in the morning? If I go ask Emily where you went, I bet she'll tell me."

"Colin, don't." I sat down on my bed. "Yes, it was me."

His eyes widened. "How? I mean—really?"

"It was luck," I lied. "I heard a rumor, and I wanted to check it out."

He scowled. "How dumb do you think I am?"

"Until last night, I would have answered that question way differently. I know you're not dumb."

He closed his tablet and looked me over. He took a breath and started to speak, then hesitated. He did it a couple of times before he finally said, "Are you a mutant?"

I burst out laughing. "I don't think so."

"Are you getting ready? We have to go help build the church float at two!" Mom bellowed from downstairs.

He regarded me skeptically. "You know, I could help you. I'm good with computers. I could be your sidekick."

"I'll keep that in mind," I said. "The best way you can help is to not tell Mom anything."

"Seriously? That's lame. Let me help."

"I'm trying to stay out of trouble, not go looking for it," I said.

"Well...promise me if something happens again, you let me help."

I sighed. "Sure." That was a promise I didn't intend to keep unless I had to. I had no doubt Colin could be helpful. He'd been using computers since he was in diapers, and he had the advantage of being firmly ensconced on Mom's good side. But I couldn't let him get involved with anything that would endanger him. If something happened to him, Mom would never forgive me, and for once, I'd agree with her.

He nodded. "Okay, cool."

"Colin! Why don't I hear the shower?" Mom yelled.

He sighed. "Bye. It's our secret."

"Bye, monkey. Thanks for keeping it quiet." As I watched him go, I realized maybe he wasn't so bad after all. Sure, he was annoying in his way, but he'd saved my bacon—literally and figuratively—and I was pretty sure he wasn't going to rat me out to Mom.

I checked my phone and found a couple dozen text messages had come in since powering it up. There was a long string of them from Emily. First she was demanding to know if I was safe, and then:

**Emily: I talked to Colin**

*Emily: You'd better call me*

*Emily: If you're not back by morning, he's telling your mom*

*Emily: Don't be mad*

*Emily: R u mad?*

*Emily: He just told me you're home and your phone is dead*

*Emily: Don't do that to me again!*

*Emily: Holy shit I just saw the news*

*Emily: Are they talking about you and Michael???*

I also had a message from Detective Fulbright that simply said:

*Fulbright: Call me.*

I ignored it and thumbed through my contacts until I landed on *Dad*. It was past nine on the west coast, so he had no excuse not to answer. After two rings, he picked up. "Hi, sweetie," he said. "Is everything okay?"

*I almost froze to death six hours ago.* "I'm fine. What's up?"

"Just working. Trying to get some paperwork done for this merger that's coming up. But that's all boring. Did you need something?"

"Well, I hadn't talked to you for a while. So I wanted to catch up."

He paused. "That's great," he said, and I didn't have to be psychic or a mutant to know he didn't mean it. "Your mother said you're helping with the Christmas play. How's *that?*"

"She's making me help with the costumes. It's okay. Colin is doing really good."

"I bet. I sure wish I could come."

"That's kind of why I called, to be honest. Colin said he thought you weren't coming."

"Yeah, I don't think I can swing a trip home this year," he said. "We're short around here at the holidays with all the management going on vacation, and I really can't take another few days off."

"But it's Christmas."

"I know, baby, and I—"

I took a deep breath. "Stop right there. You're my dad, and I'll love you either way, and so will Colin. But you've never let him down. Don't start now."

Dad was silent.

"You're not a doctor, so there's nothing out there that's so important you have to do it on Christmas Eve. Please come see him. It would completely make his year."

"I'll have to make some calls," he said finally. "I'll see what I can do."

"Good."

"So, uh, how's school?"

It was obvious from the long hesitations and flat tone that the small talk was as awkward for him as it was for me, which made me indescribably sad. I wasn't sure when my dad had become a stranger instead of one of my favorite people in the world. Out of obligation more than any real interest, we chatted for another five minutes before Mom started yelling about me getting ready. "Sorry, I've gotta go. Text me when you figure out your travel plans."

"I will. I love you, turkey."

"I love you too, papa bear," I said automatically.

I took a look back through my messages, then called Fulbright. My stomach turned in tight circles as I listened to the rings. On the third ring, a gruff voice answered. "Fulbright."

"Do you always answer the phone like that?"

"Bridget? Is that you?"

"Yeah."

"Jesus, Mary, and Joseph, child," he said. "Was that you who found Diana

Brown?"

"Maybe."

"I knew it." He sighed heavily. "I've been sober for thirteen years, and you make me want to start drinking again."

"Is that a compliment? I'm going to take it that way."

"You can't keep taking risks."

"I don't want to," I said. "I keep trying to get *you* to take them for me, but no one takes me seriously. If this happens again, and I'm pretty sure it will, how about you guys listen to me when I tell you something's up?"

He was silent for a long time. "Are you psychic? Be honest."

I laughed. "Not so much. But you're not far off."

"I've got a daughter about your age. I hate the idea of her putting herself in danger."

"But—"

"But I know of a couple of people who are lucky you did. You know, you've got the guys up here all riled up thinking they had an honest-to-God brush with an angel."

"What did you say?"

"I said you're too much of a pain in the ass to be an angel."

"That's offensive. But probably accurate."

He laughed. "I told them not to look a gift horse in the mouth, and it was probably someone who had a real good reason to not want the attention."

"You're pretty smart," I said.

"That's why I get paid the big bucks. You doing okay?"

"Yeah, I'm fine. Although I did lose my jacket."

"I think I can work something out. You did a good thing, kid. Is there anything I can do to help you out?"

"Actually, yeah. Can you check on a missing persons case for me? See if you have anything on Isaac James Watkins. He would have gone missing in ninety-seven. He's out there in the woods. I found his pack and some bones, but I didn't move it. If you go back to where they found Corey and follow the trail for a while, it'll branch off by a creek. Follow the creek and you'll find him."

Fulbright was silent for a while. "How do you know his name?"

"Don't worry about it," I said. "Please just check on it."

"Okay, anything else?"

I pondered. Could I get away with asking for a police reward? Maybe a joyride in one of the patrol cars... I shook my head. Then it hit me. "Did you ever work with Luis Salazar?"

"Yeah, I knew Sal," Fulbright said. "Young guy, hard worker. It was a damned shame what happened to him."

"So, let me run something by you."

Once Fulbright had heard out my plan, I hung up and headed for the bathroom. I took the hottest shower I could stand and stood under the hot spray until it turned cold. I braided my hair so it would dry wavy, which was as close as I was getting to a real hairstyle in the next few days. Mom hadn't been kidding. My face was ghost-pale, so I slapped on some foundation and blush to compensate. I finished dressing right before Mom yelled again that we were going to be late.

I followed her downstairs, but she stopped me before we went out the door. "Where's your new jacket? It's thirty degrees out, and I don't want you to get sick right before Christmas."

"She left it on the couch, and I spilled my drink on it last night," Colin said smoothly as he came up behind me. He handed me a light purple jacket with puffy sleeves. It was a few years old, but it was better than nothing, and way better than explaining what really happened. "I got her old one out of the hall closet."

"Colin, that was very nice of you, but you need to be more careful," Mom said.

"Sorry," he said meekly.

"And you need to put your things away," Mom said, turning to me.

I started to protest, then realized that being scolded for leaving my jacket out was much better than being grounded for all eternity for sneaking out. "Okay."

"Did you put it in the laundry room?"

"I think so," he said. "I can go check."

"No, we're already running late," she said. "I swear, you two are giving me gray hair."

I exchanged a look with my brother. *If she only knew.*

# CHAPTER TWENTY-ONE

*December 24—Three Days Found*

**B**RIDGET, WE'RE GOING to be late!"

"I'm almost ready!" I yelled back.

I went back to check my laptop again for a response. After another three days of discussion with Sal, I'd had a brilliant idea. When I'd first logged back into my fake John Smith Facebook account after finding Diana, I'd received multiple messages from her mother, Teresa.

The first had come the night Diana had disappeared and I'd tried to send a tip:

> *I don't know who this is, but I don't appreciate practical jokes.*
>
> *If you contact me again, I'll forward your information to the police and press charges for harassment.*

Well, that had been a bit excessive. The next two had come in the morning after Diana had been found.

> *Who is this? We found Diana, out at Wildwood like you said.*
>
> *Please tell me how you knew.*

Another hour later, like she couldn't stop thinking about it:

> *Is this Steven?*

She hadn't written anything since. At first, I had no intention of responding to her. But stupid Facebook was going to let her know that I'd seen her messages, and unless I let her believe there really was a social media-savvy guardian angel watching over her daughter, I had to respond. Besides, she might be the answer to a prayer of mine if I played my cards right.

Finally, I'd typed a response to her an hour earlier.

*Dear Mrs. Brown,*

*I can't really explain how I knew where your daughter was, but I'm glad I could help bring her home to you. I can't introduce myself, but I promise I'm one of the good guys. You said you wanted to repay us somehow, and this is what you can do.*

*A local police officer named Luis Salazar was killed in the line of duty almost a year ago. He left behind a girlfriend and a new baby. Her name is Veronica Lewis, and she lives in Mount Sharon. Call the police department and ask to talk to Detective Tom Fulbright. If you ask about helping Officer Salazar, he'll know what you're calling about. Between the two of you, you can make Veronica smile the way you did when you got Diana back. Just don't tell anyone it had something to do with me.*

*Remember—keep the secret. ☺ Merry Christmas!*

"Bridget!" I heard Mom thundering up the stairs and darted to yank my black-and-white patterned dress over my head. As I shoved my feet into the stiff, uncomfortable heels I'd borrowed from Emily, I saw the animated ellipse come up on Facebook, indicating a reply in progress. My heart leaped into my chest.

The door flew open. "Bridget, Colin is supposed to be there in twenty minutes!"

"It only takes ten to get there," I said.

Mom rolled her eyes and gestured for me to come with her. I grabbed my phone and purse before following her downstairs. I couldn't see right now if Teresa Brown had responded, but I had to hope for the best.

"It's Christmas Eve," Mom said. "The entire town is one gigantic traffic jam."

The snow had been short-lived. As we peeled out of the driveway and onto the main road, there was no sign of the white blanket that had covered the ground only days earlier. It was chilly, but not cold enough to need the heavy jacket I'd left with Diana.

"Colin, do you remember your lines?" Mom asked.

"I'm fine," he said morosely, staring out the window.

"Do you want to practice?"

"No."

Mom hesitated, then glanced in the rearview mirror at him. "What's wrong?"

"Nothing," he said flatly.

"I'm going to record the play so your dad can see it."

"Mom, I said I'm fine," he snapped. "Gosh."

*Bad move, Mom.* Even I could have told her that was the wrong thing to say.

She sighed and looked at me. "Save me from teenagers," she muttered.

Mom wasn't entirely wrong; the traffic all the way to the church sucked. At one minute after six, she peeled into the parking lot and screeched to a halt in the drop-off area to let Colin run inside. "I hate being late," she said as she slowly cruised the aisles looking for a parking spot.

"You can blame it on me," I said mildly. "It won't surprise anyone."

She ignored me and parked the car. "Has he said anything about Dad to you?"

"He wants him to be here. That's all." And if I had my way, Colin would be getting his Christmas wish. The last I'd heard from Dad was that he'd gotten a standby ticket, but then was stranded on the ground around lunchtime because of bad weather in Denver.

"And you?"

I shrugged. "It would be nice but it won't ruin my day if he doesn't show."

"Well, that's two of us," Mom said quietly. I didn't respond and let her think I didn't hear it.

We got out of the car and grabbed the dishes Mom had been cooking all day for the covered dish supper after the play. The night before, I'd been put to work spooning out the chocolate no-bake cookies, while Colin had put marshmallows into plastic baggies for a children's activity. It bordered on child labor, but considering we got to scrape the bowl post-baking, I wasn't complaining.

I glanced at Mom and shoved her camera bag under one of her discarded scrub jackets in the back seat. She was too busy trying to balance the plastic cake carrier to notice me.

I scanned the full parking lot as we walked toward the church, but I didn't know to look for. Dad's personal car was in Washington now, so he always rented a car when he flew back. I thought that kind of said it all, especially the way he said "I'm flying home" whenever he went back west, instead of the other way around. In any case, I didn't know what he would be driving if he'd even made it. He hadn't texted me, but if he was in the air or on the road, he wouldn't get to it.

A pair of older women in reindeer sweaters flanked the side doors. "Barbara!" they exclaimed. Mom gave them a quick hug, then held up the containers of food. "Down to the fellowship hall," one of them said.

I followed Mom down the narrow hallway and into the big room. Volunteers bustled around a long buffet table, arranging dishes wrapped in colorful plastic wrap. After I handed over a pan of macaroni and cheese, I put on a pained expression. "Oh, man," I said dramatically. "I forgot the camera."

Mom rolled her eyes and handed me the car keys. "Go back and get it. I have to get the children's church set up." Despite her exasperation, I smiled as I hurried back down the hall.

As soon as I was out of the building, I got my phone out and opened the John Smith Facebook account. I had a reply from Diana's mother.

*I don't understand any of this, but I called Mr. Fulbright like you said. He told me what to do, and I'm in, especially after what you did for Diana. I asked him about you, and he said that I could trust you. It gives me hope to know that people are still decent in this world. Merry Christmas!*

I smiled and opened Mom's car, then sat in the backseat. "Sal! Luis Salazar, I need you here right this minute. It's super important," I said, closing my eyes as I imagined his smiling face. I put as many mental exclamation points on it as I could, hoping he'd get my sense of urgency loud and clear.

"Hey, Bridget," he said. His usual smile was pulled into a crooked frown.

"I know it's Christmas Eve, but I have a job for you," I said. "You need to go to Veronica's and keep an eye out."

His head snapped up to attention. "What? Did something happen?"

"She's safe. But you're going to want to be there this evening."

Sal's eyes widened, and I saw the tiny spark of hope in him as his lips curved up. He blinked away. Operation Christmas Miracle was underway. I grabbed Mom's camera bag and hurried back to the church. Inside the choir was warming up, and Mom was running around distributing halos. I held up the camera, but she waved me off.

Donna came up and hugged me, half-suffocating me in a cloud of perfume.

"You look as pretty as a princess."

"Thank you," I said.

"Here, your mother wanted to save seats for you two." There were two programs laid out neatly on the second pew in the middle. I raised an eyebrow and moved the programs to either side of me. Donna looked at me quizzically.

"I'm saving an extra," I said.

I took out Mom's small red camera and snapped pictures as Colin warmed up. My favorite was the one of him scratching his nose that looked like he was picking it.

The sanctuary slowly filled, and the choir disappeared through the side doors to the hallway they were using as the backstage. When Mom rushed down the pew to take her seat, she frowned at the extra program on my right. "Who are you saving that for?"

"Just in case."

The pastor—or was it a priest? I could never remember—got up to say a prayer and welcome all the guests who'd come to see the Christmas Eve service and the play. He smiled as one of the high school students got up to the mic and said, "Our story begins in a time long, long ago, in a land far, far away."

Halfway through the song, the pew shifted. I caught the scent of a familiar cologne as a man squeezed into the seat next to me. I turned to see my father. I couldn't help smiling. Colin was going to be stoked.

Dad cleared his throat and straightened his sport coat. "I couldn't park," he whispered. "I ran all the way from Walmart."

"Rick?" my mom whispered, leaning out to speak across me. Her eyes went wide. "What are you doing here?"

"Bridget called and said—"

"Shh," I told them, putting my finger over my lips. Mom poked my arm and gave me an incredulous expression. I smiled and pointed to the stage. "Pay attention." She was going to have some choice words for me later, I was sure, but for now, I was pleased with myself, and I couldn't wait to see Colin's reaction.

I watched as my little brother emerged from the side door wearing his glittering angel wings. At Mom's request, he'd taken off his glasses. His eyes narrowed as he scanned the blurry crowd. He came to center stage. "Hark, good people! I bring you glad tidings of great joy," he said. He looked right at me, and I casually pointed to my right. When he followed my gesture to Dad, his eyebrows shot up in surprise.

"Come on," Mom muttered. "'Unto you…'"

"F-For unto you, a child is born." As he continued his announcement, I could have sworn he got taller, and a smile stretched across his face. I was doing pretty good on Christmas miracles.

By the time the play was over, I was more than ready to tear into the potluck dishes, but Mom insisted on helping clean up the stage first. Colin had launched himself down the stairs at our father, who was now listening to a moment-by-moment recap of the play as if he hadn't just watched it.

Under the pretense of gathering discarded programs and candles, I walked upstairs to the balcony. I jumped a little at the sight of Lena May, Peter, and Annette sitting in the front seats. When I arrived, they turned to look.

"Well, it's been a while," Lena May said. "I heard you found your friend."

"With your help," I said. "Thank you so much."

"Glad to be of service," Peter said.

"And the play was absolutely delightful. Did you see my Gabby sing?" Lena May said.

Annette rolled her eyes, but her bright red lips were curved in an indulgent smile.

Sal appeared and rushed in front of me. "It was amazing. How?"

"What was?" I asked.

"You should have seen her face. The news crew was even there. I never could have…it was…thank you." He opened and closed his hands. "I could just kiss you."

"Probably not," I said. "I'm a little young for you."

He laughed and grinned. "I just wanted to thank you. I'm going to go back and see RJ open some of her presents."

"Go. Merry Christmas."

My pocket buzzed, and I took out my phone to see a message from Fulbright.

**Fulbright: *Watch the eleven o'clock news tonight. Thanks for the suggestion. Merry Christmas, kiddo.***

**Fulbright: *PS—check your back porch.***

"Are you three going to be all right tonight?" I asked them.

Peter smiled. "We have a Christmas tradition."

"Oh, is it empty now?" Lena May asked. "Is it time?"

I leaned over the edge of the balcony. Everyone else had cleared out of the sanctuary for dinner back in the fellowship hall. "Everyone's gone," I said. What were they up to?

Annette disappeared, and when I turned to look for her, I realized the other two had disappeared along with her. They reappeared downstairs on the stage. Annette hummed a note. Then she began to sing "Silent Night." Her sultry voice reminded me of one of those old jazz singers. I could envision her slinking across the dim, smoky stage of a jazz club with a whole room watching. A few lines in,

Peter and Lena May joined her, adding harmony. It was beautiful.

I sat down on the pew and listened. My life was undeniably weird. Without a doubt, no one else I knew was listening to a trio of ghosts sing Christmas carols, but for that moment, I wouldn't have traded it for anything. Not for the most normal, mundane existence of all. Life was weird, but sometimes that was what made it wonderful.

We finally got home around ten forty-five, and Colin still hadn't shut up about Dad the whole time. I blamed it partially on the thirty-seven cookies he'd inhaled at dinner, but there was at least a little part of me that loved seeing him so excited. Maybe it would make up for getting him a completely lame Christmas present.

"He said he was coming over in the morning," Colin reminded Mom for the fifth time. "Can we make pancakes for breakfast? He likes your pancakes."

"We'll see," she said. "Now, you've had a long day. Why don't you go on to bed?"

"I'm fine." With as much sugar as he'd eaten, he probably wouldn't sleep for another three days. He ran upstairs to change into his pajamas, then launched himself at the couch and picked up the Xbox controller.

"Oh no," I said, darting around the couch to grab the remote. "We haven't watched *Home Alone* yet."

"Again?" he complained.

Mom tilted her head quizzically. "You want to?"

That had been the girls' tradition when we were little, right up until the year Valerie had died. Pajamas, popcorn, and movies. Mom and I hadn't done it since, but it seemed like as good a time as any to try again.

"Yeah," I said. "Do you?"

Her eyes gleamed with tears, and she shook herself. "Actually, I do. Just give me a few minutes to change."

Colin sighed. "I'm going to my room."

"Keep the volume down," Mom said. She walked into the kitchen and started a bag of popcorn in the microwave. After she headed to her bedroom to change out of her church clothes, I sat down with the remote and turned to the news.

I sat through some boring weather updates, and a radar update on Santa's sled before the story I was waiting for. The reporter had on a Santa hat, and she smiled as the screen shifted. "And now, for another act of Christmas kindness," she said. To my surprise, a picture of Sal appeared on the screen. "Our viewing family may remember Officer Luis Salazar, who was killed in the line of duty in January. The holidays are a difficult time of year for those who have lost loved ones, so the Byron County Police Department took it upon themselves to make sure his family had a merry Christmas."

The screen cut to a little blue house. There were half a dozen police cars parked along the street. An officer walked up the lawn and knocked on the front door. A pretty black woman answered the door with a baby on her hip. I recognized her from creeping on Sal's Facebook profile. The officer gestured for Veronica to follow, and she clapped her free hand over her mouth. The officer led her to her garage, then pressed a button to open the door.

The reporter narrated. "Another officer called ahead and asked if he could bring over some firewood after clearing his yard," she said. "He brought a few other things, as you can see."

Inside Veronica's garage were a dozen police officers, along with Diana Brown and her mother, standing inside around a pile of presents as tall as they were. They had even set up a small Christmas tree inside.

The camera panned across the presents. There had to be a hundred presents there, wrapped in bright paper and huge bows. Behind the presents was a stack of green diaper boxes as tall as one of the police officers.

The camera cut to a familiar face. Detective Fulbright said, "Something told us we needed to take care of our own. He smiled at the camera. Sometimes you gotta listen to those feelings."

Oh, that sneaky bastard.

A reporter on the scene spoke to Veronica. Sometime between shots, someone had put a pair of reindeer antlers on baby RJ, making her officially the cutest baby I'd ever seen. "Are you surprised?"

Tears streamed down her face as she tried to wipe away a streak of mascara. "Luis had some good friends on the force. They've been helping around the house, you know, fixing the car and stuff, but I had no idea they would do something like this. You know, Luis loved surprises. This is the kind of thing he would do for someone else. It makes me feel like he's still here watching out for me. For us," she added, smiling at RJ.

The camera cut back to the station. "What a great Christmas Eve surprise," the reporter said. "Next up, we're checking in with the Helping Harvest food bank on their Christmas donation drive."

I sat back and felt a dopey smile spreading on my face. Fulbright had knocked it out of the park. The thought of the gruff policeman reminded me of the other half of his message. Launching myself off the couch, I bolted to the back porch. Leaning against the back wall of the house was a big black trash bag with a red bow stuck on its side. I frowned and grabbed it, then peeked inside.

Inside the bag was my puffy purple jacket. The tag on the handle said, "*Lost and found. —Tom*"

I laughed and tucked the bag under my arm. Protect and serve, indeed. I hurried back inside and ran upstairs to stash the recovered jacket in my room before Mom came out of her bedroom.

Right as I reached my door, I heard the microwave beep to signal that the popcorn had finished. I kicked off my shoes and threw the trash bag on my bed. I jumped when I turned to see Kale perched on my desk.

"Were you going to watch me change?" I asked in a dramatic voice.

He rolled his eyes. "Don't be creepy."

"Close your eyes," I told him primly. He made a show of putting his hands over his face, and I quickly changed out of my church clothes and into my pajamas. "Okay. You can look."

"What's in the bag?" he asked.

"My jacket. The one I gave Diana. Fulbright got it back for me somehow."

"Very nice."

"So, are you going to come watch the movie with us? Or just hang out up here like a weirdo?" Again, I had a delightful vision of Kale and I curled up on the couch like two normal people. "Obviously you can't eat popcorn but you can still appreciate *Home Alone* as the fine film that it is."

"I wish I could." He smiled, his gaze on mine. Did he mean it? Did he wonder what it would be like for us to be two normal people, too? "Actually, I came to tell you about Isaac."

So much for happy dreams. "What about him?"

"I've been checking in at the police department periodically," he said. "They followed up on it and found the remains. They're working on an official identification, but it seems to be mostly a formality, considering they found his wallet in the pack."

"Have they notified his family?"

"Not yet," Kale said. "One of the officers claimed it was paperwork backing them up, but I think he wanted to wait until Christmas had passed. It's been almost twenty years. A few more days won't hurt them."

"When they do, will you let me know?"

"Of course. I just thought you'd like an update."

"Thanks."

"Bridget? Are we watching this movie?" Mom called.

I sighed and looked at the door, then back to Kale. He looked hesitant, his eyes searching me for something. Then he smiled. "You should go be with your mom."

"Oh. Are you sure?"

"I mean, this Home Alone sounds quite compelling," he said. "And spending time with you is far more interesting than sleep."

"You mean you like spending time with me?"

"Very much," he said. His blue eyes were locked on mine, his expression open and sincere. His lips weren't quirked up in that casual teasing smile he so often wore. My heart raced.

"Bridget! Are you ready?" Mom called.

*Mom, seriously?*

"You should go," Kale said. "I should go rest."

"What's that like for you?"

He shrugged. "Just like when you sleep."

"Do you dream?"

"Sometimes."

"What about?"

"Nosy girls and their insatiable curiosity," he said with a smile. He drifted toward me and brushed a light, chaste kiss on my cheek. "Merry Christmas. Enjoy it."

"Merry Christmas to you," I said. I suppressed the urge to brush my fingers across my cheek, which was somehow cool from his touch and yet burning at the same time. Talk about leaving a girl wanting more. "When will I see you again?"

"Whenever you want," he said.

And with that promise, he disappeared, and I felt strangely lonely. There was definitely an element of "OMG he's so dreamy," but it was also the absence of someone who had arguably become my closest friend. Was it weird that the person I trusted most wasn't even a person in the strictest sense? And was it extra weird that I wanted my ghostly friend—my Guardian—to come do silly, mundane things like watching movies with me? It would have been nice to spend time with him without all the life-threatening danger and ghost drama.

"Bridget!"

Mom's shout broke my reverie. Like it or not, the ghost drama was pretty much the story of my life these days. But seeing Diana and Corey get home safely made it worth it. As much as certain parts of it sucked, I knew it was right. It wasn't my inflated ego talking; there were at least two families who had their loved ones home safe and sound because of me. I couldn't save the world all by myself, but I could do something.

But for now, I was off duty. I turned off the lights and headed back down the hall. When I got back downstairs, Colin was sitting on the loveseat with his tablet in his lap. I wasn't sure if Mom had nagged him or if he'd decided on his own that it was better to hang out than to be alone in his nerd cave. Mom had made hot chocolate for all three of us, complete with tiny marshmallows floating in the foam. I wished my sister could be here. I didn't want to set Mom off, so I didn't mention it as I sat down on the couch. It had been over two years since she died, but she'd lingered as a spirit until a month ago. This was my first

Christmas without her in my life at all.

"I wish your sister could be here," Mom said, as if she'd read my mind.

"We don't have to watch it," I said as the hot chocolate went bitter on my tongue. Tears stung my eyes.

"No." She shook a blanket out over my legs, then settled in next to me. She took a deep breath and said in a firm voice, "I think she'd want us to do this."

She actually wasn't wrong. In the years that Val had lingered, she'd constantly pressured me to carry on like normal. This was exactly what she wanted, even though it would never be the same. Just because it wasn't exactly right didn't mean it was wrong, and we could still laugh even if there were tears mixed in.

"You know, we've lost a lot," Mom said. "But I'm glad for what we still have."

"Me too," I said, digging into the bowl of popcorn. "Merry Christmas."

"Merry Christmas, sweetie."

# EPILOGUE

WITH THE SUN SHINING HIGH overhead and not a single snowflake in sight, Wildwood State Park was a thousand times more welcoming than it had been on my last visit. Even so, I'd come prepared with my backpack full of pilfered snacks from the kitchen and handwarmers I'd picked up at Target while Mom stocked up on half-price wrapping paper after Christmas.

On the pretense of hanging out for coffee, Michael had picked me up from the house right after lunchtime. Hanging out with a boy was about the most normal thing I could have done, and I was pretty sure Mom was more excited about it than her spa gift card. Even I had to admit it was awesome to see Michael during daylight hours without a doomsday clock ticking.

"Is this good?" Michael asked as he parked in front of the picnic pavilion where I'd first called the Wildwood spirits to find Diana and Corey. It was considerably less frightening in daylight. The snow and ice of just days before had already melted, leaving damp brown grass and bare trees reaching for the cloudless sky.

I nodded and grabbed my folder of computer printouts. "This is fine."

"Do you want me to come with you?"

I paused. He looked oddly hopeful, but there was something about saying goodbye that seemed sacred and private. Though I enjoyed his company, I had to do this part alone. Reluctantly, I shook my head. "It'll only take me a few minutes."

His brow creased, his lips parted as if he wanted to protest, but he nodded and reached over to turn the radio up as I gathered my things.

I stepped out of the car with my backpack hanging from one shoulder. Even under sunny skies, it was still chilly, with a strong wind that nipped at my bare face and hands. I shivered and hurried toward the rusted picnic pavilion. "Kale, we're here," I said as I walked up the cracked sidewalk. I had barely spoken when he appeared next to me.

"Do you have a plan?" he asked. Resting had done him some good, giving him back the glowing intensity that made him so different from the other spirits. Where he'd seemed fragile after we found Diana, he was nearly opaque now, like a real boy if not for the way his feet didn't touch the ground when he walked.

"I actually do," I told him. "And it doesn't involve any death-defying stunts."

"I'm so proud," he said with a mocking wink.

"I can learn."

I stepped onto the elevated concrete slab, then laid my backpack on the closest picnic table. Amid the scratched graffiti was a ridged ring of wax from the candles I'd lit last time. My heart thumped in anticipation as I idly traced the ring with my fingers.

"Isaac? It's Bridget. If you're here, I have news for you," I said aloud. Then I waited, listening to the quiet rush of my own breathing and the faraway sounds of birds in the trees. "Isaac?"

It took several minutes, but he eventually appeared, hovering at the edge of the pavilion. His gaze was fixed on his feet, as if he was too ashamed to meet my eyes.

"You can come over here," I said, trying to make my voice as gentle and soothing as I could. There was a part of me that was afraid as he approached, remembering the way he'd dragged me down into his memories. I knew it would have been easier for him to meet in the woods, closer to the site of his death.

But I had no intention of traipsing off alone into the woods again, not after what had happened before.

Finally, he drifted toward me, flickering in and out of sight as he closed the distance between us. When he reached the picnic table, he crouched awkwardly so he was on eye level. Before I spoke, I glanced back at Kale for reassurance. He gave me a subtle nod, then returned his attention to Isaac.

"Are you ready to hear about your family?" I asked, my pulse quickening. As upset as Isaac had been before, I didn't know how he would take the news.

He nodded without speaking.

I opened the manila folder and put it on the table between us. As I took out the first printout, I extended my right hand to Isaac. He finally met my gaze. His face was creased with pain, his eyes downturned and full of despair. "If you want to," I said. "It's okay. I trust you." That wasn't entirely true, but I knew it would go a long way to alleviate his guilt.

He hesitated, his swollen hand hovering over mine. After I gave him a nod of assurance, he finally laid it on mine. When he made contact, it felt like I'd plunged my hand up to the wrist into snow. A shiver ran down my spine, but it was worth the discomfort to see the way vibrant color rushed up his arm. The tension flowed out of his face, leaving him looking peaceful and relaxed.

Still holding his hand, I held up the first printout so he could see it. "The police notified your mom a few days after Christmas." His grasp tightened at the word *mom*, sending a cold shock up my arm. With my arm going numb, I tried to suppress the fear creeping into my voice. The printout was from a long article the newspaper had done about him, with the bold headline *Missing Greenridge Man Found Dead after Seventeen Years*. With bright pink highlighter, I'd noted the parts where his mother, Kathleen, had been quoted. "Would you like to hear about your mom?"

He looked at me fearfully, then nodded.

"She seems to be doing really well," I said. "It says she was a schoolteacher."

"Kindergarten," he said, his voice trembling. He didn't look at the paper, like he was afraid of what it might say. Instead, his gaze stayed locked on me.

"She was the Teacher of the Year at her school in 2010. She retired last year," I told him. "After you disappeared, she adopted several foster kids." I laid down the article and showed him a picture I'd found on Facebook of Kathleen Watkins, surrounded by three smiling teenagers. "This girl came from Russia," I said, tapping the dark-haired girl on the far left. "The other two came from an abusive home. They're all in college now. They say she's the best mom in the world."

I looked up to see his eyes glistening with phantom tears. The sight of it made my throat close up around a lump of sadness, but I had to keep on. Through my own blurry tears, I scanned for the next highlighted section. "She said 'I've missed my son every day since he disappeared, but I'm glad I can finally have closure and say a proper goodbye. He'll always live in our hearts.'"

His grip tightened again. Tiny beads of light trickled down his dirty cheeks. Without a body, his tears were just an illusion, but that didn't make them any less real.

"I'm sorry," I said, swallowing my own sorrow as I watched him. "I know it's hard."

"She looks so happy. I'm glad," he said. He looked down at our clasped hands. "What about Laura?"

I set the article aside and took out another picture. "They didn't quote her in the article, but I found her on Facebook," I said. He cocked his head, his brow furrowed in confusion. Out here in the woods alone for almost twenty years, social media was lost on him. "Uh, I used a computer to find out more about her. She moved to Tennessee about three years after you...left. She got married a few years after that."

Cold sizzled through my muscles again. Fear struck me as I realized Isaac's wrist had gone livid purple again. His pain had come roaring back to life. For a moment, I felt a powerful pull like an undertow as his despair leached into me. My gaze went to Kale, and he took a tentative step toward us.

"It's okay," I said in my most soothing voice. "I don't have to tell you if you're not ready."

He shook his head. As he relaxed, the cold receded and the feeling returned to my fingers. "It's been so long. I'm ready."

With a deep breath, I took out another picture from a beach photoshoot. This one showed Laura, a pretty blonde, with her husband. Both dressed in blue and white, they each carried a small child in their arms. "This is her family. This is her husband Tom. And this is Kaylee," I said, pointing to the little pig-tailed toddler in Tom's arms. With my finger resting on the boy on Laura's hip, I squeezed Isaac's hand. "This is her son. This is Isaac."

His eyes shot to mine. "Really?"

I nodded. Though I couldn't see her social media profiles, Laura kept a public blog about her experiences as a stay-at-home mom. After hours of skimming through her archives, I'd found an old post where she'd explained her choice of names for her children. "She said she named him after someone she loved very much. There weren't a lot of details, but she said that she knew something had happened or else you would have come home. She dreamed about you promising that you would always watch over her. It was really hard for her to get pregnant, and she had a lot of health problems when she was carrying him. But when he was born, he was perfect. She says that you must have protected him. There was never a doubt in her mind that his name was Isaac."

He let out a tense sound, half-laughter and half-sob. His hand warmed suddenly, as if relief had melted through the cold sorrow. "She wasn't angry?"

"Not at all," I said emphatically. "She wouldn't have named him after you if she was."

"I missed out on so much," he said, gazing at the picture. His fingers hovered over the glossy paper, circling Laura's face. I wasn't psychic but I knew he was imagining himself in Tom's place, holding the children he'd never gotten to have. It was the same as with my sister, and with Natalie; the loss of someone you loved was only the beginning. Beyond that absence in your daily life, there were thousands of futures that had to be rewritten with a player missing.

"Here," I said, gently extricating my hand from his. I shuffled through the stack of pictures and told him about each one in turn, watching as his expression cycled between joy and grief. When I reached the bottom of the stack, I looked up at him. "I know this doesn't make up for what happened to you. I wish I could change it, but I can't."

He nodded, still staring at the picture of Laura and her family. I glanced over my shoulder to see Michael sitting on the hood of the car, arms folded over his chest as he watched me. My cheeks flushed as I turned back to Isaac. I wasn't used to having an audience other than Kale.

"It's okay to let go," I said. "You've suffered long enough."

He looked at me, eyes creased. "What happens after?"

"I'm not sure," I said. I looked to Kale, who was pointedly avoiding eye contact. Like most of my questions, he'd never given me a clear answer. But in this case, I wasn't sure he actually knew. I'd been raised believing in heaven, in a place of peace and light. Even with the crapstorm that had battered my life and the pessimism that had bloomed in its wake, I still believed. It was mostly because I wanted to believe my sister was there, because that would balance out everything she'd missed. Same with Natalie, and all the other spirits I'd met over the years. If all the girls whose lives were cut short by the Runaway Killer didn't go somewhere bright and beautiful, then life really was broken and unfair, and I refused to accept that. "I think you go somewhere good. Where you can be at peace, and you don't have to be alone anymore."

Isaac smiled sadly at me. "It's been a long time. I think I'm ready." He fiddled with the mud-stained bandana around his neck, then squared his shoulders as he mustered his courage. "What do I do?"

I looked over at Kale again, who gave me a nod. Though his eyes were oddly sad, his lips curved into a faint smile, like he was proud of me.

Leaving my backpack on the table, I stood up and walked toward the edge of the pavilion, then gestured back to Isaac. He drifted toward me, putting his hand in mine. Together, we stepped off the concrete slab and onto the flattened brown grass. The midday sun shone down on us, warming my face. In the light, Isaac's body became translucent, like he was already fading away.

"You just let go," I said. "They'll always love you, but you don't have to worry about them anymore."

His hand squeezed mine. "Thank you."

"You're welcome," I said. This wasn't my first rodeo, but it was never easy. I hadn't known Isaac long enough to call him a friend like I had Sal and Kale, but my heart ached for him. Tears stung at my eyes as I looked up at him. "It's okay to go. Go where it's warm and peaceful."

As I watched, he turned his face up to the sun. Even though he didn't have a body to feel the warmth, peace spread across his face as the light touched him. Despite the chill in the air, a warm wind stirred around us. The cool pressure of Isaac's grasp faded away, passing through my fingers like water. As he faded in the sunlight, I felt as much as heard his sigh of relief, a long-held breath joining the wind.

And then he was gone.

"Isaac?" I asked tentatively. After a few long, calming breaths, I tried again. "Isaac?" There was no answer, which was all the answer I needed. I looked over to Kale, who approached me quietly. "Did I do it?"

"You did it," he replied. "Well done."

"Thank you," I said. The warm glow of pride flowed through me even as the hot sting of tears pricked my eyes. I returned to the picnic table and took out a bundle of sage from my backpack, then lit it so the ends smoldered. Circling the pavilion, I wafted fragrant smoke to purify whatever remained of Isaac's lingering sadness. When I finished, I stubbed out the sage in the dirty ash of the grill, then returned to the car.

Michael stood there, still watching me with something that could have been awe or fear in his eyes. "Is it done?"

"It's done," I said. A lump caught in my throat as I thought of Isaac, surrounded in warmth and light. I hoped he was happy. I hoped he was finally at peace.

"Do you know where they go?" he asked, looking up toward the sky. I knew he wasn't asking about Isaac then; he was asking about Natalie.

"Somewhere beautiful," I said. "That's what I think."

He nodded thoughtfully. His voice hitched as he spoke. "I hope so." As he looked back at me, he tilted his head. "How many times have you done this?"

I didn't have to think long about it. "Thirty-four, as of today," I said. I didn't want to upset him, so I didn't mention that it would be fifty-eight if I counted all of the Runaway Killer's victims who'd been trapped here in their anguish. Once he'd been exposed, most of them had simply disappeared on their own. Natalie was one of the few I'd helped on her way by relaying her goodbyes to Michael.

His eyes widened. "Seriously?"

"Seriously," I said. If he'd asked, I could have recited all of their names. Just as I'd promised Isaac that his family would remember him, there was an unspoken promise that I would remember him. Even though I'd only come to know him long after he died, we were connected.

"That's a lot to carry," he said.

"Sometimes."

"You know you don't have to do it alone."

My eyes went to Kale. I'd never really been alone in it. But there was something in Michael's voice that caught me by surprise. Was that a hint at his feelings? Or was it just him being nice? "I'm not really alone."

He surprised me then, folding me into a hug. "Thanks for helping them," he said. I heard what he meant. *Thanks for helping her.* Whatever his feelings were, it was nice to be here with him. I leaned into the hug. With my head resting against chest, I could feel his heartbeat, reminding me that he was warm and alive.

"You're welcome," I said. "Thanks for helping me yet again."

"You're welcome." He sighed, then backed up enough to look down at me. His hands lingered on my arms, warm and solid. "So what now?"

"How about something normal?"

"What do normal people do?"

"Hell if I know."

"Well, let's give it a try."

# WHAT NOW?

If you enjoyed getting to know Bridget and the ghost gang, then please let your friends, family, and the whole world know by sharing on social media or leaving a review! Just a few minutes can help another reader find a story they may love. Thank you!

To learn more about upcoming books, short stories, and giveaways, make sure you find me online at:

## www.jessicahawke.com

There you can sign up for my mailing list and get your free copy of *Phantom Light*, the spooky prequel to the *Phantoms* series!

Here are some of the other places you can find me online:

**Facebook:** https://www.facebook.com/AuthorJessicaHawke/
https:/www.facebook.com/writerhawke
**Twitter:** @JJHawke
**Website:** https://www.jessicahawke.com

Keep reading for a sneak peek at *Phantom Whispers*,
Book 3 of the *Phantoms* series!

# Phantom Whispers

## Chapter One

I LEFT SCHOOL ON MONDAY with a stack of homework and a talkative spirit on my heels. While I had to weave through the flood of students pouring through the open doors to freedom, my spectral best friend and Guardian, Kale, passed through them like air. Even when the entire boys lacrosse team barreled through him on the way to the gym, it didn't interrupt his story.

"She had one of those silver things and was puffing on it in the lounge," he said. It was too bad that no one without the dubious honor of seeing the dead and otherwise non-corporeal could see him. Kale was a first-class hottie, with dark tousled hair and dreamy blue eyes. I wouldn't have minded if my classmates saw him walking next to me. He was even more gorgeous than my human crush Michael, although Michael had the advantage of a heartbeat.

After checking over my shoulder to make sure no one was looking right at me, I whispered, "An e-cigarette?"

"An e-cigarette," he murmured. "I'm starting to think you'll put *e* in front of anything."

I ignored him as I approached a cluster of girls blocking the hallway. Crammed shoulder to shoulder near the custodial closet on the science hall, they all looked down at someone's phone held between them. One of them screamed, while the other two laughed at her.

"Not funny, you guys!" she protested.

"Now you should go try it," the phone's owner said as she tucked the phone into her pocket. "I dare you."

My science teacher, Mrs. England, shooed them along. "Ladies, let's get moving. You don't have to go home, but you can't stay here." With a chorus of sighs, the girls spread out three across and sauntered down the hallway.

I darted around the girls and hurried outside to the bus loading area. Bus engines roared, echoing off the metal awning. Dodging a couple of boys beatboxing while a third filmed on his phone, I headed for the sidewalk that ran parallel to the front of the school.

I'd gone back to Mrs. England's classroom for an extra copy of the homework, putting me at the opposite end of the school from the parking lot. But the extra walk didn't bother me. It was a chance to let my guard down and quit pretending I didn't hear Kale chatting. After more than two years of dealing with ghosts, I had a great poker face.

"Yes, they're called e-cigarettes," I told Kale when I got past the crowd. I pulled out my phone and held it close to my mouth like I was voice-texting, not talking to myself. "It just means electronic. I'm just confused about why you think the electronic part is more interesting than the fact that the German teacher is smoking in the bathroom between classes. I'm pretty sure that's not allowed."

"She was," he said. "At least three times today."

"You watched her all day?"

"I got interested. I would smoke too if I had some of her students. So rude," he said. Then his brow furrowed. "I did other things, too. It's not like I float around your school all day looking for gossip."

"Well you should. Speaking of gossip, I found out that Brady Thomas waxes his chest," I told him. Kale's eyebrows shot up. "Yeah, as in hot wax, then rip!" I pantomimed on my chest. He winced.

As always, Kale wore light clothing that could have been linen if it was real and not just some aspect of his ghostly nature. I envied his ability to not get cold or hot, which would have been a much more useful superpower here in Georgia, where we would go from winter to summer and back again in the course of a week. Today, there was a sharp chill in the air, though the sun shone bright in a crystal clear sky.

Just minutes after the last bell, the student parking lot was already half empty. Bumper-to-bumper traffic crawled between the rows of parking spots. It was easy to spot Emily's yellow Volkswagen in her assigned spot. The loud music blaring from inside her car reached me four rows away.

As we approached Emily's car, Kale waved. "I'll leave you two to catch up. See you when you get home."

"I'm meeting with Detective Fulbright today," I said. "So after that."

He nodded. "Right. Be careful."

"Always."

With a wry smile, he faded away to wherever cute Guardians went when they weren't checking on their wayward charges or snooping on nicotine-addicted German teachers. Unlike most spirits, Kale didn't expect me to solve his problems and send him into the light. He was my Guardian, although he was annoyingly vague about what that meant. And while he had a 'gorgeous boy in white' thing going on, he wasn't an angel. After years of asking questions, I accepted that Kale was Kale, and that was all I knew. But our friendship had its limits, and he had long grown tired of my best friend Emily's taste in music and her relentless attention to detail when it came to discussing gossip and fashion.

Loud music bombarded me as I opened the passenger door. I had to move a heap of jackets and scarves into the backseat, where there was already enough clothing to outfit the entire junior class.

Emily turned down the stereo for me, which was a sure sign that we were best friends. "Hi, honey," she said. Her most recent hair overhaul had left her with dark roots that faded into dark purple ends. Blue glitter eyeshadow sparkled in the afternoon light as she turned to acknowledge me.

"Hi, darling," I replied.

She glanced over her shoulder to inspect the back seat, then looked at me with wide, dark-lined eyes. "Are we alone?"

"Just the two of us." I'd kept my ability a secret for two years, but I'd finally told Emily about it a few months ago.

Back in November, I'd helped an angry spirit named Natalie find the sicko who killed her. Natalie had been a senior at my school who had run away from home in the past, so people thought she'd taken off again. But when I encountered Natalie's enraged spirit in my bedroom, I knew better. The killer had kidnapped Emily before the police converged on him and scared him out of town. Thankfully Emily had only minor injuries, but our relationship had changed since then. It had taken her some time to get used to the new development, but she was open-minded about it now. It was nice to have someone else in my life—someone with a heartbeat—who knew what I could do.

"I want you to watch this video," she said, trying to maneuver the phone with one hand while she backed up the car. She stomped the brake as a horn blared behind us. A red Jeep was inches from the back of Emily's car. "Whoops."

"Here." With my heart leaping into my throat, I grabbed her phone. She wasn't the greatest driver to begin with, and I wanted to get home in one piece.

Cursing under her breath, she twisted around in her seat to check for cars, then backed out slowly to merge into traffic. Once we stopped again, she took the phone back and swiped through her apps. "This. Tell me what you think."

When she handed me the phone again, it was displaying a paused video in YouTube. The caption read *Uno Bros Tres: Dead Eyes Challenge*. "What is it?"

"Everyone was talking about it in gym today," she said. "It made me think of you."

That wasn't an answer, but I pressed *play* anyway. A slick animated intro spelled out *Uno Bros Tres* in glowing letters. Then the screen appeared to shatter like exploding glass before fading onto a dark shot of trees and what looked like tombstones.

The camera bounced, following two figures with flashlights. A male voice narrated. "This is Uno Bros Tres bringing you the Dead Eyes Challenge. We were tagged by our buddy Darkstar, so we're heading out to the cemetery tonight."

The video cut to three figures with flashlights. The camera had stabilized, like it had been put onto a tripod. Now it was clear that they were surrounded by tombstones, rising like teeth against the dark backdrop of night.

One of the figures, a boy with shaggy blond hair, stood in front of the camera. "Here we go." They sat in an arc around a large headstone. The blond boy took a folded piece of paper out of his pocket and read from it, "Restless spirit, come to me. Tell me what your dead eyes see. Unbroken and unfettered be; from your ancient graves be free!"

I shivered. They were just a bunch of dumb high school boys, but the thought of calling out to spirits in a graveyard was stupid no matter who you were.

Silence fell as the three boys stared at each other, then looked around frantically. The blond boy looked off camera and whispered, "Did you hear that?"

A shadow passed in front of the camera. One of the boys shouted, then the camera fell over. The audio was all pops and static, with the occasional muffled shouting breaking through. On screen was a blurry dance of black and gray, as the camera bounced along without focusing.

The video cut to a shot of the three boys sitting at a yellow plastic table that could have only been a Waffle House. All three boys were still, eyes wide and faces pale.

"So what did you see?" one of them asked. Dead leaves stuck out of his messy, dark hair.

"I didn't see it, but I felt it," the blond boy said.

The third boy snickered, apparently unshaken by what had happened. "That's what she said."

But the others didn't laugh.

The boy with leaves in his hair shook his head. "There was definitely something out there."

"You think it was real?"

They continued like that for another few minutes, but they just kept repeating that they were sure something was there without giving any details.

Finally, the video cut back to the blond boy alone in front of a white background. "Have you taken the Dead Eyes challenge? Let me know what you thought of this video in the comments, and tune in next Thursday for a new video."

The video cut to credits with embedded animations of his other videos over techno music. The two featured videos were *Home Depot Toilet Prank* and the *Sriracha Challenge*. Not exactly high art.

"So?" Emily said. When I looked up from the screen, we were on the road toward my house, with the winter-bare trees blurring by the windows.

"I don't know," I said. "It seems like some douchebags trying to get YouTube-famous."

"But was there something there?"

I frowned at her. "I don't know. I don't see anything."

"Oh." Her expression fell. "Well, it seemed like your kind of thing."

I handed her the phone back and shrugged. "Sorry, I didn't mean to ruin your surprise."

She rolled her eyes. "Girl, please. I have plenty. Let me tell you about what Eliza Jane told me in gym today."

I half-listened to her story about two junior girls getting busted for sexting. Despite my initial disbelief, my mind drifted back to the video. Could the invocation have worked? I had called out to spirits and stirred them up, but I was different.

About two years ago, I was in a car accident that killed my older sister Valerie and left me injured. They had to do surgery on my leg, and a bad reaction to anesthesia made my heart stop for a few seconds. According to Kale, I came back as a new and improved version of myself, one that wasn't completely in the world of the living. That was when my ability had started. But these boys weren't like me, as far as I knew.

Emily elbowed me, sending a sharp pain down my arm. "Ow!" I complained.

"You totally checked out on me," Emily said.

"I'm sorry, I was thinking about that video."

But instead of rolling her eyes in annoyance, her glossy lips curved into a wide smile. "I knew it was something!"

"I'm not saying it's definitely a ghost thing," I said. "But I'll try to find out more about it."

When Emily drove up to my house, a sleek police cruiser sat in the driveway. "What the…What did you get into now?"

"It's okay." I said. In case it wasn't already obvious that my life was weird, the sight of the police cruiser in the driveway didn't faze me. The car belonged to Detective Fulbright, who I'd been in contact with several times over the last few months. After my most recent adventure with the life-impaired, Fulbright had decided he wanted to check in on me every few weeks. Today was our first meeting. "He just wants to check in with me once in a while."

"You are so weird," Emily said. "And I love it."

"Thanks."

"Skype me later if you get bored."

"Got it. Bye!" Grabbing my heavy backpack from the floorboard, I got out of the car and waved goodbye to her.

Fulbright was fiddling with a file in his lap and looked up in surprise when I knocked on the window. With my heart thumping in anticipation, I dropped into the seat. Though he wore a normal plaid button down and jeans, his close-cropped salt-and-pepper hair and craggy face gave him an aura of authority.

"Hey kiddo," he said. His gravelly voice sounded like he was trying for warm and friendly, but considering the situation, it came off a little awkward. "You ready to go?"

It probably said something about me that I was hanging out with a detective instead of a cute boy—one with a heartbeat—but I'd long learned to accept the sheer weirdness of my life. "Let's go."

*Continue the story in Phantom Whispers!*

# Acknowledgements

Writing may seem like a lonely business, but it takes more of a community than most people realize.


Thanks to…

The Tuesday Sushi Club – Hildie and Olivia, my writer BFFs – for encouragement, tough love, a never-ending wellspring of wisdom, and stickers, because we all need a sticker once in a while.

Rhonda Helms – for great editing that sharpens my writing.

Clarissa Yeo – for a breathtaking cover

Carmen – my BFF, who doesn't bat an eye at the "HELP NOW" texts she inevitably receives during the process of producing a new book. You're the bestest.

Jenny – for encouraging me to pursue my dreams.

Luke – for tough love and keeping me on my toes with unexpected insertions into my text.

Facebook Tribe – for suggestions on titles. You named this one!

Marisel – for Spanish help! *¡Gracias!*

Tambra – for being a cheerleader and savvy business mentor.

Dad – for always believing that I can, and making sure I believe it too.

Mom – for always being my biggest fan.


Finally, thank you, generous readers, for sticking around for Book Two. I hope you'll be back for more, and that we share this journey of story for years to come.

# ABOUT THE AUTHOR

Jessica Hawke's first stories were painstakingly scrawled on notebook paper in second grade. While the story of the Three Little Fish will never again see the light of day, her parents felt this was a sign, and as usual, they turned out to be right. She enjoys writing paranormal and fantasy novels, since reality is overrated.

www.ingramcontent.com/pod-product-compliance
Lightning Source LLC
Chambersburg PA
CBHW020359210626
46816CB00006BB/2037